OLIVIA'S MINE

OLIVIA'S MINE

Janine McCaw

iUniverse, Inc.
New York Lincoln Shanghai

OLIVIA'S MINE

Copyright © 2006 by Janine McCaw

All rights reserved. No part of this book may be used or reproduced by any means, graphic, electronic, or mechanical, including photocopying, recording, taping or by any information storage retrieval system without the written permission of the publisher except in the case of brief quotations embodied in critical articles and reviews.

iUniverse books may be ordered through booksellers or by contacting:

iUniverse
2021 Pine Lake Road, Suite 100
Lincoln, NE 68512
www.iuniverse.com
1-800-Authors (1-800-288-4677)

ISBN-13: 978-0-595-37924-8 (pbk)
ISBN-13: 978-0-595-82295-9 (ebk)
ISBN-10: 0-595-37924-9 (pbk)
ISBN-10: 0-595-82295-9 (ebk)

Printed in the United States of America

For Gerri Cook, who loved to tell a good tale.

PREFACE

For years I had been driving up the coast from Vancouver to Whistler, passing by an old mine site on the east side of the sea to sky highway.

One summer day my husband Paul and I decided to stop and take a tour of the mine. I was fascinated by the history that had occurred at Britannia Beach, that for years, I had never taken the time to learn about.

To try to write a true account of the life and times there was beyond my scope. I'm quite content to leave that task to the historians. But the drama that occurred there, in the early 1900's set my imagination into over-drive, and I spun a tale of what life might have been like, given the situations and the times.

We attended the 100'th anniversary reunion at Britannia Beach, where I learned a little bit more about the tight knit community that once thrived there.

Britannia Beach during the 1900's was a multi-cultural community with all the challenges that entails. People were not necessarily politically correct. That part of the book was difficult to write as I don't share the viewpoints of some of my characters. But times were what they were.

Urban sprawl being what it is, Britannia Beach will soon change forever, and rumour has it, the old mine on the hill is going to get a face lift. Some of the charm of the old town may be lost, but more people may take the time to stop and learn the history of the area. Olivia would have liked that.

ACKNOWLEDGEMENTS

I could not have written this book without the love of my life's constant support and encouragement. Paul Busch, thanks for saying "Is it done yet?"

The artwork is done by Canadian artist Millie LaBelle who lives in Thunder Bay, Ontario. Millie paints incredible landscapes, and if you would like to see more of her work, you can email her at mx3@shaw.ca.

Grace Shaw, I will never truly learn the proper use of a semi-colon. Thanks for reminding me it wasn't a body part; as you patiently read through the works. I am learning about syntax for the next one.

Also, thanks to Kristin at iUniverse, the web gang at Fairfax Creative and the publicity crew at Translucent.

The story you are about to read is fictitious. The characters are figments of the author's imagination and never existed outside the pages of the book. There is however, a real Britannia Beach, with a real mine and a real history. There really was a landslide, a fire, a cave-in and a flood. A good book to read for a more accurate account of the life and times would be *Britannia: Story of a Mine* by Bruce Ramsey. Or if you happen to be in the neighbourhood, spend some time at the BC Museum of Mining located on the sea-to-sky highway between Vancouver and Squamish.

"There was a time in this fair land when the railroad did not run.
When the wild majestic mountains stood alone against the sun."

> "Canadian Railroad Trilogy" by Gordon Lightfoot
> c 1967 renewed 1995 Moose Music
> Used By Permission.

CHAPTER 1

The single rosebud he held in his hand was a mixed hue of yellows and soft pinks a hybrid common to the gardens of the Pacific Northwest.

"You know that every time I come into this garden and see the roses, I'll think of you," William Bower said, as he removed the thorns, shortened the stem and handed the flower to the beautiful young woman before him. In its life the blossom had reached for the light, twisting itself around a portion of the wooden arbour that blocked it from the sun. This gave the stem a unique curve. It was not a perfect specimen, but it was beautiful in its own right. He removed his spectacles to take a closer look at the flower. It gave him a sense of peace. The rose garden at the back of the house was his hobby, his escape, and he tended to it well.

"Nothing in nature is straight," he commented, his voice breaking slightly. He coughed, trying to cover up his emotion, bringing his other hand up to cover his mouth, his grey moustache poking out from beneath his fist. Although he was a man well into his fifties and seasoned in the ways of business and life, at that moment, he found it hard to compose himself.

"I'll miss the roses very much," she said, pausing to smell the perfume. "These are my favourites. I'll always remember how it really doesn't smell much like a rose at all, more like a peach. Look how the colours blend together, like it can't quite decide what shade it really wants to be."

"Ah, now you've hit upon it," he mused. "Perhaps that's why they remind me of you. Not because you're delicate like a little flower. Nobody in their right mind would have the audacity to compare you to such a thing."

This made them both smile, and broke some of the awkwardness of the moment.

"No," he continued, "because after this plant gathered the gumption to survive the never ending winter rains of Seattle, it bloomed forth in glory, still managing to hold something of itself back. It didn't quite let its full beauty show. It's feisty and so complex, like you. I have no idea why this bud has bloomed early in March. Perhaps it is a sign of good things to come this summer. Perhaps it just couldn't wait. Patience has never been your strongest virtue either."

"That's really quite beautiful," she said. "I never knew you could be so eloquent."

"There are a few things you don't know about me, you know," he replied.

William gazed at the young woman before him, her chestnut hair, not unlike his own, placed erratically atop her head, like some last grasp at childhood. Her slender figure cast an early morning shadow over the well-manicured lawn.

"You have always been my flower, Olivia, and you don't have to go."

"I'm a married woman," she reminded him. "My place is with Frank, in Canada."

"But Canada is so far away," he stated in a tone that told Olivia he really didn't believe it himself.

"Next you're going to say I'll be living with a bunch of savages who live on ice flows all year round. I am an educated woman you know. I shouldn't have to remind you of that. I'll be a short journey away, just north of Vancouver. You can always come see me if you miss me too much."

"And you can always come back if you miss *me* too much," he added.

The two continued their stroll though the garden. The rhododendrons were beginning to form buds. In another month, a mass of royal purple would be in full display along the pathway leading to the home, but Olivia knew she wouldn't see their full splendour this year.

"You've been to Britannia before, haven't you? You've never told me what I'm in for," she noted.

"Your Uncle Aaron asked me to investigate one of his business holdings a few years back," William replied. "He was dabbling in mining himself then, always looking for new money-makers; you know how he is. Since I was heading up there on some investment business myself, I dropped in on the town for a weekend. Despite what your mother might have you believe, it's actually quite civilized. There are over 500 men working at the copper mine. The town's not a bad size. My stomach ulcer was acting up somewhat while I was there and I was relieved to learn that there was a doctor living at "the Beach" as they call it. In fact, there is a tiny little hospital which seems to be able to handle most of the day-to-day mishaps and ailments, which is more than I can say for our own medical facilities at times. Don't get me wrong, I was rather relieved to have to spend only a few days there. I think the isolation will drive you quite insane, you being a big city girl. But you won't be any worse off than you would be in one of the smaller towns here in Washington State. Your mother's sister lives in Spokane, and just try to get out of there in the winter when the snows close the Snoqualmie Pass. Now *that's* isolation."

William sat down on the wooden garden bench he had hand-crafted many years ago. The winters had weathered it over the years, but it held for him many memories of spectacular sunsets with his children on his lap.

"At least," he continued, "you will be able to take a boat into Vancouver every now and then if you get lonesome for some city life. Vancouver's not so bad, and it's rare that there's enough ice in the Straight of Georgia to stop the boats, even in January. That's how you'll get back and forth, on supply boats, mainly."

He noticed Olivia was taken aback by this last bit of information.

"Besides," he said, taking her hand as she sat down beside him, "it's 1915 and we're heading into a new age, let me tell you. If my conversations with the Canadian government continue at the pace they are now, they'll soon be putting in a railroad there too, north-south, just like they've done here. They've got to find a better way to bring that lumber down from the forests to the pulp mills, mark my words. If they had listened to me the first time around, they'd have the confounded thing completed by now, instead of just talking about it. Great Pacific Western Railway indeed!" he scoffed. "Silly buggers."

"Now that sounds more like you," Olivia laughed.

He tweaked her nose like he had done so many times in her life, a ritual between them, and Olivia briefly wondered whether she would ever find that familiarity with him again.

"There's a man up there, McMichael, I think is his name. I'd say he's in his early thirties but he's crusty enough to be in his eighties. Swarthy character…you'll find out soon enough who he is. Don't you go spilling our family secrets to him. He's got his fingers in enough of the pie up there, from what I recall. Don't mention me. I think he'll remember the occasion we butted heads. There's no real reason for him to know you're a Seattle Bower unless that man you married goes and tells him so. I told him I'd flog him if he did, and by God, I meant it. You'd be better off to wait until we have the opportunity to harvest some of that untapped wealth up north, so that you'll be able to provide for yourself once you divorce that man. No sense handing him the money. You've got to be practical."

"Daddy," she said. "I'm surprised that such a staunch Catholic as you would even whisper the word divorce, let alone recommend it. If you want a family scandal to spice things up, open Emily's closet." She looked him in the eye. "I know what I'm doing. I'll be fine. Frank's a good man, you know that."

"Hmm, we'll see. I've spoken to your sister Emily about her gallivanting ways and she tells me it's entirely your fault. She says it all started when you taught her how to tie the sheets to the bedpost and use them to escape out the window and onto the porch roof and off into the great beyond. Something your mother has never been able to figure out to this day. Or at least she claims not to have. Perhaps separating the two of you for a while is not such a bad idea. Your sister is a young seventeen, rather naïve…wipe that smirk off your face Olivia…but she's ultimately sensible, takes after her mother. That husband of yours though, Frank, I'll never understand why he insisted on dragging you, a woman of twenty years, up to that God-forsaken copper mine rather than take the job I offered him here. You go with my blessing, my child, but not my approval. We had this discussion before you married him. They are two very different things."

Olivia smiled. "I never told him about the offer. It never would have worked. You'd have been hard on him to disprove any favouritism."

William Bower laughed in mock disgust. "Favouritism?"

"You know what I mean," she laughed back. "He would have hated you for it."

"I should have known better," he sighed. "Still, if I really wanted him to work for me, I suppose I could have asked him myself, rather than leave it to you. Freud would have something to say about that."

Olivia noticed a vacant look in her father's eyes.

"Dad?"

"Sorry, I was just reminiscing. By God, you were a frustrating child Olivia. Always going against the grain. At four you would turn your head when we were reprimanding you, thinking that if you couldn't see us, we couldn't see you. Your mother and I laughed so hard we didn't feel much like scolding you after that. A devious little mind, even then. No, out of the five of you, if there's one child I worry the least about, it's you. You're the most like me. I've often wished it was your brother Jason, but it's not, it's you. I have very fond memories of you, but I don't want just memories. Promise me you'll be careful, because I have a feeling that life is going to throw you some interesting curves.

You have the stomach for it. You will be fine. Your family loves you very much, and we'll always be here for you. Remember that. Remember to hold on tight to those you love, and that everything material can ultimately be replaced. I love you Olivia, and I trust that God loves you as much as I do and will protect you. It is hard for me to let you go, but go I know you must."

Letting his guard down was not something William Bower was want to do, even amongst his family, as he suddenly remembered. He cleared his throat and glanced at his watch.

"Get inside and say good-bye to your Mother. It's time we were off to the docks."

Olivia turned and took one last glance at her childhood home. Nothing, she knew, was ever going to be the same.

CHAPTER 2

❦

As the boat headed north towards the international border, Olivia smiled, remembering the last few moments she had shared with her father by the pier. She took a moment to gaze at the beautiful scenery surrounding her. Mount Rainier was a magnificent snow topped sight in the distance.

"What are you staring at, Olivia?" William had asked.

"The mountain. It is always different. All fourteen thousand feet of it. Every time you look at it, it's never quite the same. Whenever I lost direction, I would just look up and find it, and I knew it was to the southeast. I am not going to know where my southeast is anymore. I want to hold this vision in my memory."

"You're going up the coast to an ore-mining town. I suspect you'll be sick of seeing mountains soon enough," her father had laughed.

The Captain of the steamer the Northern Mary, Frenchie Cates, had leaned over the stern side of the vessel. Olivia noticed its home port was Britannia Beach, British Columbia. The boat belonged there, and soon she would too.

"Fitzpatrick," he had yelled. "Get yer kiester aboard m'ship. Time's a wastin'. I gotta get 'er goin' while the tides awit' me. I called ye once, me mate called ye twice, if ye aren't here, we're leavin' witout ye. *Merde.*"

"That's you, you know," William cajoled.

"Oh my heavens, I forgot..." Olivia said, astonished. "My married name hasn't quite sunk in."

"Interesting..."

"Daddy, please..." she pleaded.

"You're right. I've said my peace. Good-bye Mrs. Fitzpatrick," said her father as he kissed her good-bye on the cheek.

"Give my love to mama," she said. "I'm sorry she didn't come to see me off. Tell her to please stop crying."

"She'll be fine Olivia. She'll be busy once the baby comes."

"You know Dad, she is getting a little old for that."

William's voice became embarrassingly stern.

"There are things, Olivia, that a respectable woman does not discuss, not even…especially not with her father."

Olivia returned the tone of the voice.

"There are things, my father, that a respectable man, does not do, or at least is more careful about…"

An awkward moment of silence was slowly broken as a smirk crossed her father's face.

"Git yer kiester aboard the boat, before I throw ye in," he laughed, mimicking the Captain's accent. "Have a safe journey. Godspeed, my child."

With that, Olivia had boarded the boat the Northern Mary, waving goodbye to her father and the rather affluent lifestyle she had been raised in. The Bowers may not have been the richest family in Seattle, but they were far from the poorest. William Bower's family had been in the banking business for generations, most recently in California, and were only now going their separate ways, diversifying and using their family connections to spread the new found wealth amongst the old found few. Michael Bower Jr., Olivia's oldest uncle, remained in the banking business along with her grandfather, who had not yet retired. Mackenzie "Mac" Bower, the second born son in her father's family, was the attorney general for the State of Oregon. Aaron Bower, the next in line, was the risk taker, and had several interests, some legal, some not, including a newspaper chain, a metal fabricating plant and running Mexican tequila up through Texas.

Olivia's father had met her mother, Grace, and became betrothed to her while he was away attending university. Grace was the daughter of the mayor of Los Angeles, California. Olivia's grandfather had found that a good business match for his son William, and her uncles were envious for the same reason, her father had told her, particularly Uncle Mac, who had a few other reasons of his own to be jealous.

"One of your Uncle Aaron's football team-mates had set him up with Grace, but he wasn't sure he wanted to go," her father had told her. "So he wanted me to arrive early and see what she was like. If she was less than desirable, I was to make excuses for Uncle Aaron, meet him at the concession stand and he would sit somewhere else in the ballpark and watch the game. We were cads, no doubt about it. I got there a half an hour before the game, and there she was, the most beautiful girl I had ever seen. So I made excuses for Uncle Aaron anyway, told him she was as ugly as sin, and stole her away. I don't think he's truly forgiven me for it, to this day."

William had instantly fallen in love with Grace and would have married her whether she was rich or poor. But as it happened her family was quite well off and rich didn't hurt as his banker father had pointed out.

William and Grace's children had led very comfortable lives. There was always plenty of food and no such thing as hand-me downs. William, being the youngest in his own family, had enough of those in his life because Michael Sr. said he was "rich, not stupid" and refused to throw anything out. Of William's girls, Anne, the first-born, became a nun. She had been born with a quieter disposition and was always a bit of a loner. Olivia, the middle daughter and Emily the youngest, were both quite boisterous, and had insisted upon the requisite coming-out parties into Seattle society. What parties they had been! There had been dancing until dawn. Hundreds of guests from up and down the Pacific coast had come to wish them well. Of the boys, Jason, the oldest, was still trying to find himself, and Bill, who was definitely a Billy and would never be a William, was studying to get his carpenter's ticket. The generations of Bower bankers were not continuing down this particular branch of the family tree, William noted, with some sadness, but not surprise.

Olivia had never been to Canada before. She had met several wealthy Canadians at parties that her parents hosted every now and then at their home, so she knew they were not very different from Americans. Not like the Oriental workers that her father had hired to work on the railway lines stretching down the Pacific coast. They had brought with them completely different customs and beliefs and a language barrier Olivia had found daunting.

But she was leaving everything thing she knew behind her, and beginning a journey of her own.

A low whistle from Captain Cates brought Olivia out of her daydream.

"Yer gonna strain ye neck if ye keep gawkin' at dat pile a' rock, misses."

"The mountains on the horizon, do they go all the way to Canada, Captain?"

"Aye, up de coast as far as I've ever bin. Course, I've been doin' dis stretch of the Pacific Nor' West for thirty odd years now. It's been the liven' fer me, so I dunt see no sense in goin' any ferder. Gets too cold. Dat's Mount Baker to de *est*. Part of de Cascade Range. I tink e's one of those volcanoes, but it be sleeping."

He winked at her.

"Pretty soon," he continued, "we'll be inta de Coastal Mountains. I suppose you'll be gawkin' at dem too. Dat's okay. Visitors always do. Sorry 'bout yellin' at ye earlier. I was tinkin' I was waitin' for a man. Dat's what dey told me, eh. Told me to pick up a Mister O. Fitzpatrick. Ye can see how I was confused. Why don't ye come inside lady, it's gettin' a little cool out. Ye can meet de odder misses we picked up, and her kiddies."

Olivia studied the Captain. He must be in his early sixties, she thought. His grey beard covered the weather worn skin on his lower face. His eyes were the colour of the sea, a stormy grey-blue that she envisioned had seen many hardships over the years. His teeth betrayed the years of chewing tobacco he had enjoyed. He did not wear a traditional nautical captain's cap that her father's friends with sailboats had worn. He favoured a red wool toque.

"It is a little cool," Olivia agreed. She had bundled up in a new blue wool pea coat for the journey, but the wind was picking up. They started to make their way into the cabin. "You know Captain Cates, if I were an artist and someone asked me to paint the image of a mariner, I think I'd paint him just like you. You are just like I would have imagined. I get a sense you've been very happy at sea over the years."

"I'll take dat like a compliment Madame, *merci*."

Olivia noticed him stretch and flex his hand. He had arthritis like her mother did. He wouldn't be sailing the seas much longer.

"Please do," she said. "Captain, I'm a little confused about your accent. It's not like any Canadian accent I've ever heard before."

"Ach, yeh. It's a little bit of dis n' a little bit of dat, eh misses? Me fadder, 'e was a Scotsman. Nae just south of Edinburra 'e was. Came over 'ere on one of the Royal ships as a stowaway. Dey shudda tossed 'im o'er, but 'e could cook up a storm. Dey kept 'im when the first cook died a' scurvy. I 'eard a tale dat it wasn't really scurvy, dat me fadder just says dat cuz 'e poisoned 'im on purpose, so 'e could stay like, but I dunna. 'E met me mum somewhere down de St. Lawrence. 'Dat's a big river. She was a French-Canadian Indian. 'Er mum was an Iroquois, and rumour has it 'er dad was a Jesuit priest." The Captain put his finger aside his nose. "On the Q.T. like. So, I reckon I'm like a bottle of good Scotch whiskey…well blended. I grew up in Sept-Iles, dat's in Quebec, speakin' French and what me dad called an abuse of de English language. But I speak French real good. *Comprenez-vous?* Course I dunt get much use fer it out 'ere."

"You said there was another woman on board?"

"Aye, 'er name is Lucy Bentall. Bin down to Olympia to see 'er kin. Show off da kiddies. Lives at de Beach too, she does. I know 'er husband Marty. Good man. Some sort of mineralogist or sometin'. Knows 'is rocks. Spends most of 'is time in the caves, 'e does. Been to university and all dat. I tink 'e was even a professor once, but now 'e spends 'is days in de dark. Makes ya kinda wunder, eh misses? What's yer fella do up der?"

"I suspect he works in the tunnels too, although I don't know exactly what it is he does. He's a miner."

"Me big foot's been goin' in me bigger gob a lot today, eh misses? Ach ye well, it ain't de sea, mining, but it's an 'onest livin', I'll give yer dat."

He opened the door to let Olivia inside the main cabin. He was shocked by what he saw, a young sandy haired boy, barely more than a toddler, steering the ship.

"Ach matey," he yelled to the strapping middle-aged man on beside the boy. Whadda ye doin' lettin' de laddie at de wheel? We're gonna wind up in the Japans if ye keep doin' dat."

"Sorry sir," the first mate replied. "I was only trying to keep the lad amused for a moment. I wanted to keep his mind off things as he was telling me he was a little tummy sick."

"Come on now wee Robbie, down you get." The Captain good-naturedly took the boy by the hand. "Mon Dieu, it's 'ard to get good 'elp dees days, ye know misses?" said the Captain, shaking his head. "Ach well, no 'arm dun, as de say matey. Da waters are pretty still today, the laddie shouldn't get sickly. Misses Fitzpatrick, why dun ye take the lad to 'is mum. I tink she's in me private cabin just o'er dere," he motioned with his head. "Just go past de galley. Wait, where's me manners? I canna let ye go up der until yer properly introduced."

The Captain took his sextant and tapped on the wall.

"Hey, Lucy!" he yelled. "Get yerself round 'ere. I've got someone fer ye to meet."

The other passenger came out from the private quarters.

Lucy Bentall was perhaps one of the most strikingly handsome women that Olivia had ever met. Her red, flowing, curly hair betrayed her Irish descent, yet the freckles that she had, fell only upon her prominent cheekbones, not all over her body like most of the red heads Olivia had encountered in her life. It was as if they had been hand painted on a porcelain doll.

She appeared to be in her mid-twenties. She was tall compared to Olivia. She may have been five-ten, with a svelte frame that carried her well. She showed no outward signs of having borne either Robbie, or the tiny baby girl in her arms. She had the most piercing green eyes Olivia had ever seen. Olivia had never met many women with green eyes, and certainly not with that beautiful strawberry hair. She was dressed in a bright red Stewart tartan skirt, a heavy red Aryan cable sweater with a matching tartan coat. Her outfit stood out in bright contrast to the weathered backdrop of the interior of the old boat.

"Lucy Bentall," the Captain started, "dis 'ere is Misses Fitzpatrick. I dunna know 'er given name yet, but when ye find out ye can tell me and den if it's okay, I'll call 'er dat because she doesn't answer very well to Fitzpatrick."

He noticed Olivia's pained expression.

"Ach, I'm just 'aving fun whit ye, misses."

"Hello, Mrs. Fitzpatrick," Lucy said, extending her hand. "I'm Lucy Bentall."

Olivia shook her hand.

"Her name is Olivia, Captain."

Olivia looked at her, surprised she knew her name.

"She's Frankie's wife."

"Ah," the Captain said, making the connection.

"It's a very small town, Olivia. I already know a lot about you. Here…" Lucy said, offering Olivia a blanket, "…put this over your shoulders, and let's get outside, I need a breath of air."

"But I keep telling ye, it's na a bad sea ladies," the Captain said.

"Frenchie, that cast iron stomach of yours would stay still during a hurricane. We ladies have a more delicate constitution. Besides, I'm thinking about having a little nip of 'the tonic' and if I show you where I'm hiding my flask of whiskey, you'd be all over me and up on charges too vile to mention."

Lucy pulled Olivia along by the hand.

"Come along Livvy, let's get outside. Frenchie, be a darling and watch Robbie and Melissa while we get acquainted."

She handed him the infant.

"Lucy," he pleaded, "dis is no place for de baby."

"Well, what do you want me to do with her Frenchie? Take her outside so she'll catch her death a cold, or be swept overboard by a crashing wave? I hardly think so."

Frenchie looked at Olivia and rolled his eyes.

"She's a good one for the stories, she is," he said.

Lucy pouted teasingly at the Captain.

"Oh Frenchie, be an angel and hold her for fifteen minutes. That's all I ask."

"Ach, okay, but if de baby, being a wee girlie, has a "delicate constitution" like de two of you and gets sick all o'er me, der's gonna be trouble."

"She'll be fine. Come on Liv."

Olivia had no choice but to follow Lucy back on deck.

"How do you understand him?" Olivia asked once they were out of earshot. "It's hard for me to tell what he's saying."

"Who, Frenchie? You'll get used to him. He's a loveable old salt. Robbie adores him. Frenchie's like a big playmate for him. It's all a big adventure for Robbie. We've been onboard quite a few times over the past few years, but this is the first trip for the baby, so the Captain is a bit nervous with her. I need to get out of town when the weather is good. You'll see. I suspect you'll be accompanying me on a few of these trips."

Lucy leaned closer towards Olivia, and whispered. "I listen to every third word he says, that's the secret. It seems to work."

Lucy let out a laugh that filled the air.

"You don't seem too anxious to get back," Olivia commented.

"You've got to be kidding. Back to what? Back to countless hours of trying to get the mine out of Marty's clothes when they're permanently stained with rust? Back to worrying about whether the men are going to come out of the mine alive each day? No thanks. Honey, if I were you I'd turn around at Vancouver and go back home. You don't need Britannia Beach."

"You're going back," Olivia pointed out.

"Liv, I'm an idiot, plain and simple. More beauty than brains they say…" She let out her contagious laugh once more, "…but I love my husband Marty, and Marty loves the mine. He's a mineralogist, Frenchie probably already told you. Doesn't know the meaning of discreet, Frenchie doesn't. Marty, he tests the quality of the copper ore they bring out before they take it to market. He keeps tabs for his head office in the States. He doesn't actually work for the mine. He's on contract from the United Pittsburgh Smelters. They purchase enough of the ore each year to have someone up at Britannia year round, permanently protecting their interests. The mine used to be owned by the Americans, but a few years back a group of investors purchased it and reformed it under the laws of the Province of British Columbia. So now it's basically Canadian owned and operated. Nothing really changed much with the purchase, other than the names of the owners."

"My husband is the only one who calls me Liv," Olivia stated.

"Well, he's the one who's been talking about you, and that's what he's been calling you, so that's what I assumed you liked. You'd better get used to it, that's what everyone is calling you in that stuffy old town. You're not going to change their ways now. Anyway, we're talking about me. I'll ask about you in a minute. United Pittsburgh offered Marty a job at the head office, but I didn't want him to take it because it was too far from my family in Olympia. I get quite homesick, as you've probably gathered. I'm having second thoughts now, but he's under contract at the Beach for another two years. I'm hoping they offer him a transfer then. We'll be able to move just before the children have to go to school."

"How old are they?" Olivia asked.

"Robbie just turned four last month, and Melissa is almost six-months. They keep me busy, God bless them, otherwise I'd go quite crazy. Sometimes I don't think I was cut out for this motherhood thing. Marty and I met back when he was a student at the university. I had finished school and wasn't doing much of anything. My brother was studying there so sometimes I would go to the library with him. A lot of the photography students were always wanting to take my picture so I think I could have maybe been a model. But Marty and I fell in love and *voila*, as Frenchie would say, I now live in a town of a few hundred people with not a fashion show in sight. How about you?"

"Well," Olivia started, "nothing quite so glamorous. Frank and I grew up together, he's twenty-two, two years older than I am, and we were high school sweethearts."

"High school sweethearts," Lucy taunted, "my, my…"

"We are talking about *me*. You had your turn."

Lucy laughed at her new found friend's confidence.

"Frank's brother got a job at the mine, so he got one for Frank. Only his brother quit and Frank's still there. End of story."

"You're right. That's not very glamorous. And your family, they don't mind you going to another country?"

"My father has travelled around quite a lot. He thinks I'll be safe enough. Besides, Frank's not going to let anything bad happen to me. He loves me too much."

"How long have you been married?" Lucy asked.

"Only just…" Olivia replied.

"Ah, the sound of young love. I'm starting to like you. You're full of hope. Well, full of something, anyway. You might do all right at the Beach after all. God knows I'll be better off with you there."

"Is it really that bad?" Olivia asked.

"Oh goodness no. I'm probably being a little harsh…just a little mind you. The folks there are just so set in their ways. I suppose it's like that in any small community, really. The first thing they'll ask you is what church you belong to, and if you don't, well, heaven help you. Not that there's really a right answer. All the religious services are held together at the school anyway, just at different times on Sunday. It just gives them something to argue about. The ladies have tea Saturday afternoons, and there's an every other Wednesday night euchre game…but wait, if you're really, really popular, you might get a chance to join the quilting club." She sighed. "It gets a little boring."

"If you're bored with the town, why don't you get a part-time job? I hear more and more women are doing that these days. Surely you could get someone to watch the children for a few hours. Won't your husband let you work?" Olivia asked, innocently enough.

"Lordy girl," Lucy laughed, "my husband has nothing to do with it. The jobs they have there are for the men. It's one of J.W. McMichael's golden rules, and Liv, there are plenty of them, all beginning with the word "don't". "Don't let your women out alone after six o'clock. Don't gamble. Don't let a drop of liquor pass your lips past midnight the night before you have to work. And don't ever, ever, think of giving a woman a job that a man has a birthright to hold. I think he even made up some superstition about women working in the mines being the curse of all time. Strange isn't it? In coal mines around the world they're using women and children as cheap labour, but here, in the ore mine, it's forbidden. Unless of course you're a Jap or Chink woman, then it's okay to ask for work. They get the dirty jobs."

"Are there a lot of Oriental women there?" Olivia asked. Olivia had learned through her father that the slang ethnic terms were common in more than one sense of the word.

"Your ancestors may have been on the Mayflower," William had admitted, "but they were in the cargo hold with a lot of the criminals. We've come a long way since then, because our talents were recognized. Never ignore talent, it can make you wealthy a lot quicker than a cutting remark."

They were strong words of advice that Olivia knew to be true.

"Oriental? Well, I suppose they are Oriental. Honey, we're not so conscious about such things at Britannia Beach. They're the Japs. They have their own section of town, Japtown, and they do not associate with us white folk much. Nor with the Chinese either. They keep pretty much to themselves. I'm not saying that's right, but in "McMichaelville", that's the way things are."

"Surely it can't be that bad. You're making it sound like some old western town in a novel where the Sheriff is related to everyone, including the mayor."

Frenchie Cates voice came booming into the night. "Ladies yer fifteen minutes is up. I'm not a babysitter."

"Frenchie," Lucy yelled back. "I was just telling her about J.W. McMichael. Friend of yours?"

"Matey, you mind the wee ones for a moment. I've got to set de record right," said the Captain, bursting through the door and passing the infant to his First Mate who had followed him on deck.

"Lucy," he said, "if I tole ye once, I tole ye twice, I spit on de man named McMichael. One time, a mate of ours, one-eyed Rusty McKay, 'e tried to sneak back some whiskey for 'is own 'ome, but 'e 'ad de misfortune of takin' a wee tumble as he got off me ship. De bottle in 'is 'and, it broke on de wharf. No big problem. But McMichael, 'e got wind of it, and checked Rusty's footlocker. 'E 'ad some good stuff in der, some rye, a little vodka, may be even some Mexican tequila, I dunna, I forget. But I will ne'er forget what McMichael did next. 'E took all the bottles and 'e broke dem on de dock. Said der would be no "outside" liquor in 'is town. 'E told Rusty dat if 'e e'er cot 'im again, it'd be Rusty's bones e'd be breakin' and dat it was lucky 'e didn't fire 'im on da spot and send 'im packin'. But ye know what it was? It was because 'e makes a profit on all de booze dat dey serve at de hotel, cuz 'e owns it, and der was no way 'e would let anyone cut into dat profit. And Rusty was a good customer of de bar, so it would cost 'im a good worker and a good drinker if 'e really got rid of 'im. Worked doh, scared the liven' bejeeses oudda Rusty, I'll tell ye. Never tried smugglin' again. Well, not booze anyway. No Misses Lucy, 'e's no friend of mine. *Non*. Ye be wantin' to stay awee from 'im, Misses Fitz. Trust me. Now gadder up ye belongings, like yer kiddies Lucy, as we're pullin' inta de 'Couve to pick up a few supplies before we go up ta 'owe Sound."

"It's your last chance to jump ship Liv," Lucy said. "We'll be in Vancouver for about an hour."

"No, it's been almost a month since I've seen Frank. They only gave him the weekend for our honeymoon. I can't wait to see him."

"A weekend? Hmm. McMichael was feeling generous," Lucy commented. "Why don't you go upstairs and try to get a bit of sleep before we arrive? We can't have the young bride all worn out before she gets there. I have a feeling you're in for a few sleepless nights."

"Oh, you're terrible," Olivia laughed, "but thanks for the suggestion. I think I will. That is if you don't mind, Captain."

"Ye can take over my cabin just like Lucy does," the Captain offered.

Olivia smiled and headed inside leaving the two old friends on deck.

"Getting' a liddle cheeky der, eh Lucy love?" the Captain commented.

"When I said she'd be having a few sleepless nights, I was not speaking of the lust of a newlywed couple," Lucy assured him. "You know all too well Frenchie, that poor woman is in for the shock of her life."

"Aye, I suppose ye are right der."

The Captain looked at Lucy and winked. "Ye know Lucy, it might be best ye give me yer flask o' whiskey fer safe keepin' before you land back at de Beach and dey start askin' questions. I dunt want them to 'ave to start callin' ye one-eyed Lucy."

"Aye Frenchie," Lucy sighed. "It might be at that."

She handed him the silver flask.

CHAPTER 3

❁

The air-compression wood drills, weighing over three hundred pounds, and taking two men to operate, were running at capacity inside the secondary tunnel, but Frank could still hear McMichael's vocal blast through the noise.

"Do you like working at the Royal Columbia Mining Company, Mr. Fitzpatrick?"

Frank nodded.

"They why the hell did I see you riding up the skip car yesterday? You take the stairs up, all three hundred and seventy-five of them, just like everyone else does when you're inside the mine. And shut that damn drill down when I'm talking to you," McMichael yelled.

Frank and his partner complied, but with the other ten men still drilling into the ore around them, it wasn't much help. McMichael ushered Frank into an enclave. It was slightly quieter and provided them with a bit of privacy.

"Now explain yourself."

Frank thought about what he was about to say. He wiped some sweat from his brow, beneath his helmet. You had to watch what you said to McMichael, especially the tone you said it in. Don Smith had been told to vacate the premises and the town after he had raised his voice to the boss. Frank wasn't about to lose his job.

"I wouldn't normally do that Mr. McMichael, but my leg was sore. It was the end of a double shift for me, and I needed to get up there, because Lloyd needed some help fixing the concentrator."

"What the hell's wrong with the concentrator now?"

"Nothing serious, a bolt had come loose and Lloyd couldn't find where it belonged, so I gave him a hand. Like I said, it was after my shift. I wasn't wasting any company time."

McMichael sighed. "Okay Fitzpatrick, thanks for helping out. I admire men who give a little extra. You should think about taking that management test we're doing. I could use someone with a little initiative."

McMichael liked this man Fitzpatrick. He was young and strong and did what he was told. He had a good head on his shoulders and never took risks in the tunnels, which is why it had angered him to see him doing something stupid.

He glanced down at Frank's leg.

"So what's wrong with you? I noticed you limping earlier. Have you been to see the doctor?"

"Yes. I went over to see him before I started today. He said it's just a sprain. I twisted it the wrong way or something."

"A sprain? What did you trip on? Did John Howser leave those God-blasted rods lying about again? Because if I found out he did, there will be hell to pay. What the hell's going on in there? Those tools are worth hundreds of dollars and he's just tossing them around and leaving them wherever he damn well feels like it. I told him last week to smarten up or he'd get his cards."

"It's nothing sir, really."

"Nothing? You've been injured on the job. That's a safety concern. But you know what's a bigger safety concern? You. Riding up the bloody skip! Really Frank, did you stop to look at the angle that flatbed car goes up? There's no way to strap yourself in. It's designed for mineral transport. It's not a commuter tram. You could have fallen hundreds of feet straight down. Blood would have been splattered all over the place and your brains would have wound up in the ore. Not a pleasant thought now is it? Don't be so stupid next time. I won't have another accident here like the time that kid doctor smashed his head on the tower. On his first day here at the mine! Young man, about to be married, and he meets his maker because he's too busy gawking at the scenery. And it wasn't his fiancée he was gawking at either. It really was the scenery. Stupid man."

"Yes sir," Frank said quietly.

The whistle blew to signal the end of the shift.

"Isn't your wife arriving this afternoon?" McMichael asked.

"Yes sir, she is."

"Then you'd better go home and bathe. You stink man, you stink."

McMichael turned to hop in the exiting commuter tram, taking the miners back up to the beach site. The workers were allowed to ride the commuting tunnel trams only. There were no seats left, so Howser, a young gangly man, gave up his own.

"I want to see you in my office Howser, in a half an hour," McMichael said.

"Yes sir," Howser said with dread in his voice.

The tunnel tram had been McMichael's brainstorm. Getting in and out of the mine had been a time consuming ordeal. The old ore transport cars were constantly breaking down. By the time the men had come to the end of their physically demanding shifts, they were too tired to carry the raw materials out. McMichael decided it would be far more efficient to run a small steam powered train through the tunnel to move both the people and the ore. He did efficiency studies, and provided the owners with a budget for the transportation tram. Within the year they had given him what he wanted. McMichael was able to move twice the loads and gave them back twice the profit.

John Wesley McMichael was a Canadian, and proud of it. A comparatively short man, standing five foot seven, he was none the less solid enough that although the men had many good reasons to hate him, they never dared raise a fist to him. There was a story that his wife had died of physical violence, which McMichael probably started himself to keep everyone in line. But the truth was she had a brain aneurysm that took her life quite suddenly one summer night. He never got over it, and those who knew him before her death said that was when he had turned cold hearted. Some men die of broken hearts, some sink into deep, dark depressions. McMichael just got mean. His only signs of outward compassion ever sighted were for his two young daughters, Lara aged eight, and Christina, aged twelve. He had hired a nanny, an older German woman with grown children in Vancouver, to help look after his children after his wife's death.

The women of Britannia Beach were generally of two minds about McMichael. He was, despite his temperament, a handsome man. He kept his sandy blond hair well barbered and he was always clean. Due to the amount of physical activity he got each day, his body was as lean as it had been when he was a teenager. His smile, when he actually smiled, could warm the chill out of the northerly winds. There were those who lived in fear of his every step, of what he could and would do to the welfare of their families. There were those who craved a piece of him, and were secretly hoping that one day, he would look at them and become bewitched by their charms. And of those women, some wanted to marry him and take a new position in society, but some simply wanted to lie with him, and feel the blood pulsing through his veins, somehow absorbing his power within.

McMichael walked into his office.

"Sarah, I want you to take a letter," he began, "Stuart J. Collin, Vancouver Police Department. Dear Stuart, I have come to discover that just outside the town limits of Britannia Beach is a home that houses ladies of questionable repute. This den of sin is temptation for the many hard working single men employed here at the Royal Columbian Mining Company. The moral disintegration of their virtues and the loss of integrity of my employees aside, I fear that the gambling parlour that is also housed illegally at this address is merely a ploy to rob the men of their hard-earned cash. I trust that you will send a constable up to take care of this matter, or I will be forced once again, to take matters into my own hands. I know we had talked about re-stationing a constable permanently here in Britannia, but you know I don't feel we need a full time officer. Save your money. However if I can borrow one for a day to remove this woman and her 'staff' it would perhaps scare the fear of God into her and cause her never to return. She obviously has no regard for the law here in Britannia. Sincerely, J.W. McMichael."

He ended his dictation.

"Get it out in this evening's post. Oh wait, you can't. It's Sunday. I had forgotten, what with the extra shifts needed this weekend. I'll give it to Frenchie Cates to drop off in Vancouver when he leaves again on Monday. That will do Sarah."

It would also teach Ruby a thing or two about not cutting him in on the action, he thought. He leaned over and tapped on Sarah's desk.

"When I told Ruby Dalton to pack up her girls and move on out, I didn't mean she could set up shop just north of here, outside the town limits, and she damn well knew that. And another thing, that John Howser, you pay him up today until the end of the month. I'm sending him out of here tonight. He's a walking disaster area."

His thoughts momentarily left his business.

"Is my tuxedo ready for the wedding?"

"Of course Mr. McMichael," Sarah sighed. Sarah Lieboldt was one of the few women at Britannia to have a job, and as such, she found herself indebted to McMichael just like the men at the mine. She was a frail thing, almost twenty, lived at home with her parents, and had no boyfriend in sight. She was quite adept at exasperating McMichael with her constant inane questions and tendency to be clumsy. But when it came to math, for whatever reason, she was a genius, which more than made up for her lack of typing skills. What he was getting for a junior secretary's wage was actually a skilled junior accountant, which saved him considerable time and money.

"Isn't Sunday an odd night to have a wedding?" she asked hesitantly, knocking over her cup of tea.

McMichael glared at her. He liked to see the panic in her eyes.

"What exactly are you suggesting, Sarah?"

"Nothing sir," she replied. "I was just making a little friendly conversation." She reached for a rag to clean up the mess. McMichael grabbed some papers on her desk just before the runaway tea spoiled them. The tea had managed to nick the corner of some papers despite his efforts.

"Sorry sir," she blushed.

"I didn't realize we were friends, Sarah. I thought you were my employee."

"Sorry again sir, it's just that some of the ladies were asking…" Sarah regretted saying that as soon as the words were out of her mouth.

"Then tell the ladies, Miss Lieboldt, that my niece wanted to get married this weekend, before she sets off for Winnipeg. I had previously promised the dance hall on Saturday, last night, to the Harper family wedding party, who had as their guest, among other people, the Premier of British Columbia, who, after all that, didn't even bother to show up as you are well aware. Not much gets by you, does it Sarah? Still, it could have been a social faux pas, not to mention a political fiasco, to have bumped them out for the evening. People in this town don't always appreciate what I do for them, you remember that, Sarah. Remember to tell the caretaker at the hall I want everyone out tonight by midnight and by God the men working tomorrow had better watch themselves. That's all I need is drunk and disorderliness at a McMichael family function."

"I'm sure they'll behave themselves Mr. McMichael," Sarah offered.

"Humph," he snarled as he left the office once more, slamming the door behind him as he went outside. He paused for a moment then went back into the office. He wasn't quite finished.

"So tell that to the ladies Sarah, and if you want more time to tell them stories, that can be arranged as well."

He saw her two fingering the typewriter.

"And never mind the letter, get him on the phone."

"Now?" Sarah asked.

"In the morning Sarah. First thing Monday morning, all right?" he said exasperated.

"Mr. Michael, I was wondering, will there be any new single young men at the wedding, you know, maybe coming up for the special occasion?"

"For the umpteenth time, I don't know, Sarah."

The door slammed again. McMichael stood outside viewing the workers heading to their homes. He saw Howser coming down the hill towards him.

"Mr. McMichael, I can explain…"

"Into my office Howser. We've got a few things to discuss," McMichael said sternly.

Frank Fitzpatrick headed over to the cabins on the west side of the beach town. He had been lucky that a vacancy had come up just before his wedding and McMichael gave him the nod to move on in. Up until that point he had been staying in one of the men's dormitories, up on the hill. The cabin was tiny. It had only a kitchen, a living room, a bedroom, a bath and a pantry area, but no one else had anything better, other than McMichael, so Frank was quite content with the place. McMichael was renting the house out to him, complete with water and electricity for five dollars a month, a bargain, even for McMichael. Frank had purchased some paint from the general store and had spent the last few weeks making the place feel more like a home. Liv's father had sent some money for Liv to buy some furniture once she got there, but Frank hadn't done too badly furnishing the house on his own. He considered the money from William just another stab at his lack of ability to provide for a wealthy man's daughter.

He had taken McMichael's advice and poured himself a long, hot bath. As he stepped from the bathroom into the bedroom, he looked at himself, naked, in the mirror. One thing about the job at the mine, it kept you fit and muscular. There was not an ounce of fat on his six-foot frame. His stomach was as flat as a young fighter's. He ran a comb through his mass of dark hair, and debated shaving his day-old stubble. Olivia liked the stubble. He decided to leave it. He would ask her to give him a shave in the morning, perhaps in the bathtub, perhaps together. He supposed that if any of the men saw him primping like he was, he'd be labelled a sissy, but Frank was proud of his physique, and knew that Olivia was too. He figured something had attracted her to him, and it sure wasn't money.

Frank made sure their engagement photo her family had insisted upon was dusted off and prominently displayed on the bureau. He thought about how much he loved her, and what he would do if any of the men got out of line and tried anything. There wasn't a man there, he figured, that he couldn't kill by sheer force if he had to. He hoped Olivia would be comfortable in their home.

Lucy Bentall had helped him pick out a quilt for her, made by the ladies of the town, as a present from him. It took Lucy forever to do it, and he never did figure out why. Lucy was like a ball of fire headed towards a babbling brook. You were never quite sure what would happen in the end, but for sure there would be some steam. She was a bit brassy for Frank's liking, but he hoped that Lucy liked Liv and vice versa. It would be tough for Olivia to make friends here, he knew. She would need some female company from time to time.

An angry pounding on the door interrupted his thoughts. He pulled on his pants and went to the door. It was Howser. Frank let him inside and was taken aback when Howser grabbed him by the throat and tried to throw him up against the wall, his hands clenching around Frank's windpipe.

"What the hell did you say to him?" Howser demanded.

His adrenaline rushing, Frank gave a blow to Howser's nose with his left fist, causing Howser to drip blood, the pain taking him off balance.

"What the hell are you talking about?" Frank replied.

Frank towered over Howser, and now that the surprise attack was over, Frank shoved Howser to the floor quite easily. He had him on the ground and was inches and seconds away from punching him again in the face when he abruptly pulled back. It might have been the look on Howser's face, the look of a defeated man.

"He sacked me. You told him that I didn't put the tools away yesterday, didn't you? I saw you trip and fall."

Frank released his grip on Howser.

"You damn near broke my nose."

"Well thanks for asking if I was okay, you son of a bitch," Frank said sarcastically. "It doesn't take a genius to figure out who left them there, but I didn't tell him. He caught you, leaving them out (himself) a couple of days ago. He put two and two together."

"Geez Frankie, he's got me paranoid. I just assumed he'd figured out how you hurt your leg, and that maybe you had told him, you know, it was because of me."

"The man's got eyes in the back of his head John, you know that. He asked me about it, sure, when he saw me limping, but I didn't tell him anything and I doubt anyone else did. We wouldn't do that to you Howser, you know that. It would go against the brotherhood. He must have just figured it out. I'm no rat. We're all in this together."

"We *were* all in this together. What am I supposed to do now? He wants me out of here tomorrow. He took away my job, my home…what the hell, I might as well go on up to Ruby's and drown my sorrows. A nip of gin and a nip of a young girl's thigh. That might make me feel a bit better. There are still a few things he can't take away from me. He probably can't get it up at night, he's such a hard ass during the day. Do you want to come along and have a boy's night out?"

Frank just glared at him.

"What is with you, John?"

"Some day Frankie, when the itch comes a calling, and it will, you'll feel a little different about such things."

"I don't have any itches, John. Get on out of here before I knock you senseless," Frank said. "You know my wife's due here today. Why don't you just forget about Ruby's and go clean yourself up. Stop by before you leave town tomorrow. You've been a good friend to me while I've been here, and I'd like Olivia to meet you."

"You know Frankie," Howser glared. "I'm not gone yet. Just once I'd like to have one up on old McMichael, just once. He thinks he's the big tough guy, he thinks he's untouchable, but he's not. Wouldn't you like to see one of the brotherhood take him down a notch? This wouldn't have happened if we had all voted in the union like Bill Armstrong wanted. Then the brotherhood would have some real power."

There had indeed been a brief movement to give an official title to the "brotherhood". They got as far as sending a letter off to the union office in Vancouver before McMichael found out about it. The men never knew why they never received a call back for sure, but they had a pretty good idea. There seemed to be more than one piece of mail go missing that week. Armstrong and five of his buddies were suddenly unemployed. That would have been a tough one for Armstrong. He was ready for retirement and only had a couple of working years left.

"Maybe not. But Armstrong is gone, and there is no union. And sure, we'd all like to see McMichael knocked down a peg or two," Frank agreed. "But John, he's not worth it, really. You said your cousin could get you a job at the docks in Vancouver, maybe McMichael just did you a favour." He noticed the glimmer in Howser's eye. He was worried about his friend.

"John, don't go doing something stupid. Leave it alone. Stop by for breakfast tomorrow morning before you leave."

Frank patted his friend on the back and ushered him through the door.

"Life goes on John. You'll find another job. You'll be fine. A year from now you'll be thanking your lucky stars you're out of here. You'll see. Just don't go doing something stupid."

There was a vacant stare in John Howser's eyes as he started to walk up the hill.

CHAPTER 4

The first Japanese pioneer in Canada arrived around the year 1877. Manzo Nagano left Nagasaki dreaming of the New World, and found work on a ship carrying goods from Japan to Victoria, British Columbia. Throughout the years, many young Japanese men followed in his footsteps, hoping to make as much money as possible to bring back to their native lands. The work was hard, and the wages were low, averaging a dollar sixty-five per ten-hour day. If they stayed in Canada for a year, their bosses often rewarded them with an increase of salary to two dollars a day. By order of the crown they could not be pharmacists, lawyers, or members of the government. Because of the cost, it often took much longer than they had originally expected before they had saved enough money to return home.

In Canada, there was a general anti-Japanese sentiment during the early 1900's. There was no real reason for it, perhaps just a fear of an unknown culture invading the land. Shinichi Yada found this to be the case when he arrived in Canada around the turn of the century with his wife Fujiko. He had been a doctor in Japan, but upon arrival found that he was not able to practice medicine in this new, strange country. He found work on a strawberry farm in the Fraser Valley, east of Vancouver, and through hours of hard work and scrimping, the Yada's managed to eventually buy a plot of their own. They had two children, both adults now, a daughter also named Fujiko, who worked as a housekeeper for a wealthy Vancouver couple, and a son Hiroshi "Harry" Yada, who was now employed at the Britannia Beach mine.

It was forbidden in those days, for a young Japanese man to be seen with, let alone marry a Caucasian woman. So it was that Harry found himself like other young Japanese men, looking for a "picture bride" from back home. Ten years ago his wife Akiko had arrived from Japan in this fashion. She had heard that Canada was a wealthy land, where there was lots of food and big homes. She was disillusioned to learn that her husband was poor. There was no big house, but at least there was plenty of food.

"Oh my lord," she said, clasping her hand over her mouth as she gazed at the mining town that was to become her home. Harry had not lied to her, he had told her that he had a "modest" income by most standards, but Akiko felt that perhaps he did not speak the entire truth either. As she got off the boat with the strange white Captain she could not understand, she placed a few grains of rice in the sand for good luck. Now she was about to meet the man that she had only seen a picture of, and she was hoping the image she had created of him in her mind was not a disillusionment, like the image her mind had concocted of Britannia Beach. Akiko was an average looking woman, a bit on the heavy side. You couldn't call her beautiful, but you couldn't call her unattractive either. She fell somewhere in the middle. Her more beautiful sisters had been eagerly placed into arranged marriages by her parents, but it seemed there was no eager suitor for Akiko. Her chance to move to Canada was a chance for her to break away from her parents, which, if the truth be known, is why she agreed to become a picture-bride in the first place. Harry, on the other hand, was an ugly sort. But he was a very kind, very smart man, and in the end, Akiko knew she was fairing far better than her sisters back home. She grew to love him, and he grew to love her, although secretly the fact that she was five inches taller than he was, disturbed Harry to no end.

Their marriage appeared to be a happy one. Akiko became pregnant but lost the first baby in the second trimester of pregnancy. Their second chance proved fruitful however, and their son Jimmy was born. He was a *sansei*-third generation Japanese-Canadian. He had turned seven the day before last, and was happy playing with the wooden toys Harry had carved for him out of scraps of lumber he found around the town site. Harry had loved to carve wood since an early age. But his passion was his knowledge of chemistry, passed to him from his father's medical days. He had spent hours with his father pouring over the periodic tables, as he had once hoped to become a doctor himself here in Canada. He never made it to university, but his knowledge of the elements had landed him a job in the assaying department of the mine, and he was thankful for it. Unlike many other Japanese workers who lived at Britannia, ten to a bunkhouse, Harry and Akiko were fortunate enough to have a small home in the Japanese district of Britannia.

While Harry had learned English early in his life and was truly a bi-lingual asset at the mine, Akiko was still struggling with the language, and because of this, had difficulty at first finding any sort of work at Britannia. She had managed to earn some extra income as a night cleaner for J.W. McMichael.

"What time to do you think you'll be finished cleaning the hall tonight, Akiko?" Harry asked.

"Around two in the morning," she replied in Japanese.

"Two a.m.?" he retorted. "Well, I suppose it'll be midnight before the people are gone and you can finish up. Still, that's very late. We really have to try to find you another job."

"I do not mind," she said.

"Well, I mind. You deserve better than this Akiko. In Japan, your family was in the silk manufacturing trade. A very honourable profession. Many people looked up to your family. I want the same for you here. Perhaps we can work on our English again tonight, hei?"

Akiko sighed and went into the bedroom.

So it would be as it always was, she learning English so slowly, while her young Jimmy picked up both languages, Japanese and English so quickly. He could chat back and forth easily in both, never mixing the two. At least, she thought, he would have a good future in this strange land.

Unbeknownst to her, little Jimmy was learning something else from his father. That love of science had been passed along from father to son and to son again. Late at night, when his mother was working and his father was fast asleep, Jimmy was reading some of his grandfather's old medical texts by candlelight. He particularly liked the ones about Chinese acupuncture and eastern medicine practices his grandfather had picked up while travelling.

Harry heard a scream come from the bedroom. He rushed in to find Akiko standing with her hand over her mouth, pointing at her collection of little silk Geisha dolls she had so carefully packed and brought with her from Japan. They all had little pins sticking out from their heads, arms and legs.

"It is the devil," Akiko cried in Japanese. "It keeps happening. I take pins out, pins go back. This God-forsaken place. Maybe we should leave."

Harry went back into the livingroom and gave Jimmy a smack across the head.

"I told you to stop doing that," he said.

"I need to practice where to stick the needles," Jimmy laughed. "For when I become a doctor. I'm studying hard, like you want."

His father looked at him.

"Maybe we should practice on you, you think it's so funny?"

They stared sternly at each other for a moment and then both broke in to helpless giggles.

Akiko came out and saw them both rolling on the floor, laughing.

"Men," she sighed.

CHAPTER 5

The Port of Vancouver was busy with container ships bringing in exotic treasures from the Orient. Situated in Georgia Straight, Vancouver was the southern most point on the west coast of Canada, and as such was the gateway to the Pacific Rim. Victoria, the Capital of British Columbia, was actually situated on Vancouver Island, to the west of Vancouver, which was a geographical point many found confusing. Although Victoria was the political capital of the province, Vancouver was its major centre. Frenchie figured it was because politicians and businessmen had to be kept apart.

"Ye might get a liddle rain," the Captain said as the Northern Mary headed out of Burrard Inlet. The stay in Vancouver had been a short one, as Lucy predicted.

"Dem North Shore mountains," the Captain continued, "dey tend to sock in de wedder. Way o'er der, way east, dat's Mount Seymour. De one in de middle, dat's Grouse, and de one towards where we're headed, dat's Cyprus. I dunna know how de got dose names, but I do know 'ow de Couve did. It was named after Captain George Vancouver, who first came 'ere. I think he was Dutch, but 'e was a Captain for sure, dat's why I remember. Just a little 'istory for ye. Maybe some day, dey will name a piece of land after Frenchie Cates. What do you tink, eh?"

"I think it's very beautiful here," Olivia stated. "Not the port so much, it looks like most other ports, really, at least to me. But on the other side of the water, by those mountains, it some of the most beautiful country I've ever seen."

"And see that big mountain o'er south, that's Mount Baker we were talkin' about befer. I've seen it up and down de coast, and I tell ye, ye get the best view of it right 'ere in Canada."

Frenchie noticed Olivia removing the blanket Lucy had loaned her earlier.

"You probably tot it would be very cold 'ere eh? *Tres frois*. And yeh, in some places in Canada, ye would be right. The very east coast, dem Maritimes, dey are cold mostly all de time. Dey 'ave storms dat keep a banshee's nipples 'ard until de summer. All de way down de St. Lawrence, de big river dat runs east-west, it's de same ting mostly, maybe not quite so bad. Sometimes de river is frozen with ice. Ye go nowhere. But de summers, de are very 'ot. Very 'umid. Ye sweat like a pig, ye do. Der are lots of lakes and rivers as you go east tru Quebec to Ontario. Den ye get to the Prairies. Deys flat. Lots of wheat grows der in the summer, but it is damn cold in de winter. Dey grow lots of mosquitoes too. And grass'oppers. I dunt know what it is, but dey get more grass'oppers den anywhere else in de world, I tink. And dey 'ave tiny little flies dat bite and make ye scratch too. I went der once to see my sister, den I told 'er from now on, she 'as to come and visit me. Den ye get to Alberta, where der are not so many lakes, but der are lots of mountains, and deer, and elk and wild buffalo. De land der is very rich with minerals, which is very good, and I 'eard talk dat dey tink der maybe a lot of oil under de ground. Can ye believe dat?"

"What about Britannia Beach?" Olivia asked. "What are de, I mean, what are the winters like there?"

"Well, dey are not so bad as some places. You know what it is like in Seattle. Rain, rain, and more rain. Mostly de same 'ting 'ere. De winds dat come across de Pacific Ocean are mostly warm. Dey keep things pretty calm. But sometimes ye get a blast from Alaska, like we did in 1912. Dunt blame me for dat, dat's one of your United States of America. Den it can get really cold. Now where Lucy lives, up at Jane camp, well, we got tirty-five feet a snow one day. Sometimes if it's really bad, we dunt see Lucy fer munts. Sometimes we get a lot of snow. De Beach site, where your house is, dat's a liddle milder, counta de currents comin' off de ocean. You'll need good boots but we'll be able to find ya," the Captain laughed.

Olivia smiled. Frenchie's words were re-assuring.

"You told me you've been working these waters for some time."

"Aye," he replied.

"You probably know the history of the mine quite well…"

Frenchie noticed some hesitation in Olivia's voice.

"Misses, if ye got a question ye be best ta be like Lucy and just spit it out. I'm gittin' old, der's no time for beatin' around da bush," he winked.

"Well, I was wondering…you hear about these things so often and Frank assures me everything's fine, but then he would, wouldn't he? Have there been any deaths at the mine?"

The words were so full of uncertainty that Olivia didn't really know whether she wanted to hear the answer or not.

"No, I can't say as I recollect any of late, at least not any dat didn't 'appen just because de miner was drunk or stupid or both. Der was dat doctor who conked 'is 'ead, and died, but 'e was stupid dat dey. Dat's why McMichael, 'e has de foremen check de worker's breath before a shift ta make sure des sober befer 'e let's dem clock in. I dunna like de man, but 'e runs a tight ship like dey say, I'll give 'im dat. Always lookin' out fer safety, not like de guy who ran it befer. Der used to be more cave-ins and tings before McMichael took over. Tragic dey was, lost a lot of good men. But nottin' like dat fer a while. Not like what 'appened in Alberta. Dat was bad. De whole side of Turtle Mountain, it come tumblin' down. Killed a lot of people. McMichael, 'e read de report on dat and 'e hired some engineers from de Asbestos mines in Quebec to come 'ere and take a look-see. No misses, anyting dat happens now would be an act of God, like dey say. And den God would have to deal with de temper of McMichael, and I dunt tink even 'e wants to do dat, so I dunt worry aboud it too much."

"Do you worry about anything, Frenchie?" she asked.

"Not much Liv."

Olivia blushed when he said her name.

"Well," he said, "if yer gonna get familiar wid me, den I tink you have to extend me the same courtesy. I'm calling ye Liv. At least when it's just us girls talkin'," he winked. "Der's tings in life you can't change. You can't change de wedder. You can't change de mind of the Irish-remember dat when Lucy drives ye nuts. Ye can't change water into wine, even doh it would be a good ting if ye could. So, I try not to worry about worryin'."

"You sound like a smart man," she commented.

"No, I'm not smart. I'm born wid a lot of common sense doh, and I wouldn't trade dat for all the schoolin' and smarts in de world. I've seen many a smart man do a stupid ting, let me tell ye. I got a good memory, too. I hardly ever forget a face. Dat man who was wid ye back in Seattle…"

"My father."

"Okay. Yer fadder. 'E's been on my boat befer."

Olivia remembered her father's warning about telling to many tales about her family to strangers.

"I don't think so Frenchie. People always say that, that he looks familiar to them. It happens all the time. We've often joked that he has a twin brother running around somewhere."

"Well, den, I must be mistaken. Must be de *"deja-vu"*. Dat's what we say when ye feel like ye've seen, or been somewhere befer. 'E must have a common face, like ye say."

But Frenchie knew better.

It had been a rough night a sea some twenty odd years before, the night he carried William Bower up to the Beach. The waters were choppy and an eerie grey green in colour. It was dark and it was late, but no one aboard the Queen Mary was in a mood to sleep. The swells were crossing the deck and the winds had not let up for several hours.

As they passed through Puget Sound, just passed Port Townsend, Frenchie had heard a cry in the night. There, on the starboard side of the boat, was an overturned fishing vessel, with two men clinging to it for their lives. It was a wonder the two ships had not collided.

Frenchie instructed his first mate to take care of the boat while he tied himself to the guardrails and began the rescue attempt. To his surprise, his own passenger, the same William Bower, instantly did the same thing, and together they were able to pull the freezing men from the water. Bower bundled the men up and helped carry them below deck. They knew the men needed to be hospitalized, that they might not make it through the night, but it was too dangerous at sea to take them to Victoria, the closest centre with the right kind of medical care. Even though it meant that Bower would be a day behind for his important meeting, they decided to take refuge in Oak Harbour and transport the men over to the island the next day when the seas cleared.

It turned out that two other men had been lost from the fishing boat that night. How long they had suffered no one knew. Hypothermia had probably taken the fight of life from their bodies. No, the Captain and crew and one particular passenger of the Northern Mary were very indebted to their makers that they had been able to save two lives that night, two lives besides their own.

It was when Frenchie learned that this man Bower, was headed to meet McMichael, that he began to wish they had headed straight for Canada and not been delayed. For even in his early twenties, McMichael had been a force to reckon with. But when Bower finally arrived, there were no harsh words from McMichael. Bower apologized for the delay, told McMichael the story, and

McMichael took Frenchie, his first mate and Bower out for dinner. The first and only time it ever happened. They had talked for hours about the railroad, how it had been promised to British Columbia as part of the province joining into Confederation, and how the scandal of misappropriated election funds had delayed its becoming a reality until the "last spike" had been laid at Craigellachie, British Columbia, November 7'th, 1885. This man Bower, he knew all about the railroads, Frenchie remembered that much. And then the talk had turned to the mine, where McMichael was the foreman at the time, and Frenchie and his first mate had been politely, but decidedly, dismissed.

No, Frenchie did not forget that man's face. But that had been many years ago.

As fate would have it, it was raining as they headed north this Sunday morning, up Howe Sound to the Beach. Captain George Vancouver had named Howe Sound in honour of Admiral the Rt. Honourable Richard Scrope, the Earl Howe. Earl Howe had won many battles for the British Royal Navy, his most famous one coming in 1794, where he defeated a much larger and faster French fleet, capturing seven of their ships in the process. It was a fairly sheltered sound, being cushioned to the east by the lands of the Sunshine Coast.

Lucy had opted to stay inside and tend to the baby. Melissa had managed to pick up a runny nose despite Frenchie's constant tender loving care.

Olivia sat down beside her.

"She's beautiful, Lucy."

"She is, isn't she?"

The baby had been born with a full head of hair of the same nature as her mother's, the curls cascading over her forehead.

"I had a tough time with her," Lucy shared. "Robbie had been an easy birth, but Melissa had turned inside me. I lost a lot of blood, and the doctor didn't think I was going to make it through the delivery."

She paused for a moment and looked at her daughter. A tiny hand reached up and grabbed a strand of her mother's hair. She sneezed, and Lucy carefully wiped her tiny nose with her handkerchief. Olivia smiled. Such a tiny little sound. The baby made a face, but hardly squirmed.

"Robbie used to laugh like crazy when heard himself sneeze at this age..." she paused for a moment.

"The doctor told me that I probably shouldn't have more children, so I treasure these two with my life. I come from a small family, it's just me and my parents, so I just wanted to have a house full of children. But I need to be content with the two I have been blessed with."

Olivia truly didn't know what to say to the woman. After all, she had just met her, and she herself would not have been comfortable divulging such secrets to little more than a stranger. Perhaps, she thought, Lucy felt some sort of kindred spirit with her. Lucy had made the statement rather matter of factly, as if her life were an open book.

The boat hit the dock with a thud. Olivia grabbed a nearby rail to hold on.

"Sorry 'bout dat," came a call from on deck. "We're here ladies."

Olivia stepped back on deck. It was a dreary day at Britannia. The rain was making it difficult to see very far. She could see groups of little cottages, interspersed up the hillside like little individual communities. Further up the hill there appeared to be some dormitories, and she could make out the sign of the red cross on the larger building to the west, marking the hospital.

"Welcome to Britannia," Lucy said, as she bundled herself and her children in the blanket to protect against the rain. Robbie had noticed his father coming down the dock and ran towards him.

"Daddy!" he cried out.

"That's my Marty," Lucy said. "Marty, come here, come meet Olivia."

Olivia glanced around but could see no sign of Frank.

"Pleased to meet you Olivia," Marty smiled. He was a good-looking man, a little shorter and more barrel-chested than Frank, with an easy-going air about him.

Marty glanced around and noticed that Frank was not in sight.

"I don't know where he is," Marty offered. "You're all he's been talking about all day. I saw Howser, one of the guys, at the door a few minutes ago when I was coming down the hill, and Howser, well, he's a handful. I suspect Frank will be here any minute now."

The kind words did little to comfort Olivia. She was miles from home, away from her family, and there was no one there but relative strangers to greet her. She began to fight back the tears.

And they she heard him. The whole town heard him. He came running down the road, (more of a fast limp really, with his sore leg), waving his hands and yelling her name.

"Liv! Liv, I'm here!"

He took her in his arms and she smiled the most beautiful smile in the world.

"I'm sorry I was late. Welcome to your home, baby," he whispered. "Welcome to Britannia Beach. How was the trip?"

"Fine," Olivia said. "Everyone was really nice."

Frank could feel her shiver in his arms.

"You're wet, and you're cold, Liv, come on, let's get to the house where I can warm you up."

Olivia gave her husband a squeeze.

Frank turned and waved to Frenchie and his first mate.

"Thanks for taking care of my precious cargo Frenchie," he said.

"Our pleasure," the Captain replied.

CHAPTER 6

❦

"So how was the trip?" Marty asked Lucy, once they were back in the house and the kids were settled down for naps.

"Oh, you know, the same as usual. Mom and dad held the kids all weekend. Spoiled them rotten. Mom got Robbie a huge sack of candy. Thankfully he didn't eat it all. She said she'd save it for his next visit, and Robbie told her he'd be back tomorrow and to take good care of it. So good luck tomorrow when we have to tell him he can't go. We're going to have to take him down to the general store and get him some candy, you know that. They send their love, and dad said if you could get some time off, he'd like to enter the salmon derby with you and his buddy Roger again this summer. So I told him you would, because you will, right? He was thrilled. Says he's got a new lure to show you that will do the trick. I had a nice time. I actually got a bit of a rest. What did you do?"

"I worked some overtime, which is good, considering apparently I'm taking some time off the 4'th of July holiday to go fishing with your dad. You keep forgetting it's not a holiday up here. The holiday here is on the first of July. Don't worry, I've already got three days booked off. I told McMichael I'd work the Canadian holiday if I could take a few days around the American one, and he was happy. Harry said he would cover me the other days."

She laughed.

"And," Marty said apprehensively, not wanting to change the mood, but knowing he must, "how are you feeling? What did the doctor say?"

Lucy's smile vanished. She sat on the bed.

"He said that she's not hearing properly."

Lucy started to cry. Marty stepped forward and held her close.

"You know how she doesn't react to sounds? How she doesn't seem to hear big noises around her? Oh, I know she reacts to us when she sees us, but remember the time Robbie's balloon popped right beside her and she didn't even flinch? He said it wasn't normal. He said she's going to have to have more tests when she gets a bit older, to tell how much of a hearing loss she has. She's a little too young to tell for certain right now. He thinks it might have been because of the mumps you came down with just before, you know…" her voice trailed off.

"Oh God, Lucy. I'm so sorry."

"It's not your fault Marty, I know that, I didn't mean that," she whispered. But her voice held for Marty, a note of disbelief. "I just don't know how we're going to cope up here if she is deaf. Maybe we will have to move earlier than we planned. To get her some help. There aren't any other deaf children here. We'll need to get her into a special school."

"We'll do whatever you want to do," Marty offered, trying to console her.

"I want…I want them to be healthy beautiful children."

"They are healthy, beautiful children Lucy," he said softly, trying to comfort her.

"What are we going to tell everyone? Even my parents noticed how quiet she was, for heaven's sake. I haven't said anything to them yet. It's only a matter of time before everyone will know."

"Lucy," Marty's voice became firm. "She is a wonderful baby girl. She has a hearing problem, that's all. I don't mean to make light of it, but it's no one's business but this family's. Who cares what other people say? Who cares what other people think. Your parents will love her no matter what. They're great people. We will cope. Be strong, Lucy. This isn't like you at all."

"That's because for once in my life I feel totally helpless."

Marty didn't know how to take that comment.

"You're not alone in this Lucy. You have me, you know. The pain and the joy, I feel all of those things too."

Lucy took a deep breath.

"I know, I'm sorry Marty. I'm just not dealing with all this very well. I can't really say it's a shock because we suspected it. But still, when you have your worst fears confirmed, it's a bit hard to shake the feeling of despair."

"I knew I should have gone with you."

"No, I wanted some time alone, to think about things."

"Things like what?" Marty asked nervously.

"Oh heavens no, Marty. We are fine. I love you. No, I didn't mean that. I just meant, you know, people always expect me to be a certain way. Even you, you just said it. "It's not like you, Lucy." Well, Lucy needed to be someone else for a while. I needed some quiet time. I left the kids with the folks one night and went for a long, long walk. I needed to sort this out for myself, alone, without having to be "happy Lucy." I thought about a lot of things. I though about how lucky we really are, all of us. We have a nice life, and we have each other. And I thought about how she wasn't the only person in the world with this problem, and how doctors were learning more about the condition every day. The doctor told me many deaf people grow to lead normal, healthy, productive lives. I thought about how we'd all have to learn sign language so we can communicate with her, and how we could make it a game for Robbie, you know, tell him it was a secret language only a few people could understand. I had a good cry. A couple of good cries. Then I pulled myself together and went back to mom and dad's and pretended, at least for the time being, that nothing was wrong. So you see, deep down, I know you are right, and this will pass. It's just a little difficult, that's all."

"Still, I wish I could have shared some of that load with you. That's a lot for one person to take on by yourself, and she is my daughter as well. But I do appreciate that you want to spare everyone else some pain. You know your mom and dad will find out eventually, and knowing your mom, she's probably already got it figured out. I'll talk to them about it when I go down for the derby. Let me take care of that burden for you, okay?"

She nodded.

He brought her a handkerchief so she could take care of her tears.

She wiped her nose.

"Lordy," she said, "it's running more than Melissa's."

Marty laughed. The tension had been broken, at least for the time being.

"Tell you what, why don't you go to the wedding with Frank and Liv tonight and enjoy yourself. I'll watch the kids, give you a break. There's not a baby-sitter to be had tonight. I tried to find one. So one of us will have to go, and one of us will have to stay. Did you like Liv?"

"Yes, she seems really nice. She likes to be called Olivia though."

"Well then, it's settled. Go get your party dress out. The bright pink one you love so much. You don't get enough occasions to wear it. Olivia won't know any people there, other than you and Frank, so she'd probably really appreciate you introducing her around. Just take it easy when you do okay? No calling McMichael's nanny the 'ferocious frauline', all right?"

Lucy smiled. "But redheads should never wear pink. And I don't call her that. Well, not within ear shot anyway."

"Like that has ever stopped you before. And you know what I mean. Go easy on the locals. But do her a favour and let Olivia know who's related to whom. Have a good time. Have a few dances for me tonight."

"But what about you? Are you sure?"

"I'll have my own dances at home here with the kids tonight, and just be thankful that I have all of you. It'll be my special time with them. I did miss them, you know."

"Marty, you are a wonderful man. I love you. Thank you," she said, giving him an inviting kiss.

"Don't you need to get ready?" he asked.

"I think the bride's the only one that really has to be on time," she said.

CHAPTER 7

❦

Frank and Olivia stood outside her new home.

"What are you doing?" she asked.

"I want it to be a surprise."

"It already is a surprise," Liv said. "You are supposed to carry me over the threshold of our first home, don't you know anything?"

"Well, I can't do that if my hands are over your eyes."

"Exactly," she said.

"Okay babe. You're the boss," Frank said and picked up his bride.

"I'll cover my own eyes," Liv said, and did so.

He carried her into the house.

"A woman who knows how to compromise," Frank laughed. "I knew I had a good one."

Frank put her down and took a deep breath. Liv uncovered her eyes. She had imagined what the house would look like, in her deepest, darkest moments of uncertainty. But she was quite pleasantly surprised after all. It wasn't the Bower homestead, to be certain, but it was compact and tidy, rather cute actually. She noticed the engagement photo right away.

"Oh Frank…I love it!" she said.

"Really?"

The sincerity in her voice was actually a shock to Frank.

"Yes, show me more. Show me the kitchen, show me the bedroom…"

"Uh, Liv, this is the kitchen. It's a kitchen/living room combined. See turn around, there's the oven."

She laughed. "I'm only teasing you. It's fine, it's wonderful."

She threw her arms around Frank and gave him a tender kiss.

"I would like to see the bedroom though."

She tugged at his shirt. The tug was felt from his heart down through his loins.

"Do I need to carry you over that threshold too?" he asked, pointing at the bedroom door.

"It depends if you want to be lucky or not…" she smiled.

"Why argue with tradition?" he said, gathering her up in his arms once more.

"Do we have time?" Liv asked. "Aren't we supposed to be at the wedding event of the century?"

"Oh, we have time," Frank assured her. "I think the groom is the only one who has to be on time. And just what has Lucy been telling you about the people in this town?"

"She says, they're always late."

"Then so be it."

He took his lady into the bedroom and lay her on the bed he had carefully strewn with soft pillows.

"Have you missed me?" he asked.

"You have no idea how much," Olivia whispered in his ear, her breath heated with the passion she felt. "And you?"

She lay on top of him. He took her soft hand, with the long, slender fingers, and started leading them on a journey that started with a kiss on his lips, and carried down his body, entwining in his chest hairs, skimming over his navel, and resting between his legs.

"Isn't it rather obvious?" he asked her.

The nights had been long since they had been apart, even for this short while. How she wanted to be beside him, walking with him, telling him her deepest secrets and fears in an honesty only man and wife can share. He had been her first and only lover, and his body was a safe haven for her. The wedding night had not been their first night together, that had happened several years before while they were both young and curious. It had been an awkward journey of discovery, with desire overtaking fear as they moved closer to that first sweet release.

There were some subtle changes since she had last seen him. His hair had grown, cascading in waves behind his ears that were never there when his hair was close cropped. His arms and legs were firm and hard due to the constant physical activity. He had a kind of confidence that never surfaced around her family. Perhaps the mine was a good place for him, she thought.

He glanced at her and saw the same young girl he had fallen in love with as a teen. She still had that carefree way about her, but there had been a maturity of late, perhaps due to her leaving her family ties behind and beginning a new life. Frank was glad she was out from her family's influence. It was a time for them to begin something new, something where he would be her lover and provider.

This thought was in his mind as he gently eased her onto her back and raised himself over her where he could take her beauty in. She reached for him, their eyes meeting together, a smile crossing both their faces. So began their intimacy in their first new home, something they would never have again, but always remember fondly.

CHAPTER 8

❀

A little later than originally intended, Frank and Olivia went to the Bentall's to pick them up. They were surprised to learn that Marty was staying home. Frank said he would try to smuggle a shot of McMichael's good rye back for Marty.

When she first arrived at the wedding reception, Olivia felt like she was being starred at more than the bride was.

"Why is everyone looking at me?" she asked Lucy.

"Because you're young, married and not pregnant which is more than they can say for the bride…oh and because you're new here," Lucy laughed. The earlier events of her day were being put behind her.

"What?" Olivia gasped.

"Forget the story about them moving away and wanting to get married in front of their friends. This is an old-fashioned shotgun wedding plain and simple. But relax and have a good time because it is a McMichael shindig after all, and they don't come often and they don't come cheap. The bar is free tonight."

"Are you sure? About the bride I mean?"

"Olivia, this is a small town. I'm sure. Okay, first things first, that stern looking woman with the two beautiful girls, that's Mrs. Schwindt. She's the McMichael nanny. Those are McMichael's daughters, Lara and Christina. They are the royalty of this town."

Mrs. Schwindt, decked out in her Sunday finest of black on black, reminded Olivia of a governess her father had once hired who lasted about a week and a half. She had beaten the children once too often and had been caught by her father who promptly smacked her back and threw her out the door faster than she came in. But the two girls didn't seem terribly frightened of the woman, so

Olivia told herself not to judge a book by its cover. The youngest daughter, Lara, as beautiful as Lucy had said, had long blonde hair tied up in a French braid for the occasion. She wore a lovely knee-length blue velvet dress with lace around the collar and cuff, and a few flowers in her hair. Olivia thought she must have been a flower girl during the wedding ceremony as her dress was a younger version of the one her sister Christina wore. Christina, Olivia noticed, was a truly blossoming young woman with hair as fair as her young sister's, and a smile that lit up the room. She was on the verge of adolescence, and Olivia noticed the teenage boys hovering around her.

"See that woman over there in the green dress with the hideous hat with the bird on it?" Lucy continued. "That's Mary Alice Carpenter, the local seamstress. Had to let the bride's wedding dress out twice the past few weeks, she tells me. Notice how forgiving the cut of the gown is. The older man over at the bar is Dr. Van den Broek. She's been in to see him a few times lately. And the skinny gal over there is Diana the hairdresser. Says that the bride's hair won't hold a curl anymore. Some say that's just an old wives tale but, three plus three equals six and that's about how many months we all figure she is along. Now shhh! McMichael's nearby."

McMichael, playing the role of father-of-the bride for his niece, was pleased with the way the event was progressing. The wedding was a grand affair with plenty of food and plenty of liquor. He was a self-proclaimed frugal man, but when he did things, he did things right. He had even brought a professional band up from Vancouver to provide live music. Everyone seemed to be having a good time, he thought, as he glanced around the room. As beautiful as the bride looked today, there was the lovely Lucy, stealing the show as she always did when she walked into a room. She had danced most of the night away, with the single and married men alike lining up for a chance to take her for a twirl. As gorgeous as she was though, he couldn't explain why his heart literally skipped a beat when he gazed upon the woman now standing beside her, with the lovely long chestnut hair.

"Nice wedding, Mr. McMichael," Frank said as he passed by with a couple of drinks in his hand.

"Is that your wife Frank? Over there with Lucy?"

"Yes sir. Come on over and I'll introduce you," he said, making his way back to the ladies.

Olivia took the beverage Frank brought and put it down on a table.

"Frank, I love this song, let's go dance," Olivia begged, not paying much attention to the stranger with him. She had met so many people that night, she couldn't remember who she had been introduced to and who she hadn't. They were becoming a blur.

"Liv, I'd love to, but my leg's killing me. I'm sorry. I need to sit down for a few minutes."

"Well then," McMichael said, literally sizing her up. "I would be happy to have a dance with your wife, Frank. Olivia isn't it? I'm J.W. McMichael."

Olivia hesitantly looked at Frank who in turn gave her a hesitant go-ahead, as McMichael placed his hand across her back and led her onto the dance floor.

"Oh sure Frank," Lucy said, "throw her to the wolves her first day."

"Why doesn't he ask you to dance Lucy? I mean if he wants to dance so much? I know he likes you. I think upon occasion I've even seen him throw a smile your way."

"Because," she replied, "I'm taller than he is. I tower over him and he can't stand it."

The crowded dance floor soon made room for the new couple.

"Thank you for inviting me, Mr. McMichael," Olivia said. "That was quite kind of you. I didn't know anyone beforehand, but I've met quite a few of the townspeople tonight. Your daughters are quite beautiful."

"Thank you Olivia," he said, taking her into his arms. "I hadn't realized that I did invite you, but no matter. It is a pleasure to have you living in this town. I hope you're happy here. That's a lovely dress you are wearing. Do you mind if I ask where you got it?"

Olivia was taken aback by the question.

"It was a birthday gift from my parents. I'm not sure where they got it."

"Ah, well it's just that the workmanship is so detailed. I thought it might have come from a private clothier in Seattle. My wife had one very similar once. A gift from a friend of the family. I thought perhaps they were made by the same shop, that's all. Your parents have remarkable taste."

"Is your wife here? I don't think I've met her yet," Olivia asked innocently.

McMichael stopped dancing.

"No. She died, I'm afraid."

"I'm sorry sir, I didn't know…"

"Please call me McMichael, everyone else does around here. It's like it's my given name, not my surname."

"I think I'd better call you Mr. McMichael, as obviously I'm not very familiar with you, and you are Frank's boss. That's probably more appropriate. Again, I am terribly sorry about your wife, I didn't know."

McMichael was comforted by the sincerity in her voice.

"Well, you will be hearing many things about me over the next few days, I'm sure. It would have come up eventually. Good to hear Frank hasn't been gossiping about the boss."

Olivia blushed at that remark and McMichael noticed how the colour only made her more stunning.

"Hmm. Well then, I see the music has stopped. I'd better take you back to your husband. Welcome to Britannia, Olivia. Make sure he's not late for work in the morning. I'm sure you'll find everything you need at one of the stores in town. If not, let the shopkeeper know and we will have it brought in for you. We like to keep the money in the town, to keep people employed, so outside goods are frowned upon, just so you're aware. It was a pleasure to meet you," he smiled, releasing her, as the dance was done.

"Well he's a bit of a pompous chore," Olivia said when she was safely sitting on Frank's lap. "Let me guess. He owns the most of stores in town?"

"Nothing gets passed you, pretty lady," he said, kissing her softly on the neck.

The old steam clock in the centre of town struck midnight, letting out eleven short whistles, followed by one long blast.

"Does that go off every night?" Olivia asked.

"It does, but you'll get used to it. I hardly hear it anymore," Lucy replied.

"It's a little quieter up the hill where you are," Frank admitted. "There's been a few nights when I've wanted to stuff a sock in it."

"Last call!" the bartender yelled above the music.

"I'll go get us another one," Frank offered.

"No more for me Frank," Lucy said "I really need to get home, I should have gone hours ago. I'll never hear the end of it from Marty. I was just having so much fun with you two."

"Cut the music," McMichael said, taking the microphone from the singer's hand. "I want to make a farewell toast to the bride and groom."

The musicians stopped playing and the hall grew silent. But only for a moment.

A thundering noise could be heard outside, a noise that was so loud it caused the walls of the dance hall to vibrate.

"Oh my God, what's that?" Lucy asked.

McMichael took control over the panicking crowd. "Men, outside! I want the women and children to remain indoors. Mrs. Schwindt, take care of the girls. Keep them inside."

"What is it? An earthquake?" Olivia asked. Earthquakes had been known to occur at various locations up and down the Pacific coast.

"I don't know Liv," Frank replied. "Do what he says, stay here, I'm going outside."

The rain had mercifully let up, giving the men emerging from the hall a clear look at the horror that was unfolding before them. A torrent of mud and debris was coming down from the top of the Jane Mountain at a tremendous speed. The entire north face of the mountain above the 1000-foot mark had split from the mountainside and was sliding down towards the town site. The noise became deafening as the rock crushed what had once been longhouse number six, home to eight Chinese workers of the mine, their cries for help stymied by the rumbling force of Mother Nature. Louder and louder the noise got as the rubble worked its way like falling dominoes down the side of the mountain, toppling one structure after another and carrying parts of them in its path of destruction.

"What do we do?" Frank asked McMichael.

"Nothing. We do nothing."

Frank looked at him cold-heartedly. McMichael read his mind.

"Right now, we are safe and we are alive. She's cutting a path down the east slope. Simpson, get Dr. Van den Broek over here. He's been at the bar all night, so he's probably still there. Get him some coffee and sober him up. I want every available medically trained person over to the hospital immediately, and that includes the vet. Christianson, start knocking on doors and get every available man down here and form rescue teams. We're going to need to get up there and get help to those who need it. You, Clarkson, we'll need some stretchers from the hospital and Jeffries, get the stretchers from base camp. The dead are going to stay dead. Got that? We take care of the injured first. But we are not going up to the top camp until it is safe to do so."

Lucy, true to her nature, came out from the hall to take a look despite McMichael's instructions not to do so.

"Get back inside," McMichael yelled at her.

"Oh my God, it's going towards my house!"

She froze in horror.

"I said get back inside Lucy!"

"My babies!" she cried, and bolted into the street. "Oh my God…my family…"

McMichael ran after her and grabbed her forcefully. "I said get inside." He shook her. "Do you hear me? Lucy!"

"Yes, of course I hear you…oh my God, my little girl, she can't hear the noise…"

"Leave her alone," Frank snarled, his hatred for the man pulsing through his veins. How dare he rough up the woman. Could he not see the shock draining all but the slightest colour from her face?

"Do you really want her to see this Fitzpatrick?" McMichael asked, turning her head and giving her to Frank, a fleeting moment of compassion in his voice. "You get in the hall, and you tell that young wife of yours that you need her to keep Lucy and the other women who are in a state of shock, inside the hall. We will get some blankets brought over. Olivia's new here. She'll be able to help them without any pre-conceived notions or prejudices. I need her to be compassionate. You don't need any training for that, but it's not something all of us have. From where I'm standing, you and your wife have come out of this very lucky. So you save that attitude of yours for another time and place. I have a job to do, and right now, it isn't very pleasant. I have to count the dead. I have to decide where to set up a temporary morgue. Do you really want to be in my position?"

Frank, somewhat humbled, took Lucy back inside. There was wisdom in McMichael's words if not in his actions.

The thought of the lives of her loved one's ending so abruptly was too much for Lucy to bear. She sobbed hysterically.

"Oh my God, Marty!" she wailed. "Marty's gone…and Melissa, she just had a little cold. I should have stayed home with them. I should have brought them to the wedding anyway. Robbie wanted to come and I said no, I didn't think there would be any other children here…"

"My lord Frank, what is it? What happened?" Olivia asked.

"Mountain slide," he replied, nodding towards Lucy. "She's right. They're gone. There's no way they could have survived that. The whole two upper levels of the town…"

Frank's voice choked and he could not continue.

Olivia remembered her new friend's conversation on the boat. How these were the only children she would ever be able to have.

"What?" Olivia asked, shocked.

"I saw it, Liv. I saw the rocks come crushing down on their home. It pummelled it like it was made of paper. There's nothing left. McMichael's asked if you could stay here, with her and the other women, in the hall, as there's going to be more bad news tonight. I guess he thinks you've got a warm heart. Please, stay with her, and help the others. I need to go back outside to help."

Olivia put her arms around Lucy.

"Lucy, if there's anything I can do…"

Lucy just looked away.

What can anyone really do when your family has been taken from you in one swift act of God, Olivia asked herself? Call it Mother Nature, call it fate…call it what ever you want. Nothing prepares you for a loss as great as she was suffering.

Olivia sat her down and Lucy began rocking, in a catatonic state.

Frank went back outside. The tons of rock had crashed down to the lower level campsite, taking Lucy's home and five others along with it, and reduced them to rubble. The thunder was now silent. There was devastation everywhere. People started to emerge into the street with candles.

Akiko, who had been making her way over to the hall when the rumble began, turned around and glanced towards her home, where she was relieved to see Harry and Jimmy safe on the doorstep. Their home had been spared. She must remember to burn incense, she thought, in honour of the saving of her family's life.

"We need blankets taken to the dance hall. Go get them," McMichael barked at her, and she was only too happy to do so, to be of some assistance. She searched her mind for the English words to say. "So sorry," was what she was able to come up with.

McMichael nodded.

"I want every man available to get his flashlights and gear and assemble at the foot of the mine. Divide up into crews of four. Do not separate under any circumstances. Go up and down the mountain together. I want you to report the number of injured people to your crew chiefs. I am going to ask you to make a judgment that I hope I never have to ask you to make again in your life. If they look like they are about to die, they probably are. Leave them. If they are talking, in pain, but able to move and speak coherently, leave them for now. Take the most severely injured out first. Injured means alive, unconscious with a pulse, turning blue, or bleeding severely."

He touched under his neck.

"You feel your own pulse under your chin? That's what you're looking for. If they don't have one, they don't go. Now let's get to it."

The men broke into groups and started to make their way up the mountain.

And like a moment's rest from the tragedy surrounding him, Frank came across an extraordinary site. There at the base of the rubble, was Tan Chui, one of the immigrant workers from longhouse six. He had come down the entire side of the mountain inside a ball of debris. Like a massive snowball making its way down an avalanche, Tan had tossed and rolled down to the town. Frank glanced up at the distance he must have travelled and shook his head.

"Mr. McMichael, come see this. You're not going to believe it, but I think he's still alive."

McMichael began to walk over towards Tan. He touched his fingers to his neck again to remind Frank to check to see if Tan were indeed still alive. As Frank moved aside some wood and mud, finding Tan's head, then his throat, Tan let out a moan, scaring Frank half to death at the same time. Frank quickly pulled back his fingers from Tan's throat.

"I'd say he's alive," McMichael agreed. "Get him over to the hospital."

Tan's face was beginning to swell, his face covered with lacerations. Pieces of wood and glass were embedded in his forehead, which was bleeding profusely.

"Should we move him?" Frank asked.

"Well," McMichael paused, "we really don't have a lot of choice, we don't know how secure this area really is. Clear the rubble from around him as best you can. Keep his neck straight and slide that stretcher under him. It'll take a few of you to do it. That's why I wanted you in fours. Get some cloth and put some pressure on that forehead wound. Don't worry, it looks worse than it is. The head tends to bleed. That's the least of his troubles."

"Thanks sir," Frank said.

"No, thank you men. But that's the only time I'm going to say it to you tonight, so make it count for everything you do."

Sarah Lieboldt crept up to McMichael. He turned towards her. She was shaking, and white as a ghost.

"What is it Sarah," he asked, this time, with patience.

"I was just thinking sir, it's Monday now. Should I get the police on the phone?"

There was almost a smile from McMichael.

"Indeed it is, Sarah. That would be a wise thing to do. Don't tell them about Ruby, we'll deal with that another time. Tell them I will try to be there in a minute. And get yourself a blanket, okay?"

And as McMichael headed towards his office, he too, saw something quite extraordinary. There, candle in one hand and cart handle in the other, was young Jimmy Yada, pulling an injured man over to the hospital in his rickety old wagon.

"Do you need some help there?" McMichael asked.

"I think his leg is broken, but I can manage, I'm almost there," the boy said, rather matter of factly.

McMichael took a closer look. The boy had taken a piece of lumber from the rubble and secured the man's leg to it with some torn clothing, making a quite reasonable splint for the leg. The man, who spoke little English, made an O.K. sign with his thumb and his index finger and flashed it at McMichael.

"So you can doctor," McMichael said, highly impressed with the lad. "Carry on."

CHAPTER 9

The sun was rising lazily over the Cyprus trees as if nothing about this day was out of the ordinary. A hawk circled above the town, its massive wingspan casting large shadows on the sand. It hovered and cried, waiting to scavenge the dead and decaying if only the humans would leave. Eventually it was chased away by a majestic bald eagle, which, while equally as curious, found more sustenance with the offerings of the Pacific Ocean.

Olivia and Frank awoke from what had been a very restless sleep for both. It had been almost five a.m. before Frank was able to go to the town hall and bring Olivia back to their house, a home that had been thankfully spared from destruction.

"How are you?" he asked, brushing a delicate strand of chestnut coloured hair from her face as she lay in bed, nestled in the pillows. He was hoping she didn't want to turn around and go immediately back to Seattle.

"Fine, I think," she yawned. "Although I certainly didn't expect to spend my honeymoon like this."

It was not as if Olivia had grown up with the notion of marriage being the be all and end all of her life. Her mother had instilled in her the knowledge that the roadway of life was full of ups and downs, and marriage was just a stepping stone on the path along the way. Still, it had been what she desperately wanted, to be wed to Frank, her high-school sweetheart, and be accepted into a couple's society. She was so much unlike her older sister Anne, who had chosen to forsake marriage and children, and give her life to God. Olivia did not expect to become rich, but a life of service and poverty was definitely not for her. Some couples, her mother said, had very rocky beginnings to their marriage and wound up happy for their entire lives. Others, she had told her, looked outwardly blissful but were internally self-destructing. Olivia hoped her own marriage was coming in like the proverbial lion and would go out like a lamb.

Frank entwined some strands of her hair around his finger.

"No, I guess you didn't. I'm sorry. I'll make it up to you Liv," he said. "Tell you what, come summer, we'll go away for a bit. I hear there's a nice resort on Vancouver Island, across the water. We can get away for a few days, lie on the beach, and go to a fancy restaurant or two. Would you like that?"

Olivia smiled, but said nothing. She stretched her slender arm across her husband's bare chest, and tried to return to slumber. But the image of her new friend Lucy, and the anguish of the night before, played over in her mind, keeping her awake. She had asked Lucy to come home with her, but Lucy had shaken her head, declining the offer. Olivia felt Lucy must have wanted to be with her friends in town that she had known for some time. They would probably know how to comfort her better, appreciating the despair of the situation more. That would be only natural, after all the two women had only just met. Still, Olivia felt a kindred spirit to the woman who had unconditionally offered her friendship on the boat trip up the coast. She hoped that sometime she would eventually be able to repay that kindness.

Olivia rolled over, her bare back now turned away from her husband.

Frank reached around her and cradled her breast in his hand. He came closer, kissing the nape of her neck and holding her tightly. She could feel him pressing against her, his body getting harder with each quickening breath he took. She turned and put her arms around his broad shoulders, drawing herself nearer to him, to the comfort she was yearning for.

His lips delicately traced her face. A simple caress on the tip of her nose. Tender butterfly kisses on her eyelids. He licked her ear, and feeling her rise, he breathed softly into her lobe. She moaned softly. He reached down and touched her gently, stroking her until she responded with long sighs. She needed his closeness and continued to encourage him. He slid inside her, and what energy the two had left was now involved in a sensual cadence, each body keeping time with the other. He waited until he could feel her tighten around him, and then he began to move rhythmically, causing her to completely lose control to him. It was then that he let himself go, with an eruption that shook his entire body. The emotion he had bottled up for the last eight hours had now been sweetly released, leaving him utterly exhausted. He rolled over and finally, fell fast asleep.

Olivia held him, her head on his chest, listening to his heartbeat, until eventually sleep overcame her as well, if only for a short time.

The sun was rising through the window, rays of light coming across her eyelids. She got up and went to the window, intent on shutting the blinds so that Frank could get some more sleep. She could see down to the waterfront from her home. The streets were empty, except for a young Oriental boy passing by. She could see that man, McMichael, standing defiantly steadfast with no outward signs of weariness. He must have had a night even worse than her own, she thought. She stared at him for a few minutes, somehow fascinated by the man the town called "boss."

She looked over at Frank, who was still asleep. How peaceful he seemed right now, and how handsome he was, the blankets strewn haphazardly across his naked body. She glanced at him for a few moments, thinking about how much she loved this man, this man she had known for what seemed like forever, this man who brought her to this strange little town. She smiled. It would be all right.

CHAPTER 10

McMichael stood on the steps of his office building, surveying the damage. The night had been long, cold and never ending. Most of the men, including him, had not been home, not even to change out of their sweat-drenched, bloodstained clothing. The town was virtually silent, its people exchanging not words, but looks of either sorrow or relief, depending on whether or not their loved-ones had made it through the night with their lives intact.

He saw Harry Yada coming around the corner. His clothes were dirty and torn from the night before, which, for the immaculate Harry, was quite out of the ordinary. McMichael motioned the man over.

"Harry," McMichael said to the assayer. "There's a rumour I'm hearing circling among the men that John Howser had threatened to show me who was boss last night and was responsible for all this."

The two men looked at the ruins from the mountaintop on down.

"I somehow doubt that the story is true," McMichael continued. "You understand the language of the rocks better than anyone does. Harry, what the hell happened last night? What brought the side of the mountain down?"

"I cannot say for sure," Harry said. "But, I do not believe that this wrath was man-made. I heard the talk too. They think Howser threw some dynamite down a fissure? That's what they're saying, hei? But even that wouldn't do this kind of damage as you know. I have also heard the Chinese say that it was Buddha, avenging the landlord because they could not get any rice wine at the general store."

Harry paused and surveyed McMichael's face after his bold comment. McMichael controlled what was and wasn't stocked at the general store, and for many of the Orientals, this had been a bone of contention. There was a brief recognition of the insult in his words, but McMichael let it pass for the time being.

"Well you want to hear all the gossip, hei? I suspect the truth is somewhere in between," Harry commented.

McMichael remained silent for a moment.

"I understand they found his body near the top of the mountain."

"Yes. Parts of it anyway. His torso was entwined with that of a young woman from Ruby's when they found him. I do not think he blew up the mountain, boss. I think he was busy."

It struck McMichael humorous how sincere Harry was in his statement. But he did not laugh out loud as he did not wish to offend him.

"Harry, we haven't had any aftershocks today. Would you go up to the top of the mountain and take a look around? Let me know what you think."

Harry looked warily up the slope. A look of uncertainty fell upon his face. McMichael noticed this.

"The crews have been up and down all night Harry, I believe it is reasonably safe now."

Harry hung his head.

"Reasonably is not one hundred percent," he said.

"I am not asking you to because I want to make you the sacrificial canary."

It was McMichael's turn to watch the face of Harry, to see if he recognized the reference to the inhumane practice of sending Chinese railway workers into the tunnels with only a live bird to see if the air was poisonous or not. He knew this would get a reaction from him. He knew that Harry did not like being mistaken for someone of Chinese decent, much as some of his Chinese workers found it offensive to be thought of as Japanese. He knew the assayer to be a man with his own hidden prejudices. Harry's body stiffened. He grunted.

"They say Chinese workers were in the mine yesterday. Very bad luck, you know."

"Harry, this act of God hit us all. The Canadians, the Americans, the Indians, the Brits, the Japanese, the Chinese…it did not play favourites. The Chinese cooks always take the shortcut through the mine to the galley. Always have, and always will, and you know that. This has nothing to do with superstitions. This has nothing to do with the rice wine that, by the way, your own wife was asking me to stock the other day, never mind the Chinese. We need to set aside our differences. I asked you to go up there Harry, quite frankly because you are probably the most astute man of science I have here in Britannia, now that Marty is dead, God rest his soul. I trust your judgment and your knowledge of the rock. News of this disaster has reached Vancouver and I'm sure the authorities are going to want some answers. I don't expect you to know "one hundred percent" what happened, but we'll be able to rule some things out I suspect. For example, people will want to know if an earthquake caused this. I don't personally think so, as the damage seems to have originated from the top of the crest. We need to be able to give people answers. The true answers."

Harry thought about this for a moment. He turned and gazed towards where the Bentall home had been only a day before. They had always shown such kindness to the Yada's, not like some of the other Caucasian families living at the beach. He had heard Lucy call him a Jap, but he didn't think she really thought it was demeaning when she said it. It was almost like a nickname, unfortunately, to her. Marty just called him Harry. Or sometimes, Mr. Yada. Harry liked that. Marty often called him Mr. Yada in front of McMichael, giving him respect.

The Bentalls had invited the Yada family over for Christmas turkey this past year. Harry and Marty had drunk wine until the wee hours of the morning, discussing the uncertainties of the world's politics. Marty had told Harry that Europe was having some problems, some big, bothersome problems that weren't going to go away. Harry tried to explain the problems in the Far East. Eventually the wine bottle was empty, and Harry had run home for his own bottle, and introduced Marty to sake.

His wife Akiko had brought some colourful squares of paper over and showed Lucy how to make little animals by making folds in the paper. An introduction to origami. Akiko was able to pass the time with Lucy without talking in this way, and Lucy had truly appreciated the lesson. Akiko was a master at it, and could make the miniature objects quickly, with perfection. Lucy's took longer, and her unskilled hands made rather strange shapes, but she found the art fascinating and admired Akiko's talent. The children had loved them. Akiko strung them together and hung them from the baby's crib so she could play with them, the colours enticing playful swats from Melissa. Lucy made sure she brought more pieces of colourful paper back for Akiko on her next trip out of town, a generous gesture to show Akiko how much joy that evening had given her. Akiko had beamed ear to ear, Harry remembered.

Little Jimmy had split the turkey wishbone with Robbie that night. The bone was tiny and it hadn't taken much strength for the boys to snap it in two. Jimmy had wound up with the short end of the bone, but had remarked that Robbie needed more luck anyway, in a not so hidden attempt to save face. Perhaps Jimmy had been right about that, Harry now surmised. It was a wonderful evening, two families from different cultures sharing the celebration. Although Marty had been Harry's boss, there had been no posturing. Marty was a fair man and a hard worker. Harry was going to miss Marty. Marty was an educated man, something Harry held in extremely high esteem. Marty would have known what caused the slide. He owed it to his friend's memory to try to find out why it happened.

"I'll go with you if you think it's necessary," McMichael offered.

"It is true. I probably am the smartest scientist you have now," Harry agreed. "But I am not a coward. I will go. Alone."

"Thank you," McMichael said. And he meant it.

Harry headed up the mountain. McMichael began to walk towards his office.

"Now where the hell is Sarah?" McMichael said to himself.

He had not seen his secretary in the office when he had strolled by the front window earlier. He knew she had gone over to the hall after calling the Vancouver police for him last night, but he had been so busy, that he never had a chance to find out what had been the outcome of that conversation. It was probably a conversation that he should have had with the police himself, but there just hadn't been the time. They were most likely going to send a man up to investigate. McMichael wasn't all together certain he wanted another constable at Britannia. There had been a small force in town once, until budget cuts sent them back to Vancouver, and he hadn't been all that bothered to see them go. There had been a drop in ore prices, McMichael had laid off a third of his men, and had been able to justify a smaller community able to police itself. It was easier running the town his own way. He had elected Les Ferguson his town enforcer. Les was one tough character, who had a passion for cheap women and beer. McMichael saw to it he got everything he needed to feed his vices, and in turn, Ferguson did everything McMichael asked, legal or not. It was a good working relationship, but he had a feeling it was about to be curtailed. McMichael thought whoever they sent up was going to be staying for a while. Stuart Collin had been keeping tabs and knew the town was prospering again. The town was getting too big to police itself, Collin had warned. Until last night McMichael had proved him wrong. No one stepped out of line in town for long. The small jail they had built on the outskirts by the cemetery was rarely used more than a night. The men would sleep it off with a reminder of life's frailty near by. But this time, this was different, McMichael admitted. He needed some help, at least initially, sorting all this out. But how would he get rid of the officer when things started to get back to normal? That would be a problem he would have to ponder later, he thought to himself.

For now he had to concentrate on what the owners of the mine were going to be asking questions about over the next seventy-two hours, let alone what the authorities would want to know. The authorities would be immediately pre-occupied about the care of the townspeople, who actually, were being very well cared for under the circumstances. But the owners, well, they would be worried about liability. Thankfully McMichael had commissioned an engineer's report on the structural safety of the mountain only the month before. Having learned from an earlier unpredicted landslide at Tunnel Mountain in Alberta, McMichael had wanted to ensure that this mountain was stable and talked the mine's owners into paying for the analysis. They had been reluctant to do it at first, but had eventually agreed. They would be very pleased with that decision now. The mountain had passed with flying colours. McMichael had done all he could to provide for the safety of the people. This would, in the end, prove to be his saving grace, putting an end to the police investigation. It would eventually be deemed a force of nature, the freezing and thawing of the rock taking its toll from centuries of wear and tear. But where the hell was the copy of the report now? Sarah was the last one with it, and that, was a potential problem.

He was distracted for a moment by the sight of Jimmy Yada pulling his wagon through town yet again, this time loaded with tea pots and cups.

"Jimmy," he yelled. "Come here a moment."

Jimmy at first did not hear him, so McMichael yelled again, somewhat louder this time.

"Jimmy Yada! Come here my friend, the little ambulance driver. Do you know there are jobs for grown men doing exactly what you did here last night? You've got a bright future ahead of you Jimmy; you just keep at it and stay out of trouble. You'll be able to drive those gas-powered automobiles. Now wouldn't that be something? Now tell me, what are you up to today?"

Jimmy froze for a moment, looked warily around and started over towards the man. McMichael crouched down to the boy's level and examined the contents of the wagon. "What have you got there?" he asked.

"Tea."

"Tea?"

"Tea." Jimmy nodded.

"I didn't know you were a man of such few words," McMichael said to the young boy.

"I'm just curious. You're not in trouble. What exactly are you doing, Jimmy?"

"The people here are all upset. Because of what happened last night. I am bringing them calming tea. No caffeine."

"No caffeine?" McMichael said, amazed by the young boy's knowledge. "What is it then?"

"Herbal tea. Chamomile. My grandmother sent it to us. It was a present. She told my mother in a letter that it is very healthy. She told her it would be soothing. My mother sometimes feels lonely and upset and my grandmother thought this would help. I think it works because my mother has stopped crying so much lately. Would you like some?"

McMichael smiled to himself. Jimmy probably revealed more about his mother during that conversation than Akiko would have liked, as children often do. He hadn't noticed a change in Akiko himself, but then he didn't pay that much attention to her.

"Well, that would be fine, Jimmy. Yes. Thank you."

Jimmy took a small demitasse cup from his wagon and poured a little tea into it. McMichael took a sip. It was quite good. He might have to think about stocking some at the store.

"The water has been boiled," Jimmy stated. "It is safe to drink."

"I wouldn't expect anything less from Harry Yada's boy," McMichael said. "Would you like some money for this son?"

When he finished he gave the cup back to Jimmy, who also had the foresight to bring a bucket full of soap and water to wash it with, and a towel to wipe it dry.

"No, Mr. McMichael. I must do this for the people. For kindness. My father says it will come back to me three-fold. It will help us become centred once again." Jimmy put his hands together in a prayer-like fashion and gave a slight bow.

McMichael clasped Jimmy's hands and gently pulled them apart, stuffing a nickel into his palm regardless.

"You are quite an extraordinary boy. Your father should be proud," McMichael said to Jimmy, who bowed his head but could not hide his grin. "It is quite considerate and kind of you to share the gift your grandmother sent your family. But always take the money. You've got to cover your expenses, charity or not. Carry on son."

"Mr. McMichael," the boy hesitated. "I am going to be a doctor some day."

"Well then, we'll have to find someone else to drive the ambulance, won't we?" McMichael laughed. "You keep your eyes open for a few good men for me."

"Yes sir," the boy agreed.

Jimmy left up the street with his wagon, the nickel tucked safely in his pocket. McMichael opened the door to his office and went inside.

Sarah, who had obviously not been home, had now arrived. Her hair was tossed on top of her head, and her normally primly pressed dress was wrinkled as though she had slept in it. But other than that, she actually seemed quite in control under the circumstances. She was sitting at her desk, going over the books.

"Mr. McMichael," Sarah said. "I spoke with the Vancouver police last night. I told them there had been a landslide. They said they were sending up an officer, and that he should arrive sometime today."

"Good," McMichael said. "I suspect he will be here a while. Send Akiko up to John Howser's house to clear things out and clean it up for the constable. He can stay there while he's here."

"They said he would be moving up here..." Sarah said nervously, not sure how her boss would respond.

"Well, then you'd better tell her to clean it good. And charge him two dollars more a month than Howser was paying. No employee rates for the police. We want to make that clear."

"I believe he's bringing some doctors and nurses up with him."

"Then call the hotel, make arrangements for the medical staff to stay there. Tell them it's no charge. At least for the time being. If there's too many of them we'll have to billet them with families in town. Anything else?"

"Should we have the pastor bless the house, you know, since John's dead and all? Get rid of any evil spirits lurking about?"

"We could if we knew if the pastor lived through the night. I haven't seen him myself. And if you do find him, I think he's going to be a bit busy with pastoral care, funerals and things. Maybe you can just whip up a séance Sarah, and be done with it. On your own time of course. Which reminds me, people are going to need more candles after last night. All those vigils in the street. Get down to the store and tell Joe to put the price up five percent."

"But sir," Sarah began to plead. It shouldn't have surprised her that her boss would try to profit from the tragedy, yet it did.

"Anything else?" he asked, the tone of his voice telling Sarah he was losing patience.

"Um, no sir, I don't think so anyway," she replied.

"Good. Can you find me the engineering stability report?" he asked.

Sarah looked confused.

"The papers that the engineers left. Remember the men who were here last week? I'm sure you remember the men Sarah. They had you type a report, one that said they thought the mountain was safe and sound. They signed it, and they put a seal on it, and they left us a copy. I need that copy Sarah."

This rang a bell with her.

"Oh yes, I remember the men. Quite distinguished, weren't they?" Sarah appeared to go off into dreamland.

McMichael coughed loudly bringing her back to reality.

"Oh, the report! Ah, no sir, I've been looking all over for it. I thought you might want it. I know it is here somewhere…"

"Sarah, do you realize how important that piece of paper is?" His voice was full of exasperation.

He leaned over her desk, and a drop of perspiration fell from his forehead onto the ledger she was working on.

"Yes sir," she said, trembling. She felt herself turning red despite her wishes to the contrary. A wave of nausea passed over her. "I wish I could remember…"

She could feel the icy stare through to her bones. His eyes moved from her face to the wall behind her, and she was glad he was focusing on something else.

"Sarah," McMichael said sharply. "What is that bundle of paper you have hanging on a string with a clothespin? Over there, behind the filing cabinet. The one with the seal imprinted on the last page that I can see from here?"

"Oh," Sarah sighed, relieved. "There it is. Now I remember. I had spilled tea on it yesterday and hung it there to dry. You remember when I did that, you were going on about Ruby…"

"Lose it again Sarah, and I will hang *you* out to dry."

Sarah's eyes began to well up. The pressure of the last twenty-four hours was taking its toll on McMichael, and his rage, which often lay just below the surface, was well above it now.

"Give it to me," he yelled, no longer able to hold his own composure.

He wished that Ruby were his only problem this morning. How much simpler things were yesterday. McMichael took the report, slammed the door leading into his private office and poured himself a stiff drink of Canadian rye whiskey. He had earned it.

There was a knock at the door.

"Oh, for the love of God, Sarah!" McMichael said and stormed over, opening the door with some force. "What now?"

But it wasn't Sarah. There standing before him was a man, dressed in a crisp navy blue uniform. The man, all six-foot four of him, was of impressive stature. McMichael sized him up quickly. The stranger appeared slightly younger than he was, but McMichael sensed maturity in the man that went well beyond his apparent chronological years.

"J.W. McMichael, I presume? Sergeant Rudy Wolanski," the man said. "Vancouver Police. I've been stationed here indefinitely by Chief Stuart Collin. I believe the two of you are acquainted. He sends his regards. Now, why don't you tell me what the hell happened here last night?"

"Excuse me, Mr. McMichael," Sarah stammered, "I didn't get to announce him properly. I didn't catch his name. He just went scooting by me. And he has a badge and a gun and all…"

"There's no problem Sarah," McMichael said, his voice suddenly finding insincere friendliness. "This is the constable you said they were going to send up, Officer Wolanski."

"Um, well actually there is sir," she said.

She gazed at the stranger, thinking how attractive he was and how single she was. This man, she sized up in her own way, was quite something. He had a handsome, rugged look about him, with a scar above his left eye. The scar dissected his eyebrow, giving him a slightly roguish look. His moustache, the same sandy blond as his closed-cropped hair, was neatly trimmed below a nose that revealed it had been broken once or twice, which in her estimation, only added character to his features. He was tall, taller than most of the men in town, and just how tall she was hoping to get close enough to, to tell.

"There is what, Sarah?" he queried with some exasperation in his voice.

"Oh yes. A problem," she giggled, blushing like a teenager. "Mrs. Schwindt just called. She says you need to go to the house immediately. There is some kind of an emergency."

"Forgive me Sergeant Wolanski," he said to the man. "As you've heard, I need to head home. Some sort of family crisis I gather. It's just up the road, I will be back in a moment. Mrs. Schwindt, my nanny, has a tendency to overreact. I'm sure it will turn out to be nothing."

"Well not all the time," Sarah offered. "Remember once, the house was on fire."

McMichael rolled his eyes. "It was a small fire in the chimney flue. Nothing to write home about, Sarah."

"In that case," Rudy stated, "I'll go with you. I'm good at emergencies. It comes with the job."

"Thanks a lot," McMichael said rather sarcastically, to no one in particular, yet to everyone in the room.

"Will you be coming back to the office?" Sarah asked. "I could put the kettle on."

"No, Sarah," McMichael sighed. "I think the officer will be a little too busy for socializing today, don't you?"

The two men went outside.

"She wasn't asking about me, you know," McMichael said. "Funny she never seems to ask me whether I'm coming back to the office. Are you married, officer Wolanski? Well, she'll keep nattering on at me until I find out, so I'd rather be done with it."

Rudy Wolanski smiled for a moment, taking in his surroundings. McMichael's secretary was a nice enough woman, but not his type.

"No, I'm not," the officer said matter of factly, anxious to change the subject. "I gather you've had quite the night."

"We lost a lot of men, women and children last night," McMichael admitted. "As you probably noticed, a good portion of the mountaintop came down last night in a landslide. It happened just after midnight. Dr. Van den Broek will be able to fill you in on the details as to the number of casualties and injuries. I'm afraid I lost count somewhere after two a.m. I've arranged a place for you to stay. Sarah will get you the keys. Did you bring some medical personnel with you? Sarah had mentioned you might."

"Yes, two doctors and three nurses came up with me. That's all they could spare on such short notice."

"I'll take them. We're normally very well staffed on our own, but the whole town is a bit of a disaster area at the moment. Did they go over to the hospital?"

"Yes, a tall redheaded woman led them over."

"That would have been Lucy Bentall. Beautiful woman. She lost her entire family last night. Quite tragic. They were in what's left of that green house, mid-section. Her two children and her husband lost their lives."

"Well, that would explain why she was in a somewhat catatonic state. She didn't talk, just pointed out the direction of the hospital and wandered ahead. She was definitely still in a state of shock," the constable noted.

McMichael was truly sorry to hear that. He knew that on top of losing her family, she was now also homeless. He though for a moment about the number of people that were now in that position. He would have to do something about that. When he was allowed some time to catch his breath.

They were close enough to the house now that he could hear Mrs. Schwindt screaming at the top of her lungs. The woman did have a loud, shrill voice when she wanted to. He would have a word with her about that, again. The officer started to hasten his pace, as he could see where the commotion was coming from, but McMichael calmly waved his hand from side to side, indicating to the officer there was no need to panic.

McMichael and the officer were soon upon his doorstep where they found the nanny, his youngest daughter Lara, and Jimmy Yada, engaged in a rather one-sided shouting match.

"Mrs. Schwindt," McMichael said calmly, "what seems to be the problem? There's no need to shout, the whole neighbourhood can hear you."

Mrs. Schwindt was an older widower he had in his employ since before his wife died. At times he felt she was a bit too stern for his children, but he needed a firm hand to guide them. He was called away from his home a lot, and he wanted to keep some continuity in their lives after their mother's death. She was a big woman, her long grey hair which she steadfastly refused to cut, drawn up each morning into a tight bun. She wore her big black boots under her dress, even in the heat of summer. She was not a woman given to breaking from her rigid routine.

"This little Japanese child," Mrs. Schwindt said, pointing to young Jimmy, "is trying to poison your children by giving them heaven knows what."

The young boy was doing his best to try to understand why Mrs. Schwindt was so upset. He looked at the two men and shrugged.

The nanny noticed the officer.

"You should probably take him away. To jail," she said indignantly.

Jimmy's eyes grew wide.

"Relax Jimmy, there will be no jail for you today," McMichael began, embarrassed. "Mrs Schwindt, young master Yada is giving Lara tea. TEA. Do you hear me? And furthermore, I told him it was perfectly fine to give anyone he liked some tea."

"Herbal tea," Jimmy corrected him.

"Herbal tea it was."

"Chamomile," Jimmy said to the officer.

"You see Mrs. Schwindt, I'm afraid you owe our little doctor here an apology, and perhaps even some lunch."

McMichael tussled the boy's hair good-naturedly.

"Jimmy, why don't you take a break, hmm? Just leave your wagon and play with Lara for a while. Mrs. Schwindt will make you more boiled water when you are finished if you'd like to continue around the neighbourhood." He turned to the nanny.

"Now if you don't mind Mrs. Schwindt, the officer and I will return to more pressing matters."

"Can I keep the nickel?" the boy asked, keeping it tucked safely in his pocket.

"Of course you can, Jimmy," McMichael answered.

"I forgot to say thank you," Jimmy said

"You earned it."

He once again saw a smile on the boy's face.

As they began walking back to the office, McMichael told Rudy the story of the boy's heroics the previous night.

"Not to worry, I am not employing child labour," he assured the officer. "Jimmy just likes to try to help people, and most of the people, Mrs. Schwindt not withstanding, seem to appreciate his efforts. He is the son of the assayer. He's quite a remarkable lad, really. Bright boy, I must say."

McMichael wasn't sure how much more he wanted to tell the officer about the town and its people. Let him discover it on his own, he thought.

"Well then, there you have it. Welcome to Britannia, Officer Wolanski. You're Polish, I assume?"

"Does it make a difference?" the officer asked.

"Not to me," he said, "but this is, after all, a small town. People are a bit set in their ways. Nationality is always a topic of conversation around here."

"I see that. I can handle it," the officer said.

"I'm sure you can," McMichael agreed. "We're a bit unusual here in Britannia that there are many cultures all trying to live together. Your own neighbours while you're here are Ukrainian, I believe. I hope that's okay. I may have to move some of the European families around if this talk of war continues. You'll have plenty to do here Officer Wolanski, particularly after payday. It gets a little rowdy on Fridays, down at the bar. If they get into trouble, do what you want with them over the weekend, but remember I need them back to work on Monday unless they've murdered somebody."

"I'll try to keep that in mind, J.W."

"Stuart Collin calls me J.W.," McMichael corrected him. "You can call me Mr. McMichael, or just McMichael."

Rudy had just gained some valuable insight into the character of the mining boss.

"Fine, Mr. McMichael. And you can call me Sergeant Wolanski, not Officer Wolanski, or just Wolanski, all things being equal."

"Sergeant?" McMichael questioned. "I think there's just one of you. Who exactly are you in charge of?"

"There's one of me for now," Wolanski threatened.

Down at the dock, McMichael could see Frenchie Cates lowering his boat's flags to half-mast. His boat would be used as transportation for many of the bodies that needed to go to their families in Vancouver and beyond. A few wooden boxes were already being lined up to be brought on board.

"I don't know where you want to begin," McMichael said. "I'll leave that to you. When you've got a feel for the situation, come back and I'll show you the engineering report."

"And here our friend Chief Collin said I'd have a hard time doing this investigation without you watching over me constantly," Rudy commented, sizing up McMichael.

McMichael looked the sergeant directly in the eye and set him straight.

"When it comes to the mine, that's my business. You want to go in there, you need an escort, just like anyone else. You are not an employee. We do tours for the families on holidays if you're so inclined. You want anything else in there, you'll need a warrant."

"Oh, that's how it's going to be, is it?" the sergeant remarked.

"That's how it's going to be. Having said that, anything that happened in the disaster last night, you've got free reign on. I'll make everyone and everything available to you with reasonable notice. I've got nothing to hide."

"I appreciate that," the sergeant said. "I understand the old police office is still empty. We've made arrangements with the provincial government office to take over the lease. I'll need the keys to it. I gather a set was left here with a caretaker in case of emergency. Perhaps the caretaker can do a quick clean of it. Tomorrow would be fine. Send me the bill of course. For now, I'm going to take a walk through the town, survey the situation and talk to a few people. I think I'll start with the doctor, like you said. Van den Broek, right? I'll find him at the hospital I trust? No need to show me the way, I'm sure I can manage."

The sergeant paused for a moment, gathering his thoughts.

"Oh," he added, a smirk crossing his face. "You never asked whether anyone else came up with the medical staff and myself. Now that I think about it, I believe there was. I believe a newspaper reporter was on board. Nosy people, reporters. Always snooping around, digging up dirt, and getting paid for it at that. But I don't have to tell a man like you that, do I Mr. McMichael? You might want to go spend some time with him. Maybe have your man Ferguson show him around? Oh yes, Mr. McMichael, I know all about your Mr. Ferguson."

Sergeant Wolanski watched McMichael for any outward reaction, but there was none.

"This man McMichael, he's a cool operator," the lawman thought to himself. "Good-day, McMichael," he said aloud.

Sergeant Wolanski began a solitary walk over to the hospital. His initial meeting with McMichael went pretty much like his own boss had told him it would. He wasn't here to be friends with McMichael, and that was just as well. The mining boss didn't leave a good first impression upon him. Arrogant, stubborn and full of himself. He had heard all the stories, and wondered how one man could have gained so much power in one tiny little town.

Once out of sight of the sergeant, McMichael felt the need to loosen his collar. He could see a stranger with a camera making his way up to the mine. Wolanski was right, it was time to go find Les, tell him to let the photographer take a few pictures of the slide, not the operations themselves, and then find a way to get the newsman back on Frenchie's funeral boat and out of town that night. It was inevitable that the Vancouver newspaper would want some pictures, but McMichael didn't want them hanging around longer than necessary.

Meanwhile, back at the house and once out of sight of her boss, Mrs. Schwindt turned on Jimmy once again.

"Get out, you filthy little foreigner," she said. "And don't come back."

"But I want to play with Jimmy," Lara protested. "We were having fun."

Jimmy looked at the big, overbearing woman before him.

"What is wrong with you?" he asked innocently, which only infuriated Mrs. Schwindt more.

"Get out of here now," she said, waiving a long bony finger in his face.

Lara started to cry.

"Now look what you have done," she said to Jimmy, grabbing Lara by the hand and taking her inside. Lara turned around to look at the boy. She managed to free her hand from the nanny to wave her fingers in a good-bye motion.

Jimmy waved back. He stood for a moment outside the home and thought about what had just happened. He couldn't figure out what he had done wrong, or why the woman didn't like him very much. Lara liked him. McMichael seemed to like him, and McMichael, he had heard, didn't seem to like a lot of people. It must just be the old woman, he thought. His mother often said in Japanese to his father, when she thought Jimmy wasn't listening, that McMichael had a bee up his bum. Jimmy figured that was what made him buzz around yelling at people so much. That must be it. Too many bees in that house.

Sarah, disappointed that the officer was not immediately coming back inside the office, had decided to go home for some lunch. She hadn't eaten since the night before and even McMichael couldn't begrudge her some time to eat. As she glanced up the road, she caught sight of the young male reporter, and her pace quickened. Who was this new man? So absorbed with this thought, she almost ran into Jimmy as he came towards her. But the young boy's head was hanging down and he seemed troubled, which was quite unlike the friendly little boy she had come to know. She instantly stopped.

"Is everything okay Jimmy?" she asked.

He glanced up at the woman. It was Sarah. He liked Sarah. He smiled at her. "Yes mam," he said. "Would you like some tea? It's herbal."

CHAPTER 11

The disaster of the spring began to be less painful as the months passed. The rains of winter finally let up, and the summer months were warm and dry. The townspeople were moved from what used to be the upper camp, to a safer spot on the sister mountain next to the peak that had cracked. New buildings sprang up where the demolished ones had once been. McMichael had seen to it that temporary dormitories were built first, to house the women and children who had no where to go. The men were housed separately, sometimes sharing a bunk, until the individual homes could be re-built. Neighbours helped out neighbours with gifts of shelter, food and comfort. They finally had a church, that all the denominations shared and a second hospital had been built. It was a steep climb up several hundred stairs from the Beach town, to the upper town, so McMichael tried to make the new upper town as self-sustaining as he could. There was a second school and a second community swimming pool. There was even a second general store that stocked the same goods as the lower Beach store. By autumn, things were getting back to normal for most of the people.

Christina McMichael walked past the mine entrance on her way to school, pausing to wait for her girlfriend as she did every morning. There was a balmy breeze, and she took off the knitted sweater coat Mrs. Schwindt had insisted she wear.

The fact that she was a beautiful maturing teenage girl did not pass by unnoticed by the group of men, including Frank, standing out side the mine, preparing to start their shift. They took a little extra time gathering their helmets that morning. Her blonde hair was done up in a pony tail that reached below her shoulders.

Peter Renister, the new arrival from the city, who was barely out of his teens himself, let out a low whistle.

"You looking for a honey pot to tend to?" Frank asked. "There's a whole honey wagon waiting in a secret shaft in the tunnel."

"Maybe," Peter said with bravado.

"Well, seeing as you're new and all, I'm going to set you straight. That's the boss' oldest daughter," Frank explained. "She's just girl, and she's off limits."

"And if you like your job and value your life, you'll remember that." Les Ferguson said approaching the crew, his voice eerily threatening.

Peter's jaw dropped.

"Ah, good morning Les," Frank said. "Working with us today are you?"

Les glared at Frank. Then he turned and looked at Christina and stared. He couldn't take his eyes off her.

"We've got another honey pot for you down the shaft, if you're man enough," Frank said, attempting to break the tension.

"Oh, I'm man enough," Peter boasted. "I can do the whole wagon."

"John," Frank called out to the foreman John Cruickshank, "take Peter down to meet the honey pot, and leave him alone with her for a while."

"Okay," John nodded. "Take the diamond drill today Frank. I want you doing some core samples."

Peter glanced at Frank and back at Les. Les was still pre-occupied.

"It's okay," Frank assured him, "and John will make sure your time is covered."

As John led Peter down into the shaft, Frank and the remaining men broke into laughter.

"I remember the day you met the honey, Fitzpatrick," an older man said. "You, a married man and all."

The men laughed some more. It had been a time-honoured ritual for the new man in the mine to be lured to the charms of the honey pot, the not so affectionate nickname of the toilet bucket.

The men reached for the candles to clip onto their helmets, stuffing a few extra ones in their pockets. It gave them the light they needed to work down the dark shafts. About five minutes later, Peter came up the shaft carrying the honey pot as far away from his body as he could. His sense of bravado had vanished.

"Oh come on Peter, get closer to her," Frank shouted, causing more laughter.

The shift whistle blew, interrupting the joviality and finally breaking Les' concentration on the girl.

"What are you laughing at?" Ferguson asked. He had been so obsessed with Christina that he was oblivious to the conversation that had gone on around him.

"Give it a rest Les," Frank said. "Come on boys, let's get to work."

The men picked up their tools and headed into the mine. Les made no effort to move as again, he stood and watched Christina, assuming all the men had gone into the mine. However Frank had an uneasy feeling about the whole situation and stayed behind. Frank didn't like the way Les was staring at Christina, who, unaware of all the fuss, was still innocently waiting for her friend.

"Is there something I can do for you Miss Christina?" Les leered, noticing her young forming breasts from beneath her school issued blouse.

"No," Christina said, "my friend's just a bit late."

"Well maybe you can spend some time with your Uncle Les," he sneered.

"You know Christina," Frank said, his voice causing Les to jump out of his skin, "I think maybe your friend might be sick today. You're going to be late, you should go on off to school. Our whistle has gone off, which gives you about ten minutes to get there."

"Okay Mr. Fitzpatrick," she said, thankful for an excuse to leave.

"Knock it off Les," Frank said, and turned back towards the mine.

"Who do you think you're talking to?" Les sneered.

"I think I'm talking to a man who's way out of line. She's well more than half your age. I don't care if she's the boss' daughter, she's just a child, and the way you're looking at her isn't right."

"She's no child." Les said. "Peter looked at her. You all looked at her. You can see that she's no child."

"She's a pretty young thing Les, I'll grant you that," Frank said. "But there's a difference between grown men acknowledging she's a pretty young thing, making a few good natured comments that she'll never hear, and what ever is going on in your head. You watch her every day. I've seen you. We've all seen you. We see you looking at her from behind the shed. We see you following her home. So I'm telling you straight, I don't care if you're McMichael's little henchman or not, if you ever lay a hand on her we'll find you. I will personally find you and make you pay."

"Oh, you think so?" he growled. "You better watch your back Fitzpatrick, you're a marked man. I'm going to watch you. Any wrong move you make, McMichael is going to know about. You so much as walk home with a drill bit in your pocket, and he's going to know about it. Your days are numbered here, I promise you that."

McMichael came from around the corner.

"Is there a problem here boys?" he asked.

"No sir," Frank said. "Les was just telling me I'd better get my ass down the shaft. I'm a few minutes late sir, I'm sorry. It won't happen again."

McMichael looked at Les.

"Good man Les," he nodded. "Fitzpatrick, I want to see you end of the day. Come straight to my office. I'm going to hold your cheque, this being payday."

McMichael walked off in the direction of his office.

"What the hell does that mean?" Frank asked Les.

"One Irishman to another?" Les mocked. "Have a nice life."

Frank spent the morning drilling for core samples. The conversation with McMichael had unsettled him, a fact that hadn't gone unnoticed by John Cruickshank.

"Something wrong Frankie?" John asked. "You're not yourself today. The wheels in your head are turning, but the drill's going pretty slow."

Frank told John about having to go to McMichael's office after work.

"You're a good worker Frank, most days. I wouldn't worry too much about it. Tell you what, after lunch, I want you on the widow maker with the new kid, Peter. Teach him how use it. That'll give you something different to focus on."

John was referring to the wood drill that weighed 300 pounds and took two people to move. The machine was loud, and the old timers all became sick after years of use. They developed silicosis, from breathing the tiny, sharp silica shards. Silica is a common component of the earth's crust, and the fragments were released by the constant drilling. Over the years, miners lungs had been known to become full of scar tissue from the constant cuts, and in some cases, it had proved fatal, hence the name of the drill. Peter turned out to be a good learner, taking direction and keeping an eye for safety. Frank was happy to work with him. His constant questions helped keep Frank's mind off the meeting he was destined to have later that day. At three o'clock, John came around with the pay cheques and handed them out. All except Frank's.

"Sarah must have dropped yours," John said, offering an excuse to the men who had noticed Frank didn't get one. "You know how she is. She did that to me a few weeks back. Tell you what, drop by the office and check, then come meet the boys and me down at the tavern for a beer. The beer is on me if she can't find it."

"Thanks John, I'll do that," Frank said, and headed over to the mine office, his feet heavy with a sense of dread.

"He's waiting for you, go on in," Sarah said as Frank walked through the mine office door.

Frank found McMichael standing, waiting for him just as Sarah had said.

"You wanted to see me?" Frank asked.

"What the hell was going on out there this morning?"

"What do you mean?" Frank answered.

"You know what I mean."

"Les was just on me to get back to work. The whistle had gone, and I was a bit late like I said."

"And…?"

"And?" Frank replied back.

McMichael took a calculated walk over to the window and turned his back on Frank.

Frank wondered what McMichael wanted to know. He couldn't tell him about the conversation that had taken place without fear of repercussion. McMichael and Ferguson were thick as thieves, and he knew Ferguson would deny everything. Frank hoped by being elusive, McMichael would eventually tire of him or fire him, and be done with it.

But McMichael continued to say nothing. The silence was gnawing at Frank.

"Les and I had a bit of an argument, a personal matter, that's all."

"Hmm," McMichael said, and then more silence.

"Was Les out of line?" McMichael eventually asked.

"I thought so, yes."

"And did you set him straight?"

"Well," Frank began, "that's not so easy to do. But yes, I had words with him if that's what you're asking. Look, it's not going to interfere with my work, if that's what you want to know."

McMichael went to his cabinet and pulled out two glasses.

"You like rye, Frank?"

"Yes sir. I'm normally a beer drinker, but yes, I do like rye on occasion."

"I think Canadian rye is the best rye there is."

"Yes sir," Frank said.

McMichael poured two glasses.

"Sit down," he said to Frank and motioned to the seat in front of his desk. "I'm making this an occasion." McMichael took the seat behind.

"Frank," McMichael began, "you are aware that Les, from time to time, is called upon to do, let's say, some extra work for me. He has certain personality traits, including an unscrupulous love of money that makes him the perfect man for the job. I'm not telling you anything you don't know. He has no conscience, which is why he's so successful at what I call upon him to do. People know he has the authority, my authority, to do these things. And he gets a bonus, to carry out these things that I need done."

"Yes sir," Frank said, sipping the rye. It was smooth, obviously from McMichael's private stock. He hadn't had rye straight up in years, but he could imagine acquiring a taste for it.

"Well, I'd like to offer you a chance to make a little more money."

Frank looked nervously at the boss.

"I don't know if I'm cut out for that line of work," he replied. "I've got a wife to think about. I don't think she'd like me being an enforcer."

"I didn't know your wife was your boss," McMichael said. "I thought you were your own man."

Frank took a drink and swallowed hard. His male ego had just taken a beating. McMichael had seen him flinch and took note for future reference. Frank's wife might be Frank's Achilles heel, and that was always something worth knowing.

"Relax," McMichael stated. "I don't want you to muscle in on people Frank, that's not your style. I want to talk to you about John Cruickshank. He's going to retire soon. His doctor says he has to. Throat problems. You've probably noticed him coughing, wheezing, and basically getting tired really easily. Dr. Van den Broek says he's got six months, maybe a year to live if he keeps working. So he's out of here."

Frank was shocked to hear this. John had never let on he was sick.

"We'll be looking into some new jack drills that use air and water. They're supposed to be a lot safer. They're being tested in the States now. If they work, we'll get some. The problem with silica is you can't see it. You don't know you're breathing it in. According to Dr. Van Den Broek, the silica gets into the lungs and the body tries to fight it by building up scar tissue. But the scar tissue doesn't let the lungs stretch, and you can't breath in as much air as you need. It doesn't happen over night, they say it takes twenty some odd years before it gets really bad. It's too late for John, but it'll give the newer guys some time. Hopefully by then we'll have some new protective gear, like I said. John's been working in this mine for over forty years. The mine has been his life. His kids were born and raised here. He'll be moving back to the city at the end of the month."

McMichael noticed Frank's glass was empty and refilled it.

"I called you into my office Frank because I'm considering you for the foreman's job."

"Well thank you, Mr. McMichael. That's quite an honour. I'm just sorry about the circumstances."

"It's part of mining life. An occupational hazard if you will. John knows that. He recommended you for the job Frank. So there'll be no hard feelings between you. But I want to make this clear, I need a man I can trust in that position, Frank. You'll be required to rotate shifts and supervise the men. I need to know what goes on in there on a day-to-day basis. I need someone who's willing to tell me what's going on with the crews. If someone's late, I want to know. If someone's slacking off, I need to know. If someone's crazy, I have to know."

There was an awkward silence again.

"You mean if someone is a danger to people outside of work as well?" Frank asked.

"Exactly. The person who gets the job will become one of my confidants. Tell me Frank, if you were in my position, what would you want to know? Where would you draw the line between your camaraderie with your co-workers and the responsibilities of being in a position of authority?"

Frank thought about the events earlier that morning. How much of the conversation had McMichael heard, he wondered? Frank wanted the foreman job. It was an impressive promotion and the extra money would certainly be welcome.

"I suppose I'd want to know my co-workers, friends and family were safe," Frank said, testing the waters. "And I would hope I had the judgment to know when the guys were just shooting off their mouths and when they were a real concern. I'd have to get along with both you and them. I'd still be spending most of my time down in the tunnels with the guys, not with you. I know you're looking for someone loyal. Loyalty is fleeting, Mr. McMichael, but I'm pretty much a stand up guy."

"Loyalty fleeting? You're quite observant. It is indeed. It's often bought and sold."

The two men locked eyes.

"I don't like the way he looks at your daughter, sir." Frank finally said. "Not that me or the other guys are always looking at her or anything, don't get me wrong. But he is. Ferguson just gives me the creeps."

"I heard the entire conversation this morning, right from Peter's wolf whistle." McMichael admitted. "The foreman's job is yours Frank, as long as you keep an eye on that particular situation. You stayed behind, were late even, because of your concern for my daughter. That's what makes you a better man for the job than anyone else. John is right about that. And you're right about Ferguson. Les is a crazy bastard, Frank. But I still need him. At least until I see which way the waters are flowing with this Wolanski character. But I won't let anyone harm my family. My daughters are precious. You keep your ears to the ground and your eyes on Les. You start Monday. He pulls any crap with you, you come tell me."

"Thank you sir. And thanks for the drink."

Frank offered his hand to McMichael, but McMichael just nodded at him. Frank took it as a sign the meeting between the two men was over.

"Oh, and Frank," McMichael said. "Pretty young thing, I can live with, but watch your own mouth while you're at it."

"Yes sir," Frank said, closing the door behind him.

Sarah had his cheque in hand as he left the inner office.

"Congratulations," she said to him. "John says to get yourself down to the bar, the first round is still on him."

Frank nodded.

"No one knows that John Cruickshank is sick Frank," Sarah said. "I think he wants it kept that way."

Being payday, Frank knew Olivia wouldn't be expecting him to come straight home. It was a tradition for the men to knock a few drinks back once they got their packet, so he headed on over to the bar as was his usual way. As he stepped through the door, a round of good-natured applause greeted him. Apparently everyone already knew about his promotion.

"Cheers to the new boss," John said, handing him his drink.

"Cheers to you John," Frank said.

Les Ferguson sat by himself in the corner and watched the men for a while. He waited until Frank went into the bathroom, then followed him in.

"Let me guess," Frank said, "you're not here to congratulate me."

"You better watch it," Ferguson said. "This don't mean a thing. You'd better spend less time watching me and more time watching your wife."

"What was that?" Frank asked, his ire up.

"You think Christina is the only one getting cat calls these days? You should hear what your buddies say about your wife when you're not around. We used to all look at Lucy, but now she's locked up crazy-like in the hospital. Who do you think all the guys are looking at these days? It'd be that pretty little wife of yours. The one with the long, dark brown hair that, when it's not all tied up, goes all the way down her slender back."

"Watch it, Ferguson," Frank said.

"Or what? What are you going to do to me? Hit me? I'd like to see you try. Then I'll knock you out of commission for a few days and there will be no one around to stop me from going over to your house and spending some time with your Livvy."

John and the boys were startled by the sound of the bathroom door coming crashing down to the floor inside the bar, Ferguson's back firmly attached to it. Sergeant Wolanski had co-incidentally just stepped into the bar to check on things, it being payday Friday and all.

"What's going on here?" the sergeant asked as Frank walked towards the exit.

"He fell," Frank said, his voice still full of anger.

Sergeant Wolanski grabbed Frank by the shoulder.

"You look like a sensible man," Wolanski said, taking him outside. "Let's get something straight. Les only thinks he enforces the town. Maybe he's got McMichael to back him up on that. But I've got a few more rights than Ferguson does, no matter what McMichael wants to think. I didn't see what went on in there. But seeing as you're not drunk, I don't think it was your typical bar room brawl. Which pretty much tells me it was about a woman. I see the wedding band on your finger. I've also seen Ferguson stalking a certain teenager around town, and I've only been here a few days. So I figure the fight was about one woman or the other. How close am I?"

"Pretty close," Frank admitted. "It was both. Are you going to arrest me or something?"

"Like I said," Wolanski offered, "I didn't see anything."

"You know how it goes," Frank said, "he was making up stuff about my wife. The guy's crazy."

"So what you're telling me is you are actually listening to a man you believe to be a crazy? And you got all worked up about it? Don't believe everything you hear," Wolanski said. "It'll drive you crazy and before you know it, you won't have a wife to worry about. You'd miss that. Take it from me."

Frank thought about what the lawman was saying, and offered his hand.

"Frank Fitzpatrick," he introduced himself.

"Rudy Wolanski," Wolanski offered back. "Now get out of here before I start remembering what I did or didn't see."

CHAPTER 12

This particular year, autumn proved to be the season of renewal, and everyone was looking forward to Thanksgiving. Lucy had spent a great deal of time in the hospital coming to terms with what had happened to her. She had stayed there until after Christmas, not wanting to face the world until the holidays were over. McMichael had tried to reach her family stateside, but there had been no response from them, and he didn't know, under the circumstances, whether it would be a good idea to find out what had happened to them or not. But Sarah had refused to let it go, telling him that Lucy's family deserved to know what had happened to their daughter. He thought they must have heard, as the news of the disaster spread quickly, and maybe there was a family reason that had stopped them from being in contact. But there was Sarah, constantly dropping little hints about it, in that off-hand way she had, that no, they were a very close family, and this was very strange. So finally he had sent Frenchie off to find them down the coast. The news had not been good. Lucy's parents had been killed in a freak accident. Lightning had struck their home, starting a fire, and it was late at night and they never woke up. He dreaded telling her about it, but again Sarah had insisted, and he had done so. It was never easy delivering or receiving such news, but Lucy had been particularly a tough one for him to have to approach. She barely had any emotion at all when he broke the news. It was as if all life had already been drained from her. He wanted to shake her into some kind of emotion, but of course he couldn't and didn't.

Olivia had written home and assured her own family that she and Frank were safe and sound. Letters came from her family with some frequency, and she was delighted when she got them. She had received several letters from her mother, who had given birth to another son. This one they named Daniel and they were both doing just fine. Anne had gone to a convent in Olympia, and also wrote her often. She was teaching at the local Catholic school and finding it to be quite rewarding. Emily had met a young veterinarian and they were to be married this summer. The invitation had arrived in the mail. Billy, her mother had written, was building family homes in Seattle for a local construction company. No sign of him settling down yet, he was enjoying playing the field. Her mother never mentioned Jason. Olivia wondered if he was in some kind of trouble, or in jail. She would have to ask her father some time. Perhaps he was stationed somewhere in the Army, she thought, and they just didn't know where he was, or couldn't say. Olivia had read that the United States were actively recruiting for the army. It would be just like Jason. He never could settle down and he would have found the armed forces inviting. America's involvement was in full force and they needed men desperately. Yes, she thought. That's probably where her brother was.

Canada was drawn into World War I automatically when Britain entered the war. This was a prosperous thing for the mine, as the demands for copper were enormous, and more men were being hired to keep up with the growing demand. As a result, the town too was growing. For most of the residents at Britannia, it was a war that didn't immediately involve them, the action being in Europe, which for all intents and purposes seemed so far away. But as time passed, more and more young Canadian men were volunteering to fight for the allies. As the young men left for the war, the older workers were having to put more time in at the mine.

And so it was that Olivia found herself glancing at a calendar and realizing that she had indeed been at Britannia now for over a year. There had been no vacation time off for the men, the mine was at capacity, so she still hadn't had her honeymoon at the resort as Frank had promised. While there was always housework of some sort to keep her busy, she was growing restless. She had made a few casual friends, but she found that the townspeople, for the most part, had grown up together, and because of this, seeding deep friendships was a bit of a challenge. Now that more young families were moving up, she was hoping that would change. Frank had encouraged her to join one of the women's groups, but she found, like Lucy had initially said, for the most part they were not her cup of tea, the gossiping aside.

"I'm still worried about Lucy." Olivia said to Frank one night as she was preparing bread dough for dinner.

"She's been through a lot Liv, she needs some time."

"It's been a year now Frank, and she's still wearing all black."

"She's in mourning, Liv, you know that, and you know you can't put a time limit on that."

It was times like this that she was glad she had married such a kind, understanding man, although lately, she had seen a few cracks in the façade. Frank had been putting in some extra time at the mine at McMichael's request and his demeanour was changing. He had become overtired and irritable. McMichael was hinting that he was going to create a new, well-paying job as a mine manager, and Frank was taking the bait, afraid to turn any request down from his boss.

"But I saw her headed to the quilting bee the other afternoon. I remember her telling me how much she hated that group. I suppose I should be thankful that she's making the effort to get out, but oh, I don't know, somehow it doesn't seem quite like the Lucy I first met on the boat."

She took the dough and started to knead it, pushing and turning and pulling it towards her with some force.

"You're right Liv," Frank agreed. "She wouldn't do that if she were back to the old Lucy that we knew and loved. Not that I spent much time with her or anything, but Marty always said she was a handful, and most people seem to agree. Maybe she needs her own welcome wagon. Why don't you invite her over for Easter dinner? You know we've never done that, had her over for dinner, and the holidays are the loneliest, or so they say. Maybe it will be a new start for her, and a new start for your friendship."

As Olivia continued to press the dough outward, she heard her dress tear. She looked down to see a small rip in the seam. Maybe it wasn't such a small tear. Frank had heard it too.

"Gaining weight there Liv?" he grinned. He came and put his arms around her waist. "Are we pregnant yet?"

They had been trying since they were married, with no success.

"No," she sighed. "We are just gaining weight."

She noticed a change in Frank's expression, and his voice had a bit of an edge.

"Better cut down on the snacks there Liv, don't want you turning into your mother."

Olivia was taken aback.

"My mother is a beautiful woman."

"Yes, she is," Frank said. "But she's not exactly a small woman now, judging by the last picture she sent."

"You're making it sound as if she's huge. She's had a few children, Frank. That's what happens to women when they've had a large brood. And my father would never say anything like that to her, shame on you for saying such a thing to me, about my mother or me."

"Well, I'm not your father Liv. All I'm saying is you've got a great body and I'd like you to keep it that way."

He undid the ribbon holding her hair into a bun.

"I've got some time before my shift," he said, "why don't we take advantage of it?"

"I don't think I'm in the mood," she replied, pushing his hands away.

Rejection was not something Frank was used to from Olivia. He clasped each of his hands over her own and drew them up to his chest. A motion, Olivia felt, more of control than warmth.

"Look, tell you what, go down to the store tomorrow and buy yourself a couple of new dresses." Frank said, trying to make amends. "It's about time I treated you anyway. I haven't bought you any new clothes since you've been here. I can't have the other women saying I'm too poor to buy you anything new."

It occurred to Olivia that in this instance, Frank seemed to care more about what others thought of his love for her than what he himself thought his love for her. She wondered when that had happened. How it had happened.

"I'll make do with what I have until the summer," she said solemnly. She always maintained her pride. Her father had once told her gifts received from guilt were not really gifts at all, because giving was meant to be a joyful emotion. "I'll pick some up when we go to the wedding. I don't like the dresses they have at the store. They're too plain. You wouldn't want the women saying you're too poor to buy me anything that wasn't plain."

She regretted the last remark, but her feelings were hurt.

"What do you mean?" Frank asked.

"They're all the same, flower prints, all of them. All cut the same, all sewn the same, it might as well be the Britannia Beach ladies uniform. I wouldn't feel special in them Frank. And you know what? I like to feel special from time to time."

"No, I mean what do you mean about us going away?"

"What do *you* mean?" shot back. "You know my sister is getting married in June."

"Liv," Frank shook his head, "I won't be able to get any time off. We're going full steam as it is."

"Well, I've got time a plenty. And if you can't go, I'm going to go myself."

"Oh no you're not," he said sternly.

"Oh yes I am," she rebutted. "I am going stir crazy here. Weren't you listening to me? I need to get out of this place for a few days. I am bored, Frank! We were going to go away for Christmas, but that didn't happen because you wanted us to spend our first Christmas together here in our home. Fine. It was lovely. But you haven't even had a full weekend off since. You are always working. Maybe you can't make time to take me away, but I can make time to take me away. Frenchie can take me down."

He grabbed her by the wrist.

"What, you want a weekend away with Frenchie?" he said.

"Of course not. Frank. You're hurting me! Let go!"

"Don't argue with me Liv. I'm your husband. If I say you're not going, you're not going."

"You let go of me right now, Frank Patrick Fitzpatrick," she said. She had never heard him speak to her like that before.

Frank released his grip. She moved away from him.

"Look," he said, "just go down to the store tomorrow and see what's there. We'll talk about the wedding when it gets closer. And I'm sorry about the Frenchie remark. It's just I see the way some of the men look at you, and sometimes I get jealous."

"You know what? I think I'll go down to the store right now and maybe I'll spend all your grocery money and buy something totally useless," she said, putting on her winter coat and hat, making sure the door slammed loudly behind her as she left.

"You do that," he said. But his disposition had returned to normal. He knew he shouldn't have said what he said and he knew she needed some time to cool off.

The air outside was quite cool and there was still a little snow on the ground from a late snow they had experienced last week. She felt her foot was getting wet and noticed a small hole in the toe of the boot.

"Maybe I'd better get some new boots first," she thought to herself.

His money. While it was true she had never earned an income and always survived on the allowances the men in her life had given her, she thought about how wonderful it would be to have money of her own, to save and spend as she pleased, without having to explain anything to anyone. Even Akiko Yada, she thought, earned her own living, as meagre as it may be. She wondered if it gave Akiko a sense of pride, or whether Akiko felt only the burden of financial necessity. She knew Akiko worked long, hard hours. Harry must make a good salary at the mine though, she thought, so it couldn't be just the need for the money. Maybe, she thought, Akiko got a sense of self from it.

Olivia may have been naive in thinking that Harry was paid as an equal at the mine, but she was becoming less naive of her current lot in life. She reminisced about the days she would spend with her friends in Seattle, drinking a cup of coffee at a local café. She had rarely been invited out for a simple cup of coffee the whole time she had been at Britannia. Why was everyone so unfriendly?

"Come to think of it," she said to herself, "I haven't actually invited anyone out for coffee myself."

That was a revelation. It wasn't that she never wanted to go have coffee with the neighbours. It's just that she never found, no, never made, the time.

She had overheard Mary Alice talking to Mrs. Schwindt about her once when Mary Alice had thought she was out of earshot, and Mary Alice had said that she was a little standoff-ish. Maybe there was some truth in that after all, she thought. Mrs. Schwindt had replied that Olivia seemed to think she was hoity-toity, being from Seattle and all, so Olivia decided to keep clear of the two women, which probably just added fuel to their fire.

Olivia opened the door to the mercantile and was greeted by Joe Cicceretti, the shopkeeper.

"Good afternoon Olivia," he said. "Some sugar for you today? It's on special this week."

"No thanks Joe, not today. Do you happen to have any ladies boots on sale?"

He took her over to the display. What they had was either too expensive or too old fashioned for her taste. Drab black ankle lace-ups. Maybe when she was sixty, she thought.

"Can I take a look at the Eaton's catalogue? Maybe they've got something. I need a new dress as well. I saw a few I liked the last time I was browsing through it."

"I'm sorry Olivia," he said. "Mr. McMichael made us get rid of the catalogues. He said it was affecting his profit margin. Not enough of one. We've got a lovely selection of floral print dresses Mary Alice Jones has made special though, what with spring just around the corner. I'm sure you're familiar with the design, all the ladies have them."

Olivia ignored the sales pitch.

"How can he get rid of the catalogue? Doesn't he know it brings us the latest fashions, like all the women in the cities are wearing? So he's not making a two hundred percent mark-up. At least he's making some money from it."

"Well, some is not all, and you know J.W. It's all or nothing. He likes to control the prices, and you can't do that with Eaton's printing how much everything costs. We're just too small a town to get a big bulk volume. Now how about those dresses? Beautiful empire waists…all hand tatted lace around the collar…"

"No!" Olivia shouted.

Joe was taken aback.

"I'm sorry Joe, it's just I'm in a bit of a mood, is all. Tell you what, why don't you get me some of that sugar that's on sale, I can always use more, and I'll head off on home."

"All right then," Joe said, silently taking her money and nodding her a goodbye.

"I am just a ray of sunshine," Olivia thought to herself.

Leaving from the store, Olivia noticed that the wind had picked up. She wondered if they were in for yet more snow, as the sky was a threatening colour. Just ahead she saw a woman draped in a long black hooded cape, bundled up from the cold. The woman's feet were covered in stylish long black leather boots that rose up to her knee. Olivia smiled for a moment. Grieving as she was, Lucy still had style. A red curl peeking out from beneath the hood confirmed her identity. Maybe there was hope for Lucy yet.

"Lucy!" she shouted.

Lucy turned around.

"Come have coffee," Olivia said. "Please."

The wind took a brief rest, allowing both women to catch their breath.

"Okay," Lucy said, much to Olivia's surprise. "I'd like that."

The two women walked into the café. More than one head turned when they saw Lucy heading toward a little corner table for two by the window.

Lucy wiped a tear from her eye.

"Don't mind me, it's just the wind, it always makes my left eye water. I'm not crying. See, the right one is dry. How are you Olivia?" Lucy asked.

"I should be asking you that."

"Oh," Lucy said, "everyone knows how I am. I'm the talk of the town. Crazy Lucy. They've always called me crazy Lucy, but it's taken on a whole new meaning lately. How are you? How have you settled in? I'm sorry it's been so long since we've talked."

"I'm going quite mad," Olivia admitted.

For the first time in a year, she did what she needed to do. Olivia sat with Lucy and told her how much she was missing her family, how bored she was getting, how sometimes she found the town depressing, and how she wished something exciting would happen to her so she wouldn't feel quite so useless. She told Lucy all the things she couldn't tell Frank.

For the first time in a year, Lucy did the same thing. She told Olivia she was slowly coming to grips with her new life, a new life alone. That meant getting out more, which was why she ventured out on this rather blustery day.

"Where did you get that cape?" Olivia asked. "It's lovely."

"Frenchie picked it up somewhere for me. I didn't ask him to. He just showed up with it one day. Brought it to me at the hospital. It was brand new. He said "Lucy, I ran inta a factery sale down de coast. Dey 'ad too many so I took one off der hands." I have no idea where he really got it. I think he paid for it himself, bless his heart. It is lovely though. I wish it wasn't black, but it is lovely. And his gesture means so much to me."

"But black is the only colour we've seen you wearing," Olivia pointed out to her friend.

"It's all I wanted to wear for most of the year," Lucy admitted. "I was really living the crying widow scenario. But when I finally got out of the hospital, I decided I needed to stop grieving so much. Start living life a bit again. I wasn't quite up to making a trip out of town, especially since my parents were killed."

"I heard about that. I'm so sorry," Olivia interrupted.

"I was talking," Lucy said, and Olivia thought she saw a slight smile. "I thought I might like to get something new, something a little nicer, so I went down to the store for some new clothes but all they had were these stupid flowered dresses."

Olivia laughed.

"I don't think I'm quite ready for florals," Lucy said. "But maybe something in beige."

They laughed some more.

"Liv, I would have liked to talk to you like this before. I've seen you many times. But I just wasn't ready. The day I met you was the day it all happened. My life came to a halt. It wasn't you, I know that now, it was just the memory of that night that I was associating with you, and with Frank, and with the town…"

"Where are you living now Lucy? Are you up in the upper village? I really don't know, I'm sorry."

"No, down here. I'm staying with Margaret, one of the nurses I became friends with over at the hospital. She's older than I am, but she has an extra room, and is kind enough to let me stay. It's not forever, but it's fine for now. Like I said, I haven't ventured out much, but I'm ready to now. I've been to the women's afternoon gatherings, including the quilting bee, and that helped."

"I was a bit worried when I heard that," Olivia admitted.

"They said you were going for a while but hadn't been in lately. You know Liv, I learned something. I learned that the women really actually had wonderful things to say if I took the time to listen. And since I wasn't in the mood for talking, I did a lot of listening. It turned out they were bored and frustrated with the isolation here, just like I was. Just like I still am. The difference is that they had learned to be content with it. I don't know if I'll ever be content with it, but my anxiety seems to be in a calmer place these days."

"So what's next for you Lucy?" Olivia asked.

"I really don't know," Lucy admitted. "I have some insurance money, but it's not going to last me forever. I'm thankful Marty had the foresight to take out life insurance. He even took it out on the children, which surprised me. I didn't know he had. Still, I'm going to need to find a job to support myself."

"A job?" Olivia said. "Are you going to leave?

"No, I don't really have anywhere else I want to be, now that my parents are gone. I'd like to find one here in town," she replied.

"That sounds wonderful. Doing what?"

"That's the problem, I'm not quite sure. I have no skills. I can't type. I don't know bookkeeping. It's not going to be easy."

"Maybe Mr. McMichael can find you something?"

"Mr. McMichael thinks the widow Bentall is quite insane."

"Oh, I'm sure that's not true. Frank said that McMichael always liked you. He said he was always complimenting you, telling everyone how lovely you are."

"Oh, I'm sure that part's true. He came to visit me a few times at the hospital. It's fair to say I wasn't my best, especially when he was breaking the news about my parents. He doesn't look at me quite the same way anymore."

"I'm sure he still thinks you're lovely. Frank says he has quite the crush on you and that the men are taking odds on, well, the two of you getting together some time."

Lucy laughed.

"No. That won't happen. I just don't find him attractive. I know a lot of women do. He's a handsome man. But…"

Lucy's thoughts wandered for a moment.

"You'll find something, for work I mean," Olivia assured her. "Listen, since you want to get out more, why don't you come for Easter dinner? Maybe we can come up with some job ideas for you, together? Frank and I would love to have you."

"I'll think about it," Lucy said. "It happens to be my birthday this year. Easter, I mean. Could there be some cake, do you think?"

"I think that could be arranged."

"Then I think I will accept your kind invitation. Thank you Liv."

"That's wonderful Lucy," she said, and gave her friend a hug.

Olivia returned home humming a light melody, closing the door quietly behind her.

Frank sighed in relief.

CHAPTER 13

The full moon was shining its light through the window as Akiko swept the floor in the mining office. The clock, striking one, reminded her that it was getting late. Finishing, she closed the door to McMichael's office, pausing to spell out the lettering on the nameplate on the door.

"J. W. M. C. M. I. C. H. A. E. L.," she spelled, reading the name out loud as she did every night. "J. W. McMichael."

She had learned her English ABC's the hard way, listening as her husband taught them to Jimmy when he was young. Even today, sometimes when she got stuck, she would sing the letters out. This was her classroom, alone at night at the office where she could practice reading and speaking as she cleaned. No one was usually around to criticize her or think she was slow.

She wiped away some of her long black hair that had escaped her ponytail and hung in her eyes. It had been a long day and she was growing tired. One more room to clean and she could go home. She always left Sarah's office to the end. Some days Sarah's office got a little out of control, but Akiko had been there long enough to wipe up the spills and know what not to throw out, and occasionally, what to keep when it had been thrown away.

Sarah, being Sarah, was extremely appreciative of this, and often left Akiko a little something in their secret hiding spot, a brown cardboard box tucked out of sight under Sarah's desk. It began one night when Sarah had returned to work to retrieve her purse. She startled Akiko when she came in, and she could tell Akiko was hiding something behind her back. Sarah noticed Akiko's meal beside her.

"Having a little snack, Akiko?" she asked.

Akiko nodded ashamedly.

"Not to worry," Sarah smiled. "You're entitled to a break just like everyone else is. I won't say anything. What do you have behind your back?"

Akiko realized that Sarah might have thought she was stealing something, so she took from behind her back what she had been afraid to show her. It was a child's picture book.

Sarah saw the pain in Akiko's eyes and knew that she was reading the book for herself.

"Oh, she said. That's a good book. I read it to Mrs. Cook's children when I was baby-sitting them a few years back. I think it's wonderful that you are learning to read English Akiko!" Sarah said. "Do you have any more books?"

Akiko shook her head.

"Baby Jimmy," she said.

It was the first time Sarah had heard Akiko say anything in English, ever.

"Well, your son Jimmy's grown quite a bit since then. Why don't I get you a copy of one of his primary readers from the schoolhouse so you can read together?"

Akiko shook her head and Sarah saw a tear coming from her eye.

"Well then," Sarah said, "maybe you'd just like to learn by yourself, hmm?"

Akiko pointed at the pictures and then moved her fingers under the words.

Sarah understood what the woman so desperately wanted her to know, but couldn't say.

"Words and pictures," Sarah said. "I understand, Akiko. That's how you learn. That's how we all learned."

A smile passed between the two women, signalling the beginning of their silent friendship.

Sometimes Akiko would leave some cookies or some tea for Sarah's morning coffee. But Sarah, oh sometimes Sarah left some wonderful things for Akiko, and this was one of those nights. Inside the box, Akiko found one of the McMichael banned Eaton's catalogues, an old one, but new to Akiko. She had never had the opportunity to look through one before; although she knew what it was. There was some jam from Sarah's morning toast on the torn corner, and the book had been well thumbed through. Akiko smiled. There was a little note attached in what Akiko had come to recognize as Sarah's handwriting. Akiko began to spell and struggled as she sounded the words out. The note said simply:

> Words and pictures
> From Sarah

Akiko opened the catalogue. How wonderful! There were pictures of everyday common things, everyday adult common things, all laid out like a child's picture book. She pointed at the pictures and tried to make out the words beside them. "D-r-e-s-s," she spelled, then "$8.95."

Akiko reached into the pocket of her apron and found the piece of cake she had brought from home. She slipped it into the box. She reached in her pocket again and found Harry's measuring tape. She had seen Sarah looking at some bedroom curtains in the catalogue and remembered that Sarah said they were lovely but she could not afford them. She didn't understand everything Sarah said, but Sarah had pointed to the pictures of the curtains and sighed woefully. Akiko had figured it out.

The next day, while Sarah was at work, Akiko rose early and went to Sarah's parents' house. She measured the bedroom window she knew to be Sarah's from the outside of the house. What good, she asked her self, was having all the silk she had brought from Japan, rotting in a cedar trunk?

Three day later, Sarah cried when she came in one morning and found hand sewn silk curtains, exactly the size of her bedroom window in her home, folded neatly and placed in the secret box. They were the same colour as the one's she had seen in the catalogue. There was a note, which in handwriting not unlike a child's said:

C-U-R-T-A-I-N-S
From Akiko.

CHAPTER 14

The tenor voice was loud and booming, and more than a little off key, as Olivia made her way down to the wharf. It was a beautiful Easter morning and many of the women were wearing their spring best, including new Easter bonnets for the occasion. They had been conveniently on sale the week before at the general store. Still overpriced, but on sale just the same. The wind picked up a little, and Olivia's newly white-gloved hand reached to steady the hat Frank had bought her. It was quite a nice hat actually, for having been picked out by a man who took little interest in the latest ladies' fashions.

"Oh, I'se the b'y that builds the boat, And I'se the b'y that sails her'.
I'se and b'y that catches the fish, And takes 'em home to Lizer.
Hip yer partner, sally Tibbo'! Hip yer partner, Sally Brown!
Fogo. Twillingate, Mor'-tons' Harbour, all around the circle."

Olivia could see Frenchie on his boat, swabbing the deck. He was wearing a light grey suit. Olivia had never seen him dressed up before. She believed that might even have been a new Easter toque that sat upon his head. Grey, to match his suit.

"What on earth are you singing Frenchie?" she asked.

"Ah, good Easter morn' to you Liv. Nice to see you. It's a Newfie folk song I'm singin'."

"A what?"

"A Newfie folk song," he repeated. He read the blank look on her face. "A traditional song from de est coast de Newfoundland. We call dem Newfies."

"Ah," Olivia said. "A sea shanty?"

"Ach, yes. Dat is it. A liddle bit of de pirate song. For us pirates. It's traditional I tink. I dunt know who wrote it, cuz I was tinkin maybe 'e could write a song about de ouest coast, but nobody knew. But I sing it anyways cuz I like it."

"You seem in a particularly good mood today. And all dressed up. You're looking quite handsome, I must say."

"Aye lass, I am. I've been invited for Easter dinner at da widow Wolfe's. I tink she kinda fancies me."

"Oh, I see," Liv said. "And do you fancy her?"

"Livvy I'm old, I'm losin' me teeth and me hair. I pretty much fancy anytin' dat fancies me."

"Frenchie!" Olivia said in mock disgust.

"I'm sorry Livvie darlin'. I was only kiddin'. She's pretty fine, she is, the widow Wolfe."

"Dat's…I mean, that's better. You've got me talking like you Frenchie!"

"Dat'll happen to you when you've been here a few more years, 'tis sad to say."

Olivia laughed.

"Did you get it?" she asked.

"Shhh!" Frenchie said, laying his finger upon his lips. "Der's ears everywhere. Dis is almost contraband you know. But yes. 'Ere are de packages you asked me to bring you. Tuck 'dem in yer bag der. If anyone asks, I ne'er saw dem befer. Riskin' me life fer ye pretty ladies, I am."

"Your secret is safe with me Frenchie," she said. "Thank you. And good luck tonight. Be careful of that dirty mop. You wouldn't want to get your suit dirty before this afternoon."

Frenchie did a little jig around the pail.

"I'll keep dat in mind. Ya dunt know the words to dat squid jiggin' song do ya? Ya know, in case I need to sing to her during the appetizers like? Suppose not. Okay den, Weez 'avin de calamari. Da widow Wolfe, she calls it calamari, but I knows dat it's squid."

Frenchie waved good-bye to her.

"Have a nice day. Oh, and yer fadder says hello! I ran into him when I was in Seattle. Never forget a face, do I."

Olivia smiled.

"Are you sure you don't want to come to church with me Frenchie?"

"Tanks for the invitation, but we dunt want to get de widow jealous now, do we? Especially not before de turkey dinner."

"Frenchie, does the widow Wolfe have a first name?"

"Uh, yes…but…okay I can't remember. But dunt go tellin' 'er dat. Okay, dat wud be bad."

"It is *so* bad!" Olivia laughed. "What do you call her?"

"I call her "luvvy." Seems to work."

"Frenchie, that's so sweet. Tell you what, I will find out her real name and let you know, okay? To repay this favour."

"Oh, dat wuld be magnifique, Liv."

Olivia waved goodbye and started walking towards the church. It was the first Easter service in the new building, so it was quite an occasion in itself.

McMichael was coming out of his home with his girls and Mrs. Schwindt in tow. He noticed Olivia, and waited for her, letting the three go ahead. The girls had received new jumping ropes and were anxious to try them out. Even Christina had one, although he supposed it would be the last year she would want one. She was growing up too quickly, he thought. Next year he would buy her a lady's hat. She would like that. He had given Mrs. Schwindt a new hat for Easter, black of course, with a small veil as she had insisted.

"Wouldn't you rather have one of those colourful new straw ones?" he had asked her.

"No. I want a black one with a veil. Jesus died. I am wearing it for his funeral."

He reminded her that Easter was a time of celebration, that the time for mourning was over.

"That's okay, I will wear the veil up then," she said.

"You still want the black one?" he tried again.

"Yes, someone will die sometime and I will be glad I have it," she replied.

He glanced again at Olivia. He thought she looked quite lovely, her hair tied up under her hat. He could see the slender nape of her neck above her coat collar. She was quite a striking woman, he thought. He felt his heart speed up.

"Frank working?" he asked, as she caught up to him.

"You know he is," she said matter of factly.

"True enough. May I escort you off to church then? I assume that's where you're headed."

"That would be nice, thank you. There was something I wanted to ask you, if this isn't an inappropriate moment."

"Well, ask me and I'll decide."

"Do you have any jobs going right now? Anything a woman could do? I thought I saw a sign in the general store the other day."

"I'm sorry Olivia, that job is taken now."

He saw her face fall.

"It required some heavy lifting anyway, not really suitable for you, I don't think. Still, if anything comes up, I'll be glad to let you know."

"Well, actually it's not for me."

"Frank's not planning on leaving the mine, is he?"

"No, I was asking for Lucy."

She thought she saw McMichael wince, just a little.

"Ah Olivia. That's a tough one. I don't know if I can employ Lucy."

"She thinks you think she's crazy."

He coughed.

"Well, that's probably a good sign then. It's not that I think she's crazy Olivia, I just don't know if she's well enough yet to consider employing. I visited her in the hospital a few times, as I'm sure you're aware. She wasn't at all stable in her mind."

"She's been out of the hospital for quite some time now."

"I know, but she's delicate. She went through quite an ordeal."

"Lucy Bentall is not delicate, as you well know," Olivia protested. "Forgive me Mr. McMichael, but people do learn to move on after a loss, even such a tragic one. Consider your own circumstances."

McMichael stopped in his tracks. That was bold for her to say to him. Their relationship was one of acquaintance at best, and he was her husband's employer. He was not used to this kind of personal attack.

"I beg your pardon, Mrs. Fitzpatrick?"

"Again, I'm sorry sir. But you had to learn to move on with your life, when your wife died, and you did. Look at the girls, they're happily skipping up the street. Not that they don't miss their mother, of course they do, but they have learned to cope. Lucy will learn to move on to. She's already coping."

"Are you suggesting I get Lucy a skipping rope?"

This infuriated Olivia.

"Don't patronize me, Mr. McMichael. I really don't appreciate it. If you didn't believe Lucy needed help, you wouldn't have done all the things you did for her in the hospital. Well, now she's out and she needs a different kind of help."

McMichael never had women, or men for that matter, speak to him in this manner. He found it fascinating that she had the courage confront him. He felt himself drawn to her, and didn't want to push her too far.

"Give it some time then Olivia, shall we? Let's see how she does over the summer."

"She needs a job now sir."

"I'm not the only employer around here Olivia."

"You might as well be."

"Are you arguing with me?"

Olivia laughed. She actually laughed at him, and he found it exciting.

"I prefer to think of it as negotiating."

"Well, enough negotiating for today then, all right? But if you ever want a job, please do come see me. I can always find a job for a woman with some…tenacity."

They had reached the church and the girls and Mrs. Schwindt were waiting outside.

"Would you care to sit with us Olivia?"

"Thanks for the invitation Mr. McMichael, but I'm waiting for Lucy. I see her coming now."

"Fine then. Have a wonderful day. Give my regards to your husband," he paused for a moment. "You know, perhaps you two ladies could volunteer for the war effort, form some sort of ladies league. It would certainly keep you busy and it would be good for the town as well."

"I think Lucy's looking for more than just something to keep her busy. She needs something to keep her spirits up. And she needs an income."

"I was thinking more for you, Olivia. Still, you never know what will come of it. Food for thought, no?" he asked.

CHAPTER 15

The aroma of the turkey filled the house as Olivia pulled the bird from the oven later that afternoon.

"Can I help?" Frank offered.

"Yes," Olivia said, "you can help by getting away from that lemon pie, and setting the table."

"Caught in the act, hmm?" Frank said.

"Yes, and get moving please, our guests will be here any minute."

"Guests? What guests? You said guests, plural."

"Yes, Lucy will be here shortly. Set the table for four please."

"Liv," he laughed, taking her in his arms, "what have you done? Who else is coming for dinner?"

"That nice Sergeant Wolanski."

"You invited the policeman over for dinner?"

"Yes. His name is Rudy."

"Why?" he asked.

"Because that's what his mother called him."

He playfully spanked her.

"That's not what I meant, and you know it. I know his name is Rudy. Why did you invite "Rudy" over for dinner? What are you up to? A little matchmaking?"

"Maybe."

"Oh Liv, I don't think that's a good idea. Couldn't you have left it alone?"

"No. I'm just giving her a little encouragement, that's all. When we were talking, she never said she wouldn't marry again."

"You asked her that?"

"Not in so many words, but we were talking and lets just say she never said she would, but she never said she wouldn't. Don't you think he'll like Lucy? I think he'll like Lucy."

"Oh, I'm sure he'll like Lucy. I don't think that will be the problem."

"So then, what is the problem? You said you met him once and that he was nice, right?"

"Yes but anyone who doesn't throw me in jail when he should have is probably nice to me."

There was a knock at the door.

"Oh well," Olivia laughed. "It's too late now! Could you get the door please?"

Frank went to the door and let Lucy in.

"Can I take your coat, Lucy?" he asked.

"Only if you swear you won't laugh."

Olivia and Frank looked puzzled. Lucy took off her coat. She was wearing one of the floral dresses from the general store.

"Lucy! You've got a new dress! You look great," Frank complimented.

Olivia howled in laughter.

"He just doesn't get it," Olivia laughed. "He's a lovely man, but he never will."

"What?" Frank asked. "I was giving the lady a compliment."

"Thanks anyway Frank. I appreciate it. Liv is laughing because this dress, well, it's not quite me. It was the strangest thing. After church, McMichael asked what I was doing for Easter dinner, and I said I was coming here for my birthday and he marched me down to the store and insisted I have a new dress for my birthday. So I tried to say thanks, but they weren't quite my style, but he glared at me, (you know the way he does that), and what can I say? Here I am."

"I told you he likes you," Olivia smiled.

"Liv, that's not it. Trust me. You should have seen the dresses he had made for his wife. Beautiful silk blouses. Skirts of the finest brocade. She lived like a bloody queen. And that's saying something, coming from an Irish lass. Still, they say it's the gift that counts and it will help get me through the spring."

"Thanks so much for coming," Frank welcomed.

"No, thank you. I think Margaret was glad to get rid of me. I think she has invited a special man over for dinner. She was busy making stuffed snails, and fussing about. I don't know where she got them. Frenchie must have smuggled them in for her."

"He probably did," Olivia agreed, a secret smile crossing her lips. Margaret! The widow Wolfe. It all made sense.

"You know, you two ladies should open your own store and keep all the ladies in the height of fashion," Frank laughed.

"That's not a bad idea Frank," Olivia said.

"I was kidding Liv. That's all I need for my chances at that new manager's position, you opening a store and giving competition to McMichael's place."

"Well," she said, "I was talking to him earlier…"

"You were what?" Frank asked incredulously.

"At church," she continued. "He thought maybe the women could get together and do something for the war effort."

"Oh Liv," he said, his voice calming. "That would be fantastic. You were telling me you wanted something worthwhile to do. See, I do listen to you."

"And make you look good in front of the boss, because you married a wife who knows how to play up to him."

"Ah, I married a smart gal, it's true," he said, kissing her.

"Frenchie brought me up a copy of the Vancouver newspaper," Lucy offered, "and I read that the men going off to war need some winter items like gloves and hats sent over to them."

"Well that shouldn't be too hard to organize," Olivia said.

"But there's also a need for good used clothing for war torn families. Maybe we can ask for donations of any good clothing item, new or used, for the war effort."

"Something for the families that are left behind here in Canada," Olivia said. "You know, a lot of women's groups are sending things overseas to the servicemen, but I bet you're right Lucy, there are probably many families here in Canada who have lost their bread earner to the war. With little or no income coming in it must be very hard for them."

"It's like what happened to a lot of us here when the landslide happened. Luckily there were people here that cared. Not everyone is so fortunate."

There was a knock at the door.

"Frank, will you get that?" Olivia asked.

Frank glanced warily at his wife.

"Lucy, I hope you don't mind, but Rudy Wolanski is joining us for dinner. He didn't have anyone to spend the holiday with, so I invited him along."

"It's kind of like an orphan Easter you're having here," laughed Lucy.

"You don't mind?"

"Of course not. Maybe you should make it an annual event."

Luckily it never dawned on Lucy that Olivia was trying to do a little matchmaking. Lucy was in an incredibly talkative mood, having found her voice once again, and enjoyed having a new audience. To say that she had captured the ear of the sergeant would have been an understatement. Rudy, like most men at the Beach, was falling under her spell.

"We have a little something for you Lucy," Olivia said, "for your birthday. I'm sorry I didn't have time to wrap it up properly."

She handed Lucy the two bags she had received from Frenchie.

Inside the first bag was a red Aryan sweater, similar to the one Lucy had been wearing the day Olivia met her.

"Thank you," Lucy gasped. "It's beautiful! I haven't had anything this lovely to wear since everything was destroyed."

"Well, Olivia wanted to get you something special," Frank said, "so she called on our friendly neighbourhood smuggler, who was only too happy to help."

"Frenchie!" Lucy laughed.

"Wait, there's one more," Frank said, handing her the second package.

"Now, I know you said you'd wear beige, but I hope you'll like this just as well," Olivia said.

Lucy grinned ear to ear and opened the bag. Inside was a long, matching red Tartan skirt, similar to the one she had previously owned.

"We don't mean to offend you or anything, because we don't know what clan your family belongs to, we just wanted one to match the sweater," Olivia admitted.

"Oh, it doesn't matter," Lucy said, tears forming in her eyes. "I'm Irish, not Scottish anyway. I just wear them because I love them. I love the colours."

She gave Olivia and Frank a big hug.

"I really can't believe it. Thank you both so much. You have no idea what your thoughtfulness means to me," Lucy said.

Not to be out done, Rudy reached into his pocked and pulled out a tiny, wrapped box. He held it out for Lucy.

"What's this?" Lucy asked, taking the tiny box into her hand.

"Well, I hope you don't think it too forward of me," Rudy said, "but I knew it was your birthday. Olivia had told me it was a bit of a celebration, so I just wanted to pick you up a little something."

"That's very nice, you shouldn't have," Lucy said, opening the gift.

Inside the tiny box was a little tiny paper origami bird. The type that Akiko had taught her to make only a year or so ago. The kind she had made for her children in the past. A wave of emotion came over her. She bolted out the front door, the tiny bird clenched in her hand.

"What did I do?" Rudy asked.

"I don't know," Olivia replied.

"Shouldn't you go out there?" Frank asked.

"I think she wants to be alone," Olivia said. "Her coat's still here. It's cold outside. I don't think she'll go far. I'll watch her through the window. Let's give her a few minutes before we go running after her. Something has obviously upset her, but I think it's something personal. It must have triggered a memory for her."

Lucy placed her head against the porch post and started to cry, unaware that she was being observed. No one followed her outside, she knew. She was all alone again. There was no way anyone inside the house could have known the significance of the tiny sheet of folded paper. None of them had been there, with her family and the Yada's. She placed the little bird on the railing.

"Maybe it really is time to leave after all," she said to herself.

She thought she had turned a corner in her sadness, but now she once again had doubts. She took a few steps off the porch, determined to take her leave and leave the bird and the memory behind.

The wind picked up at that moment and lifted the tiny paper ornament into the sky. She was certain then that Akiko had made the piece, as it was aerodynamically perfect. It swirled around and around and headed out towards the ocean. Then the wind died down and the little bird landed in the sand. Lucy looked out toward the water, afraid of the thoughts that were running through her head.

The world around her was perfectly still for a moment. There was no noise at all, not even in the lane. The town clock began to chime in the background, but in her mind, it remained silent because she did not want to hear. It reminded her of the silence her daughter must have known, and for a brief moment, Lucy felt like they were together again. She held her head in her hands. The wind picked up again, startling her. An unseasonable gust whistled by, stinging her ears, and she was suddenly acutely aware of her surroundings once more.

She stopped sobbing. She closed her eyes and let the wind enter her lungs, forcing life back in them. She raised her head to the heavens, her arms embracing a new spirit that was filling her. She opened her eyes.

The paper bird had taken flight again, given new life, but this time it was not heading out to sea. Its direction had been reversed, and it was making its way, gust by gust, back up the mountainside until Lucy could see it no more.

"That's what I must do," she thought to herself, "make my life back up the mountain, step by step, making sure I take a moment to catch my breath along the way."

She turned around, went back up the steps and into Olivia's house once more. As she reached for the doorknob, she checked her face with her other hand. Her eyes were drying. She tossed her red curls behind her back and held her head up high and she opened the door.

"Is it time to cut the cake?" she asked. Not waiting for an answer she went into the kitchen where she had earlier noticed a candle, brought it into the livingroom and placed it in the desert herself.

Olivia smiled and lit the candle for her. "I think it would be bad luck to do it all yourself," Olivia offered.

"From now on, I'm in charge of my own luck," Lucy said, "whether the candles are lit by myself or by others."

"Welcome back Lucy," Olivia said, wiping a tear from her own eye.

Olivia, Frank and Rudy never did learn the significance of the tiny paper bird that night. All they knew is that somehow, someway, the Lucy of old was returning.

CHAPTER 16

McMichael stepped onto his front veranda and sniffed the air, much like a dog would.

It was June, and all signs of winter had long since passed. There was a warm breeze coming across the Pacific this morning, signalling the arrival of summer. The tall, white dogwood, which had been in bloom most of April and May, was also losing its petals, making way for the summer blossoms.

Still, McMichael thought, there was an air of discontent that he couldn't quite put his finger on. His home was peaceful now, but in a few hours the daily shouting between his daughter Christina and their housekeeper Mrs. Schwindt would begin. Perhaps it was because Christina was a teenager and rather moody that she raised the ire of the nanny on more than one occasion. One would come to expect that. Christina had started insisting that Mrs. Schwindt be referred to as the family housekeeper, not the nanny, as she felt she was far too old for a nanny, and McMichael thought that she was probably right about that. Mrs. Schwindt it seemed however, preferred to be called the nanny. She let him know that in so many words. He sensed that was only the tip of the iceberg. More and more lately McMichael had noticed a change in Mrs. Schwindt's personality. True, she had always been a touch cantankerous, but that side of her was growing now, and it was rare that any of the McMichael's would see her crack a smile, or laugh the throaty cackle they had all made fun of from time to time. If things kept going the way they were, McMichael admitted, he would need to make a change. He was not looking forward to either the change or the decision that would have to precede it.

The streets were empty as he made his way to the office. The lights were already on, so he knew that Sarah had beaten him into work that morning.

That in itself was not a good sign. Sarah was chronically late. She stayed late to make up for it, but getting Sarah in for seven a.m. for five consecutive days in a row would signal the beginning of Armageddon. Here it was, six forty-five and the office was open for business. He opened the door and found Sarah sobbing at her desk.

"What the hell is wrong with you now?" he asked, which of course only threw her into sobbing fits as she tried to stop but couldn't.

"Sarah, you're going to hyperventilate if you keep that up," he said. He walked over to the calendar and looked at the date.

"Well, it's not a blue moon month, so you can't be asking me for a raise."

Someone had once told Sarah that McMichael gave out raises 'once in a blue moon', so like clockwork, she waited until the calendar would show the double full moon, and gather her courage to ask her boss for more money. McMichael had overheard her talking about this to a girlfriend, and he found it quite hilarious. She would work herself up into quite a state the few days leading up to it, so he always knew it was coming. But she had been fine yesterday.

McMichael went into his office and began to go through the correspondence Sarah had left on his desk. At the top of the pile was a letter from the provincial government thanking the community for the tremendous contributions the ladies of Britannia Beach had made for the war effort. He had to hand it to them, once Olivia and Lucy got it into their heads to set up a committee to gather clothing for needy families of the men stationed overseas, they distributed more than the groups in the city had managed to do. McMichael had relented and let the women use a storage room out back, and stood in awe as they inventoried their clothing stock far better than his own stock was kept. He made a mental note of that. Sarah volunteered to handle their correspondence on her own time, so he had said she was free to use the company stationary for her letters if she needed to. He supposed that's why the letter had arrived here, at the mine, instead of at the post office. Still, it was nice to see the government recognizing their efforts, and he thought perhaps he would have Sarah organize a tea party for the ladies. Nothing fancy, just cookies and tea, but a chance for celebration all the same. He went back into the outer office.

"For the love of God Sarah," he asked. "Did someone die?"

She was gazing out the window and the tears were flowing again. McMichael could see Sergeant Wolanski and Lucy Bentall having a conversation on the corner.

"Is that what this is all about?" he asked.

Sarah nodded.

McMichael had been through this with Sarah several times as she constantly fell in love with men who at best did not return her feelings.

"Why are all the men in love with Lucy? What is wrong with me?" she asked.

McMichael thought about this. It was true that most of the men in town found Lucy incredibly attractive, and he could see why. But he himself, contrary to popular belief, did not. He could think of other women in town who enchanted him more. Particularly one.

"Lucy is a beautiful woman, it's true. But not all the men are in love with her."

"You are," Sarah said.

He laughed out loud.

"I am not!" he said indignantly.

"But you bought her a dress."

"You told me to!" he shouted. "You told me it was her birthday and I needed to buy her something to cheer her up, so I did."

"You bought her the dress because you love her."

"No Sarah! I bought her the dress because you told me she didn't have anything to wear since her things were gone and that she needed something new. I like Lucy, she was a friendly to my wife. I appreciate that. Most of the women in town were jealous of my wife. If I loved Lucy, I would not have bought her that dress. Lucy Bentall hates that dress. I knew she would hate that dress. But I thought you were right, that she needed something, and I thought it would be a nice gesture. That's it. Really. That's it!"

She looked at the dress she was wearing that was also purchased at the General store. McMichael realized he might have put his foot in his mouth.

"Look Sarah," he began, "that remark wasn't meant to be personal. That dress looks quite nice on you, it's more your style. You're more demure. Lucy Bentall is many things, but demure isn't one of them. Now getting back to the matter at hand. Did Sergeant Wolanski ever make any indication to you that he had feelings other than friendliness for you?"

"Well, no..." she began, "not exactly."

"Not exactly?" he quizzed.

"Not in so many words, no..."

"He didn't lead you on?"

"No."

"He didn't ply you with alcohol and rob you of your virtue?"

"Oh stop it," she laughed. "Now you're being ridiculous."

"Love, Sarah," he began, "is a mutual thing. If you don't both feel that way, then it isn't love. Now isn't there a chance that you got a little too carried away with your crush on the policeman? Just like you did with the young red headed miner? And the veterinarian? And come to think of it, the dead doctor? I mean, I seem to recall you were crazy about him until you found out he was getting married."

McMichael took a deep breath. It dawned on him that he was probably going to be having the same conversations with his oldest daughter very soon, and perhaps Sarah was good practice.

"It will happen Sarah, you just need to find the right man."

Sarah wiped her eyes and smiled.

"Quit looking at me like that Sarah," he said. "Don't get any ideas. I am not the right man. Don't even entertain that idea."

Sarah laughed.

"Then can I have a raise?"

"No," he said. "Listen Sarah, Lucy has a way with clothes, with fashion. Why don't you ask her to help you, if you're not comfortable with your appearance. Now don't make a face, I'm not saying that there's anything wrong with you. There isn't Sarah. But maybe she can help you feel better about yourself. Why don't you ask her?"

"I don't know…" she hesitated.

"Then ask Olivia. You like Olivia right? Olivia is," he paused, "a woman of great grace. I don't know much about her own family, but I get a sense there's some culture there. She has a certain confidence that is very becoming to a man. Who knows, maybe she has a brother."

This pleased Sarah.

"Okay," she sighed. "Maybe I'll talk to the girls."

"You do that," he said. "And having solved that world crisis, perhaps we can turn our thoughts to our overtime budget. I need to check on the status."

"It's already on your desk sir," she said.

Sometimes, McMichael had to admit, women could be so intuitive and surprising.

CHAPTER 17

Frenchie Cates sat on the deck of the Northern Mary; a cup of freshly brewed black coffee in his hand. The sun had come up over the mountains earlier in what was the most spectacular pink and yellow sunrise he had seen in quite some time. He thought of the old adage, pink sky in morning, sailors take warning, which seemed to be true everywhere in the world except the West Coast.

"Tis gonna be a bonny day 'ere, non?" he said aloud, although no one was near.

It was still pretty quiet for a Thursday morning. The men had already rotated from the graveyard shift to the day shift at the mine. A little early for the rest of the townspeople to be out and about, the streets were relatively empty. He pulled his brown wooden pipe out of his flannel coat pocket and lit it. His Maggie wasn't too happy about his pipe smoking, so they had come to the understanding he would only smoke aboard his boat, not at her home, which he was spending more and more time at. She had banned chewing tobacco altogether, and this was a compromise he was more than happy to live with, rather than live without her. Things were going pretty well between him and Maggie, he thought. They might even have a future. He was tempted to get down on one knee and propose. They were both mature adults and who knew how much time they really had left together? But then he thought that Maggie would think it was too soon, that he was only after her money, and he decided to wait a bit longer. Maybe another year. Besides, if he moved in with Maggie, where was Lucy going to go? Frenchie couldn't throw her out onto the street after all she had been through, but the tiny house would be too small for the three of them. No, the Northern Mary would be his home for a while yet.

His friend Sharkey Miller's crabber was just coming up to the dock. Sharkey and his crew must have stayed out all night. That was odd, given the weather had been clear and Sharkey normally returned before sunset.

Frenchie turned his head and saw Frank standing up the dock, watching the world go by. That too, was a bit odd, given the fact that the morning crew had just started and he should have been at the mine, bossing them around or whatever it was he did. Frenchie had heard the boys saying that Frank himself was pretty odd these days. The way they told it, the good-natured young man with whom they had shared many a brew was disappearing. Some said the foreman's job had gone to his head. They never called him Frankie anymore. Some said the grudge Frank had against Les Ferguson was becoming an obsession. Some said he was having trouble at home with his wife. Even the ladies were saying that. Saying he wouldn't even let her visit her family. He never drank with the other miners down at the pub anymore they said, not even on Friday.

Frenchie gave him an acknowledging wave. Frank nodded back. That was the extent of their relationship. Although Frenchie was quite fond of Olivia, he had never had the occasion to get to know her husband, and that suited him fine. Frankie was in deep with McMichael, Frenchie had heard, and that was reason enough for him to keep his distance from Frank.

Sharkey's boat was now in, and he was tying her up to the dock.

"Where ye bin?" Frenchie asked. "I was gittin' worried when ye didn't git in 'ere last night. I was givin' ye till noon befer we got a search crew out dere fer ye."

"It was a good haul yesterday," Sharkey said. "We decided to take it on into the fisheries in Vancouver. They're paying top dollar right now. If anyone around here asks, we had rudder problems and needed to take her into the shipyard, that's why we went south."

"Gotcha," Frenchie winked.

"You got any ale Frenchie?"

"Now Sharkey, ye know der's ne'er bin any of the devil's brew onboard de Northern Mary," he said, nodding his head towards the top of the dock where Frank was still standing. He lowered his voice. There would be no whispering winds carrying this conversation up the dock.

"I tot ye were unloaded."

"It was a really good haul Frenchie. We had enough to take to Vancouver and also some left for our own interests, let's say. Not too much mind you, given the mysterious rudder problem and all. Just in case anyone is too curious. And not short of your own special cargo either. In case you were wondering."

"Twelve for twelve?" Frenchie smiled.

"Double it up this time."

Frenchie smiled wider. He loved to eat crab, and although twenty-four of them were probably too much for him and Maggie and Lucy, he was sure there were some deals to be made for the rest. He'd get that Japanese woman, Akiko, to come down and give his galley a clean. She'd be more than happy to take a few off his hands while they were still alive and kicking. And a couple would go to Olivia and Sarah, just because he still loved the ladies, much to Maggie's chagrin.

"At dusk?" Sharkey asked.

Frenchie nodded.

"No…wait," he added. "Mon Dieu, where is my 'ead? I'll be 'eadin' down de coast dis afternoon. I've got some special cargo of me own to take down south. Let's just wait for Frank to get lost and we'll make de swap."

He glanced up the dock. Frank had finally left.

"Well der you go den," Frenchie said. "Let's make de trade."

Sharkey went below on his boat and brought up what appeared to be a large cotton mailbag. Frenchie took it gingerly.

"Des still a snappin'," he smiled, taking it below and coming back up with a box marked Coastal Marine Supply held tightly in his arms.

"Dunt know what it be, inside 'ere. Must be some of dem boat parts ye ordered," he said loudly, just in case Les or Frank were lurking around.

"Careful, it's kinda 'eavy."

As he passed Sharkey the box, the unmistakable rattle of bottles could be heard.

"Must be bottles of teak oil," Sharkey laughed. "My deck has been getting rather weathered lately. I have to do something about that."

"Tought so." Frenchie laughed back. He leaned closer to Sharkey. "Only dis time, it's not teak ale, it's teak scotch. I 'ad a good haul too! I still owe ye one fer the salmon you got me a few months back. We be even stevens now, okay?"

Sharkey was grinning ear to ear as he slunk back to his own boat.

Frenchie went inside the galley and poured himself another cup of coffee, and came back up on deck. He had just sat comfortably in his chair when he saw Lucy walking by.

"Lucy!" he yelled.

She turned and looked at him.

"Lucy! Come 'ere," he yelled again.

She came down to the boat.

"Whatever is it Frenchie?" she asked.

He paused for a moment, his eyes shifting side to side.

"Okay Frenchie," she said. "Spill it. I know you're dying to tell me something."

"Lucy, did I ever tell you de story 'bout one legg'd Davey McClegg?"

Lucy started to laugh.

"No, I don't believe I've heard that one."

"Well, ye see, 'es a buddy o'mine back est. I mean east. I'm tryin' to learn to talk better for Maggie. Anyways…down on 'is luck a bit Davey McLegg was. And one day 'e gets de idea to try to rob one of dose trains dat carry de mail. 'E tinks der is money on board and 'es been 'earin' de stories about Jesse James, bang, bang, shoot 'em up, you know. So 'e works out a plan dat seems like a good idea, but 'e forgets e's got a wooden leg, and 'es a stubborn man and 'e wants to do it all 'iself. But dat is a bad idea eh, cuz 'e can't ride a horse and 'e can't run away. So 'e tries it. De robbery I mean, and de lawmen on de train shoot him bang, bang dead. At least dat's what I 'eard. Dey say dat if 'ed only 'ad some 'elp, 'e might 'a pulled it off. Might of bin a rich man. Sometimes ye need to trust people and tell dem yer plan and 'ave a liddle 'elp. Sometimes ye need yer friends."

"Frenchie," Lucy said slowly. "What are you getting at? You're not asking me to help you rob a train are you? Because it seems to me that all of your friends wind up losing body parts."

"So you're not worried about de robbery part?"

"Frenchie!"

"Okay, den. No robberies. I do need yer 'elp doh. I promise Lucy, no missin' body parts. You 'ave my word. Besides you'd be no good fer a story cuz I can't rhyme anytin' wid yer name. But come closer cuz I 'ave a plan and I already got one odder 'elper, so we'll have an accomplice like. We might even need one more."

Intrigued, Lucy came closer and Frenchie whispered in her ear.

She listened, slightly alarmed at first, but as Frenchie's plan unfolded, she felt herself filling with excitement.

"Frenchie," she said. "You tell your other helper that Juicy Lucy is in!"

CHAPTER 18

Olivia held the dirty envelope she had pulled from the trash. It was unopened, addressed to her in her mother's handwriting, and it had been thrown away. She sighed.

Tears started to run as she opened the letter.

Olivia,

It's been so long since we've seen you; I can't wait to see you when you come down for Emily's wedding. She's so excited she's started sleepwalking again. You remember when she used to do that when you were younger, and you would have to go get her in the yard and bring her back to bed! It's hard to believe my first batch of babies are all grown up. You haven't met your new baby brother Daniel yet. He's already walking and talking. He's learned a few choice words from your father, I'm afraid. And speaking of your father, don't tell him I've told you this, but he is just giddy knowing that you'll be home to see us soon. He always says he loves all his children equally, but between us women, I think he might just love you a teeny tiny bit more. Have a safe journey.

Love Mother.

Sobbing, Olivia took the letter and threw it back into the trash, carefully placing some garbage over it so Frank wouldn't discover she had found it.

Something inside her at that moment finally gave way.

The last few months had been unbearable. Frank was working overtime almost every day at the mine, and she loved it. She loved it when he wasn't around. He had asked her to quit the ladies group and she had done so, not because she wanted to, but because it pleased him and it was easier to please him than to argue with him. He wanted her to stop seeing Lucy, so she had told him she would. Lucy came by for a short visit once or twice a week anyway because Lucy didn't care what Frank did or didn't want. She would stop by in the afternoons when Frank worked the day shift and early in the evening when he was working nights so he wouldn't find out. Olivia found herself envying Lucy's freedom. She knew it was because her own marriage was failing. She just didn't know how to go about changing it. She couldn't pinpoint exactly when it had all started to go wrong, but it had been just around the time Frank got the promotion to foreman. While she didn't actually see Frank spending much time with McMichael, she figured he must have been with him a lot at work and perhaps McMichael's abruptness was rubbing off on him. Frank had seriousness about him she hadn't seen before. When they were in their teens he had been so carefree. Who knows what the two were getting up to? Frank used to despise McMichael, but lately? She didn't know; it sometimes seemed as if he were trying to emulate him. But why? All for this promise of a new job, this more important job McMichael kept dangling over Frank's head. She would try to engage Frank in light-hearted conversations about work, but he would ignore her, or worse, tell her she couldn't possibly understand.

He had become very controlling, she recognized. That, combined with Britannia's isolation, often made her feel more like a family pet than a wife, only able to go out when the master lets it. She remembered fondly the days when she was a teenager, rebelling against everything, certainly not afraid of male authority. Frank had always been a part of her schemes and what fun they had together. She had snuck out of the house late at night more times than she could count on two hands. She would inevitably get caught, but she would stand up to her father. Her *FATHER!* They had some royal battles in their time, but it would always blow over. She would take the punishment, usually more chores, and use the time to daydream about her next great caper.

Her arguments with Frank however, were nothing like her jousts with her father. They would simmer on the boil, not cooling down for days or even occasionally weeks. On more than one occasion he had raised his fist to her, and she was afraid it was only a matter of time before a blow landed.

She remembered one occasion distinctly. The idea of the store had been in the back of her mind since Easter dinner. One night, when Frank seemed in a light-hearted mood, she brought up the subject again. At first he laughed. Where would they get the money? Where would they get the land? What would he do when McMichael fired him? He had a grand chuckle about it all. But when he realized that Olivia had good plausible answers for all these questions, his tempter raged to a level she had never seen before. She had gathered the courage to tell him that if he struck her, she would leave him, and he backed off. But he kept her on a very short leash from that point on. Since he was afraid she might leave and never return, the allowance he had always given her, her mad money as he would call it, was taken away. He would give her only enough money for the groceries and asked her to provide him with a receipt. Going to her sister's wedding was out of the question he had told her, the excuse always being that there was no money, despite the hours of overtime he was putting in. He wagered she wouldn't go alone, that would be too much to explain to her family. She was trapped.

So despite being a woman from a very fine home, despite being a very clever woman, despite being an educated woman and knowing what she knew she needed to do to make herself happy, she still couldn't bring herself to actually do it. She *loved* him, she told herself. She had made a very serious wedding vow. Although she wanted to pull that letter from the middle of the trash can and put it on top so that he would know that she knew it had arrived, she left it there. She sat alone in the kitchen and cried.

There were two knocks on the door. She knew it was Lucy. Lucy always knocked twice, that was the pre-arranged signal, but she didn't get up to let her in. She didn't want any company. She had however, left the door unlocked as everyone in the town did, and Lucy, who had seen a light on, let herself in anyway.

Olivia looked at her through tear stained eyes.

"I need to borrow some of your clothes," Lucy said.

"What? Lucy, they won't fit you."

"Don't be ridiculous. They're not for me. Sarah wants to try some new styles and she's about your size. Stop crying okay?"

"And you need them right now? Right this minute?"

"Well, it's either that or listen to her go on and on about needing to improve herself so she can get a man, and not knowing how to do it without some fancy magazines to look at. I swear I don't know why the woman has suddenly adopted me, but she has."

"Aren't you going to ask me what's wrong?"

"I know what's wrong. The same thing that has been wrong for months. You want to go to the wedding and you think you can't. So you've got yourself all worked up again."

Lucy grabbed a paper bag from under the sink and went into Olivia's closet and began to pull some dresses out.

"I think I'll need another bag."

"Lucy, I don't know about this. Why are you taking my underwear? That's a little personal."

"I won't let her wear it silly. I just want to show her she has options. Sarah needs to visualize. I need to let her know there are more than white cotton fillies out there. I've done laundry with you, I know you have some different coloured ones. Mine are a little too risqué for our impressionable Sarah. They're silk. Akiko makes them for me. But these little pink ones, they'll do just fine."

Lucy turned to Olivia.

"I have tried to knock some sense into you woman, for the past two weeks. Just go. Do you hear me? Just go! I will take up a collection for the fare and Frenchie will take you down to Seattle and back. You'd be fine. I go down with him alone all the time. He's not going to try anything; you'll be in no danger. It's your sisterly duty to go to the wedding. All the ladies feel just terrible about it and would love to help you out by helping with your expenses. They figure Frank's not going to help with it."

"They know about this? Lucy, how do they know about this?"

Olivia knew only too well how they knew about it.

"Well, they just know, that's all. And they think it's a shame. Your own flesh and blood and your husband won't take you to the wedding. He could get the time off Olivia. Sarah says he has plenty of time off coming to him. In fact, she nagged McMichael about this and he offered Frank time off."

"She nagged McMichael? He knows? Lucy, Frank will kill me. First I become a charity case for the ladies and then this? Are you trying to get me killed? He'll be absolutely furious if he finds out."

"In answer to your questions, yes, she nagged McMichael. That's what Sarah does for a living. And he must enjoy it on some level or he'd fire her, which of course, he never does. He fires everyone else. Yes, McMichael knows. He told Sarah as he always does that she should mind her own business. Then later that day Frank was in the office and McMichael said that he appreciated the extra work Frank had been putting in, but that Frank was looking a little tired, and would he like a little time off this weekend? Frank said no. He said *NO*, Olivia! So then Sarah asked McMichael later what he was going to do about it, and he said he was going to take his own advice and mind his own business. And then Sarah said McMichael smiled, which she found rather peculiar. And since he was in such a great mood, Sarah said she asked him for some time off for herself and he gave it to her. He gave the time off to *her*. So you see Olivia, Frank will not find out from McMichael that McMichael knows, so there's no need to worry about that. I'm just telling you what Sarah told me for your own good. Your eyes need to be opened. Next, the ladies do not consider you a charity case. You had been so kind to so many of them that they would like to do something a little special for you because they never see you anymore. That, Olivia, they all can see themselves, without my saying anything to them, thank you very much. They got to know you when we were collecting for the war and they miss you. Even Mrs. Schwindt says nice things about you. Can you honestly say you've ever heard her say nice things about anybody? Mary Alice wanted to make you a new dress for the wedding. Okay, I talked her out of it, but at least she offered. If you are embarrassed by their show of goodwill, then I won't ask for their help. But lastly, and you listen girl, what bothers me the most is that there was an icy tone to your voice when you said Frank would kill you. So help me Hannah, if he lays as much as a finger you, and I find out about it, and find out about it I will, I swear I will kidnap you and take you back to Seattle myself. After I've rope tied him and strung him up on Mrs. Schwindt's clothesline naked, hanging by his ears."

Olivia laughed. She could see Lucy doing that.

"It's okay Lucy. I'm just being over-dramatic as usual."

"Ah, but Olivia, my dear friend. You are not the dramatic one. You are the very self-confident, smart, easy-going one whom everyone adores. Have you forgotten who you are?"

There was a silence between the two women.

Lucy said no more, leaving with the bags of clothes in hand.

Olivia sat back down and thought about Lucy's last remark. It was true, she knew that. She was becoming someone else. Someone she didn't like very much. People change, she thought. Frank had changed, that was for sure. She had changed. She had always been an extrovert, but had become rather shy when faced with the prospect of being the new person in town. Then the extrovert in her rose again, and she found herself doing more and seeing more, making friends and fitting in. Now, almost calculatedly, she was withdrawn again. Perhaps, she thought, she and Frank would change again and everything would be fine. After all, she still loved him, she told herself.

CHAPTER 19

Sarah came out from the mine office and stood on the veranda. She glanced impatiently up and down the street.

"Oh where is Frenchie?" she asked herself.

Out from the cabin of the Northern Mary came Frenchie, who looked up towards the mining office.

Sarah waved her arms in a big circle, ensuring he noticed her. Everyone would notice her, he thought.

He waved back.

Lucy walked up to Sarah and handed her the bag of clothes.

"Here you go," she said to her. "Where is everyone?"

"McMichael is up looking at the concentrator. It's broken down again. Can you believe it? He is so mad. I swear I saw steam coming out of his ears. He and Frank will be working on it for hours. Go! Quickly!"

Lucy ran back to Olivia's house and this time, didn't even bother knocking.

"Olivia! Come quick," she said, barging through the door.

Olivia looked at her friend. She had never seen Lucy out of breath before. Something had to be terribly wrong.

"What's happened?"

"It's Frenchie. He's out cold. I need your help."

"Shouldn't you get the doctor?"

"No, he's probably drunk too much. Frenchie. Not the doctor. He was celebrating something, that's for sure. I need your help giving him some smelling salts or something. Last time I gave him too many and his nose bled for days. Come quick Olivia, Maggie's down there and she's panicking and I don't know what to do. You have to help me. Please!"

"Okay, okay," Olivia said, grabbing her coat.

Lucy took her hand and the two of them ran down to the Northern Mary, where indeed, Maggie was waiting on deck. She didn't seem too upset though, Olivia thought upon observation. Sarah was there too.

"He's in the cabin, starting to come to," Maggie said. "He's a bit groggy though, if you two could check on him while you're here, I'd appreciate it. He's headed down to Vancouver this afternoon and I don't know if that's such a smart thing. Lordy, I can't find Dr. Van Den Broek anywhere. It would probably be best if someone had a look at him, just to be sure. I'll stay up here and see if I can see the doctor go by."

Olivia and Lucy went into the cabin. Frenchie appeared to be fine. He got up under his own power and went outside leaving the ladies behind. Olivia noticed him secure the lock on the outside cabin door. He kissed Maggie before she turned and headed up the dock. It looked like a goodbye kiss. Olivia also noticed the two brown paper bags that were full of her clothes, the clothes Lucy had taken, were on the galley table.

"Lucy, what's going on?" she asked hesitantly.

"Your friends have officially kidnapped you. You are going to Seattle. We are stopping in Vancouver tonight, and you will be in Seattle in time for the wedding this weekend."

"But Frank will be furious!"

"Maggie will take care of that. She stayed ashore."

"Maggie is in on this too?"

"We're all in on this. Maggie, Frenchie, Sarah and me, and one other person who shall remain nameless."

Olivia ran for the door.

"Oh, it's locked," Lucy said. "So you might as well just sit back and enjoy the scenery. Frenchie will unlock it when we're well at sea. We will have a grand time, the four of us. Yes, Sarah is coming along too. It's her first trip away from Britannia ever, and she's very excited. I am amazed she kept this a secret. She needed time off too, you see, which is why she told McMichael about the wedding and that you had invited her along if Frank couldn't come. She's cunning, our Sarah. I'm beginning to see a whole new side of her."

"But how will I pay for all this?" Olivia asked.

"Trust me, everything has been taken care of. Just don't cry please," Lucy said.

Oddly enough, Olivia didn't feel like crying.

"What are those in the sink?" she asked.

"Crabs," Lucy said. "I hope you're hungry. I'm getting a little sick of them myself."

Back at Britannia, McMichael was standing alone outside the assaying building. He had watched the whole caper go down, beginning with Sarah waving her arms in the air like a crazy woman.

"Mind your own business," he said to himself, but he was smiling. It was the only smile he had cracked since the news of the concentrator going down.

Maggie came up the road and approached him.

"Is Frank around?" she asked.

"He's trying to get the concentrator up and running again. Is it an emergency Margaret? The damn thing has been down half the shift. I'll never get the ore I need processed on time if I'm not at full capacity."

"No," she said. "Would you just see that he gets this letter as soon as he's done, Mr. McMichael?"

She handed it to him.

"So now I'm in on it too?" he asked her.

"I really don't know what you're talking about sir," Maggie said. "Just give him the letter, hmm?"

"Why must I hand him the letter, Margaret?"

"Well, you are his boss."

"I think I've been chosen."

"Well, if one's wife has suddenly had a change of plans, wouldn't you want the husband to know? And if he weren't around wouldn't you give the letter to someone who would see him and could be trusted to give it to him? And if that person happened to be his boss, so be it."

"And if the husband is angry and the boss knows what is happening between the two of them, then the wife now has someone to help keep her safe, no?"

"I could give the letter to Sergeant Wolanski if you'd rather," said Maggie.

"Not my man Les? I'm sure Les would love to deliver the news to Frank that his wife has run off. Loves to get under Frank's skin making remarks about Olivia, Les does. Delights in it actually."

Maggie pulled the letter back.

"Ah, so I'm right then. No, I'll give Frank the letter Margaret, no worries."

"This is a small town, Mr. McMichael. Everyone knows everyone. Everyone knows everything. You're right. I've heard that Les likes to continually wind Frank up about Olivia. But really, everyone knows your man Les delights in stalking your daughter, although he's not quite so obvious about it now. I suppose it was noble for Frank to give Les what he had coming to him that night in the beer parlour, but two wrongs don't make a right as they say. The boys all loved Frank that night, it was Frankie this and Frankie that, but they're not so crazy about Frank now, are they? Everyone knows you're planning to send Christina off to that fancy private school in Vancouver. You really don't have to you know. What's that going to solve? We're all watching out for her, not just Frank. But you didn't have to put the rest of us on your payroll. We watch out for her because we care about her. She's a pretty lass, just like her mother was, God rest her soul. Let her stay here with her family and friends. Don't send her away with strangers. Think about it, Mr. McMichael."

"It's too late Margaret. My mind is made up. I'm going to Vancouver to take a look at some of the schools very soon. The girls will stay with Mrs. Schwindt while I'm away. I'm surprised you know all this. The grapevine appears to be well informed but I can assure you it doesn't know everything."

"Well, it also knows you fancy Olivia more than you ever fancied Lucy," Maggie added with a big grin on her face, getting back to the task at hand. "We see the way you smile when you look at her. So you see Mr. McMichael, we know that if anyone wants to help keep our Olivia safe, you'd be the one. That is, if we were at all concerned."

"Everyone knows this, do they, Margaret? Everyone knows everything?"

"Everyone."

"Ah, I see," he said mockingly. "Then there's no need to remind everyone that she's a married lady."

But he's not denying it, Maggie thought to herself, once again placing the letter in McMichael's hand.

It was almost sunset before Frank came down to give McMichael the bad news that the concentrator was on its last legs.

"You'd better keep that concentrator running Fitzpatrick, or you can kiss that promotion good-bye. If that concentrator goes down for any length of time, I'll be laying off people, starting with you."

McMichael handed him the letter.

"What's this?" he asked.

"I don't know," McMichael said. "Margaret Wolfe asked me to give it to you."

"It's probably an invitation of some sort for the wife," Frank said.

"It's got your name on it," replied McMichael.

Frank, not knowing any better, opened the letter with McMichael standing by.

Frank's face turned three shades of red, and McMichael could see beads of sweat forming above his brow.

"Something wrong?" Michael asked, knowing that Frank was about to lie to him. He watched Frank's face carefully, so he would know how to read him the next time he did so.

"No sir," Frank said, saying nothing more, his shifting eyes betraying him.

The letter was from Olivia's father.

CHAPTER 20

❁

Frank was awoken by the sound of a steel tray being slipped across the floor. His head was foggy and throbbing and he could barely see out of one eye. He looked up at the ceiling and realized he was not at home. He was still wearing the clothes he had worn the day before. At least he was still fully dressed, he thought.

"Your breakfast," a voice said, "if you can stomach anything."

"Where am I?" Frank asked.

He sat up on the cot and it suddenly became painfully aware of his whereabouts. Rudy Wolanski was staring at him from behind the opposite side of the bars.

"Jail?"

"You don't remember too much about last night, do you?" Wolanski asked.

"I remember going down to the bar," he admitted.

That had been strange enough. Having read and re-read William Bower's letter over and over, getting madder with each turn, he had decided to go have a beer with the boys. When he got there, the tables were all full and he remembered no one making an effort to move over to let him sit with them. He wound up sitting at the bar in the space normally reserved for Les Ferguson.

"Well let me fill you in on a few more details," Wolanski said. "You were at the bar all right, although by the time I got there you had been thrown out. What was that all about?"

Frank held his head in his hands and tried to think about it some more. Les had come into the bar demanding his seat. Frank was feeling no pain by that time, he recalled. The seat next to him had come available and since it was the only vacant one Frank actually motioned for Les to sit there, but Les was insistent on getting his usual spot. So Frank had moved.

"I remember talking to Les," Frank said. "I must have got into another fight with him. So where is he? Shouldn't he be in here too?"

"No," the sergeant said sternly. "Think some more."

Wolanski walked out of the jail leaving Frank alone.

"Rudy, what are you doing? Let me out," Frank said.

It was nightfall before the officer returned, bringing Frank some more food.

"Are you letting me out now?"

"That would depend on whether or not you remember what got you here in the first place."

"I don't remember much," Frank admitted. The night was an alcohol-induced blur.

"Well let me try to help you along," Wolanski said. "You were in the middle of the street just before midnight, yelling out death threats. Does any of that ring a bell?"

"No. I remember sitting with Les. He must have said something to get me going."

"See, now that's the strange part," Wolanski said. "I was asking around and it seems that you and Les were getting along just fine in the bar."

"Rudy, why were you asking around? You know I'm not a bad guy. It's Les who is dangerous."

"Because right now, I'm not Rudy to you. You're in my cell. I'm Sergeant Wolanski. Which means you might be a bad guy, I don't know at the moment. What's going on with you at home?"

Frank felt his blood rushing to the top of his head.

"What's that got to do with anything?"

"What's this about your wife being smuggled off to Seattle and you receiving a letter?"

"How do you know about that?"

"Okay Frank," Wolanski said, losing patience. "You can play dumb all you like, and you can sit here in this cell forever if you want. I heard you threaten the lives of your wife and your father-in-law. So did half the town. So I've been asking around. I know a lot about your home life. We had this conversation once before unofficially. Do you remember? When you and Les had the fight and I asked if it was about the young girl, your wife or both? We had a discussion about letting things you can't control eat away at you. When you're ready to tell me the whole story, I'll tell you the rest of mine. You might want to get that blanket down off the top shelf. It'll be a colder night for you tonight, seeing that you're conscious and all."

"If I'm not at work tomorrow McMichael will make you let me out," Frank said.

"Give your head a shake, Frank. You're not that important to him."

"I'd never really do anything to Olivia. I love her. I was just mad at her since she ran off."

"Well that's a start," the officer said. "Just be thankful it appears she has just run off for the wedding. Keep acting the way you're acting and she'll be going away for good. I speak from experience. I was terribly jealous of my wife, with no reason. I kept pushing her. It was just one more thing she didn't want to deal with. She had more on her plate than I knew. She eventually had enough of it and left for good. It wasn't pretty. It was a hard lesson to learn. I'm trying to give you some advice. Whether you take it or not is up to you. The time you have with your wife is precious. In the brief time I have known you, I have seen a change in you, a change in who your friends are. You might want to turn yourself around and go back on that path you first came here on. I believe you when you say you won't harm her. I think it was the drink talking. I don't know if I believe you when you say you love her. I don't even know if you respect her right now. You're certainly not acting like it. I'll be watching you, all the same. Now about the other one…"

"I don't know if I can make the same promise about her father. I hate him."

"Well, I don't know if I can let you out then. You think about that. Remember, I know about that too."

Frank spent three nights in jail before the sergeant relented and let him out. He had a lot of time to think. He thought about what Rudy had said, but while the officer's intentions were virtuous, Frank did not take his advice.

McMichael had said no foreman of his should be spending time in jail and that while Frank was going to be lucky enough to be able to keep his job this time, there would be no next time and any thoughts of a promotion were out of the question.

Frank began to simmer on the boil once again.

CHAPTER 21

"So tell me again about this store you want to open," William Bower said, "and why you can't do it? Is there a need for one? Have you done your homework?"

The wedding reception for Emily was in full swing. It had been a beautiful wedding, and Emily had been absolutely thrilled to see Olivia. There had been over two hundred guests invited. Olivia looked almost as radiant as the bride in a new blue taffeta bridesmaid dress, stylishly cut, that her parents had surprised her with. Feeling a draft, she adjusted the matching shawl across her shoulders. When she first saw the dress, she was concerned that it might be too small, but the stress of the past couple of months had actually brought her back down to her normal weight. Lucy had commented that she wasn't eating enough, and now Olivia saw that her friend had been right. If she had dropped that much weight unconsciously, she thought, she had better pay better attention to her diet when she returned. She patted the back of her newly coiffed hair. She still couldn't believe she had actually been to the beauty parlour earlier that morning. What a treat! Of course there was a salon back at the Beach, but she never had the money to go on a whim.

"The problem is Mr. McMichael. He owns everything. He controls everything. There are a lot of things we can't get at the store, that the people could really use, but he won't bring them in."

"Like what?"

"Like the Eaton's catalogue. It's a catalogue that's available across Canada. He had it for a while, but he couldn't fix the prices, so he stopped carrying it. There were a lot of items available in it that the women wanted but couldn't get in town. Household furnishings, all the modern appliances and lots of clothes for the whole family. If I had a store I'd definitely offer it to the customers. The best part about it is you have this wonderful inventory and don't have to carry the stock. The customers order it through the store, and when it arrives, they pay for it. Eaton's has a full return policy. It's true the margins are small, but there's really not much risk involved. It takes a while to get here, but at least it's a possibility for everyone."

"What else?" William asked.

"Well, we're pretty much held hostage as far as food supplies go because there's only one place to shop, so to speak. Take for instance the Oriental community. They would like to see more spices brought in. By the time McMichael brings them up from Vancouver, the prices are so inflated they can't afford them. But there's no where else to go unless they want the expense of visiting the city. They wish he'd stock more dried goods, particularly dried fish."

"Bit of a monopoly is it? I thought that was illegal," William replied. "Do you think you could run it, and staff it, and keep the customers happy? Seriously?"

"Yes, Lucy will help me, she needs a job."

Olivia explained to her father the events that had transpired in Lucy's life.

"Everyone loves her; she'll make a wonderful clerk. I could start her part-time if I had to, until things got going."

"And McMichael, he won't give her a job?"

"He thinks she's too fragile."

"And is she?" he asked.

"What do you think?"

William looked across the room and saw Lucy deep in conversation with his brother Aaron. Since Aaron had little time for silly people, no matter how beautiful they may be, and he seemed to be deeply engrossed, William assumed she wasn't at all fragile. The fact that she was drinking scotch one for one with Aaron and seemed no worse for her efforts, also didn't go without notice.

"And what about the bookkeeping?"

"I thought I'd do that."

William laughed heartily.

"I don't recall math being your strong suit Olivia. You're more the creative type. Oh don't pout, it's much more lucrative being the entrepreneur. What about that Sarah girl? Isn't she a bookkeeper?"

"Yes, but she's McMichael's bookkeeper."

"Ah, I see. Well you never know, maybe she's ready for a change. He doesn't actually own the town Olivia. He just likes to control it. I think your idea has merit. Let me have a quiet conversation with your Uncle Aaron and see what we can do. He mentioned he was looking for a new venture up north. Maybe this would be the thing for him to get his feet wet, you never know."

"But McMichael wouldn't rent me the property so I could go into competition with him, and he controls everything, just like you said. And then there's Frank's job to consider. Perhaps I'm not being realistic here."

"I gather Frank doesn't have the desire to enter into this business with you?" her father asked.

"No, he'd probably divorce me. He's afraid McMichael would fire him."

William forced himself to remain expressionless. The worst of that outcome, he thought to himself, would be that Olivia would have to return to Seattle.

"But it's something you'd really like to do?"

"Yes father," Olivia admitted. "It is. I know I can do it."

"He's not going to be happy about it."

"Frank?" Olivia said. "I know. But I need to do something for myself."

"I meant McMichael. How to you plan to handle that?"

"With my head held high, like a Bower always does. I learned a lot from you, from the conversations at the dinner table over the years. I know I need to be determined. I know I need to be tough. I just don't have the money to do it. Frank's got me on an allowance that barely buys groceries."

"You don't have a joint bank account?" her father asked. "Your mother and I have one, that way she can get what she needs when she needs it. He doesn't trust you enough for that?"

"No," Olivia said. "I don't have a bank account at all."

William Bower held the rage he was feeling deep inside. His daughter was being treated in a manner unbecoming a Bower by that husband of hers, and he wasn't going to stand for it. He hadn't liked Frank much before the wedding, and now he liked him even less.

"Well then maybe we should send your brother Jason back with you to take a look around. Since he came back from the war he's been dabbling in real estate for your Uncle Aaron. He's good at it too. He wants to get into developments with your brother Billy, on the land acquisitions side. I think they'll make quite the go of it. He's a changed man since he returned, Jason is. He has a totally different outlook, a different value of life."

Olivia looked over at her brother Jason who was attempting to dance with Sarah. He had lost a lot of the extra weight he had been carrying around since his teenaged years, and for the first time in her life, she noticed that her oldest brother was really quite handsome. Since his leg had been injured during the war (he really had run away and joined the army), his mobility was somewhat challenged. He needed to use a cane to steady his walk. But there he was, making a brave attempt at dancing with Sarah, who of course was quite smitten with him. The unusual thing was, this time the object of her desire seemed to be equally enamoured with Sarah.

"I take it McMichael has no idea you are my daughter yet?"

"None that I know of."

"Well then, let's try to keep it that way. I want you to pretend your brother is just an acquaintance you ran into on the boat, nothing more. Do you think you can convince your gang of merry kidnappers to keep to the story?"

"Well," Olivia sighed, "Sarah might be a problem, she'll want to tell everyone about Jason. The rest will think it a great adventure. Lucy will love the intrigue of it all and Frenchie's a pirate at heart."

William laughed heartily as he saw Lucy getting more drinks for herself and Aaron. "I think you might have that observation backwards, my dear."

"Thank you for allowing them to come and enjoy the wedding," Olivia said. "It was kind of you to invite them."

"Not at all," William said. "Without them, there would have been a very important person missing from the wedding party. I am eternally grateful to all of them. Now if you will excuse me, I see Frenchie wants to dance with your mother…again. I'd better go help her out, or I'll never hear the end of it."

Olivia had a truly wonderful time with her family and her friends. When she came home four days later, she found Frank acting quite sheepish. She eventually learned about the letter he received from her father, but not the contents of it. Whatever it said, it seemed to have put the fear of God into Frank. It also unfortunately widened the distance between her and her husband. He was cold and distant, and began spending more and more time at work, preferring to spend his nights there, or alone on the couch.

"Well," Olivia thought pragmatically, "if I'm going to be on my own, then at least I will have a job to keep me busy. And I'll be able to afford a lawyer, should it come to that."

William had indeed sent Jason along to scout out the possibilities of a store, and Olivia's dream was becoming a reality in a series of clandestine manoeuvres.

McMichael was away in Vancouver, taking a look at private schools for his daughter. He was still determined she was going to one despite Maggie's efforts to convince him otherwise. It was a stroke of luck that he was out of town, but out of town he was.

Jason, upon his arrival, had said to anyone who asked that he was a war vet just taking a little time to recuperate from his injuries. Aside from spending some time at the café with Sarah, who everyone knew chased after every new man in town, he kept a low profile. He took a look around, found an old building that was vacant and quite suitable and took note of it. He did not make contact with Olivia. He never ran into Frank, not that Frank would have recognized the skinny man he had become, particularly with his beard and moustache that he sported pre-war now shaven clean. Frank had never paid much attention to him back in Seattle. He thought Jason was a bad seed. Jason returned to Seattle within a couple of days, slipping out with the same lack of fanfare that had greeted him. Sarah had decided that if keeping Olivia's secret meant she could see Jason again, then that was what she would do.

William and Aaron had decided between them to put up the money for the store, and leased the property directly from the government, who of course, were always more than willing to help out the Bower brothers of Seattle any way they could. There was a lot of ore moving across the U.S.A. on the railroad William had been instrumental in building. The facility they rented was technically owned by the post office, not the mine. The paperwork would not fly by McMichael. The space had been used as a storage facility before the new post office was built.

Next, the brothers arranged for a line of credit between the store and the Eaton's Company, and copies of the fall and winter catalogue were to arrive as soon as Frenchie could get down to Vancouver to pick them up.

This would all have been impossible to do had McMichael not been away for quite some time. All Olivia knew from Sarah was that he had originally taken Christina down to her new school and that something had come up, causing him to be away indefinitely.

Although excited by the prospect of running her own store, Olivia was nervous about what to tell Frank. Her feelings ran from great excitement to absolute dread and back again as she saw the store taking shape. It had been almost impossible to keep the opening of the store a secret from him, but with McMichael away he had been even busier at the mine and hadn't been paying her all that much attention. Frank had noticed the premises rented but assumed that his boss knew all about it. Now however, there was no getting around it, he was going to find out. Tomorrow. Jason had assured Olivia that it would all be taken care of, but Olivia was nervous all the same. Lucy had decided she wasn't leaving Olivia alone, and moved in, taking over the couch and claiming she had "internal women's problems" and couldn't possibly be left alone for a few days since Frenchie had taken Maggie down to the city. This also forced Frank back into the marital bed, his back icily turned to Olivia's.

The initial stock of wares for the store came up by a private barge hired by Aaron Bower, leaving Frenchie out of the picture on that one, and quite frankly, relieved. Catalogues he could hide, but not an entire store of goods. Aaron's men unloaded the crates into the building in the wee hours of the morning to keep the prying to a minimum. William Bower had paid the big burly longshoreman handsomely for the job, and there was just one more thing he had to do now that dawn had broken. There was another letter to deliver to Frank Fitzpatrick.

CHAPTER 22

❈

William glanced out the window watching the rain come down, turning his back to the man in his office. His attention had been somewhat wanting of late, as he was concerned for the well being of his daughter in Canada, he told his guest.

"It can be quite un-settling, having your children away from you, even if they are grown," the man agreed.

"Maybe there's something to be said for arranged marriages after all," William admitted.

"Married herself a bit of a challenge, did she?" the man asked politely.

"You could say that. He's not a bad man per sé, at least not in the beginning, but the wrong man, I knew it from the start, but her heart was set on it. And now it seems my initial lack of enthusiasm was justified."

"The hearts of our daughters we never want to break," the man agreed.

"My first daughter married God. I know that is a hard act to follow."

"And your youngest?"

"My youngest married a professional man who owns acres of farmland. A veterinarian."

"But the middle one?"

"The middle one I worry about. I never thought I would."

"In some regards, I'm lucky," the man said. "I only have two daughters, no middle one."

William smiled. He turned back around to face his guest.

"I'm sorry you had to come all the way down here to see me and that my secretary couldn't fit you in until today. I've just been rather busy. Now what can I do for you John?"

"I was hoping you would be able to entice your government to put more pressure on the CPR," the man said. "I've been talking to the officials on my side of the border but they're asking for numbers on the amount of trade that would be done as a result of a north-south extension."

"And can't your government come up with some numbers? I would think that would be obvious."

"They have all the Canadian figures, but they are Canadian after all. You know Canadians. We never want to be the first ones in. They want to see some American figures for a comparison."

"I think John, that the economic benefits would be greatest shipping south, America being the largest market potential for them. It stands to reason they'll be able to export Canadian goods to the lucrative U.S. of A, and that some measure of goods will also be imported back. Surely they realize that?"

"They do indeed. But in order to justify the expenditures, they would like to see an estimate of revenue potential flowing both north and south."

"And revenue for your personal interests?" William asked.

"Of course," John agreed. "That goes without saying. But my industry is certainly not the only industry that would benefit from a more efficient transportation route. We've seen how the east-west link has entered both countries into a new industrial revolution. This will by no means be on the same scale, but yes, there is money to be made William, and better you and I have some of it than others."

"Well John," William said, "we tried this before the war but obviously each country had its own concerns going. Perhaps it is time to make a few calls and see how the rails are lying, so to speak. I don't know how tied to your own job you are, but if this goes through, we could use a few good men assisting with the building of the railroad. They will be lands to acquire and men to employ and money to be raised and spent. I admire your entrepreneurship, I'll give you that. Too bad the middle child is married. She's a beauty."

John laughed.

"I'm afraid I'm not quite ready to take the plunge again William. Arranged marriages aside."

William smiled.

"I would be forever indebted to you William," the man said, shaking William's hand. "If there's anything I can do for you in return, you only have to ask."

"You may live to regret that remark. Give me a couple of weeks John, and I'll come up and we can discuss it further."

"I'll have a room at the hotel prepared for you. It will be wonderful to have you back again. Nice seeing you William."

William watched as John Wesley McMichael left his office.

CHAPTER 23

The curious were lined up outside the new Beachcomber Market long before Olivia was ready to open the doors. She heaved a big sigh. It had not been a good morning so far. Frank had been speechless when he learned of her new enterprise. He reacted like she had betrayed him, and in reality she had. The only thing he said to her in the hours since he read the letter from her father, was that she would never receive a cent from him again, and he would never step foot inside the store.

There were two knocks on the back door, and Olivia hurried to let Lucy in. She had brought along a bottle of champagne just for the occasion.

"If you think I'm going to smash this bottle over a piece of furniture to christen the store, you're crazy," Lucy said. "The bubbly is for us Olivia, let's toast to our success."

Olivia warily took a glass from Lucy's hand.

"Tough night?" Lucy asked.

"You could say that, yes. But it's not like I didn't know it was coming."

"I'm proud of you Olivia," Lucy said. "Aside from providing me with a wonderful source of employment, I'm proud of you for standing up for yourself."

She raised her glass.

"To you, to your father, your uncle, your brother and the rest of your wonderful family."

The first few hours had been incredibly busy. As word of mouth spread, more and more people, mostly the women, came by to take a look at what was being offered. They were already almost sold out of the silk stockings they had brought in, in a variety of sizes and colours. Some costume jewellery on consignment from the city was also almost sold out. It appeared the ladies of Britannia wanted to spoil themselves a little. Lucy and Olivia closed the store at five o'clock that night. It had been a good day.

The night had been eerily quiet at home, Frank working until midnight and then sleeping on the couch. Just as well, Olivia thought. The silence was better than the fighting.

The doors at the Beachcomber opened again at nine a.m. the next day. Lucy had arrived right on time.

Olivia saw Jimmy Yada standing beside the counter.

"Can I help you Jimmy?" she asked.

A customer was a customer no matter what age.

"My friend old Mr. Li would like to know if you could bring in some dried goods for him. He would like some dried mushrooms, and also asked if you could bring in some green Chinese tea, because he says his is getting old like him. I don't know why he wants it, he's got a ton of the stuff in his kitchen."

"How old is Mr. Li, Jimmy? Do you know?"

"He told me he is eighty-three."

"Eighty-three! That's remarkable. You talk to Mr Li a lot do you Jimmy? I didn't know you could speak Chinese."

"I can't, but he actually speaks English to me. He just pretends he doesn't know any. There's a lot of that going on."

Olivia looked over the list.

"Do you spend a lot of time with him Jimmy?"

"Yes. He is teaching me about the things in my father's Chinese Medicine book. He told me that when he was younger, he too ran a store just like you're doing now. A store with herbs and teas and things. My dad said it was an apothecary."

Jimmy stumbled a bit over the last word.

"I want to be a doctor some day, so I find his knowledge very valuable."

"Very valuable indeed," Olivia smiled. She found Jimmy's vocabulary amazing for a boy of his age. "You tell Mr. Li that I think I will be able to help him out, but it may take a little time, maybe a couple of months, to get some of the items on this list. And tell him to come in and say hello sometime, if he feels comfortable."

"Okay Mrs. Fitzpatrick, I will," Jimmy said, leaving the store.

"Lucy, why don't you put the kettle on?" she said, turning her back to the door momentarily. She could hear the door chimes indicating someone else was coming in. She turned and smiled.

"What the hell do you think you're playing at?"

J.W. McMichael stood in front of Olivia.

"Ah, you're back. Don't yell at me Mr. McMichael, or I'm afraid I'll have to ask you to leave."

McMichael was flabbergasted.

"You, ask me, to leave? Need I remind you who owns the lease on this property?"

"Well actually, the government does, Mr. McMichael. At least that's what it says on the tenancy papers. You might run the town but you don't own it. At least not this building."

Lucy, still in the back, was concerned about the loud voices she was hearing.

"Are you all right Olivia?" her voice rang out.

"Quite," Olivia replied.

"Oh, that's just perfect. You have Lucy working here too? Well, it will be a shame to have to put you both out of business."

Lucy came back into the store, carrying two cups of tea.

"I gather you won't be joining us, Mr. McMichael?"

McMichael came up close to Olivia. She could feel the fire within him raging, as their eyes met defiantly.

"Who gave you the money to do this?" he sneered. "Apparently I am paying that husband of yours far too much. That will soon change."

Olivia laughed aloud.

"Frank? Frank doesn't have the money or the gumption to open this store, Mr. McMichael. You weren't the only one who was kept in the dark about this. I can keep quite a secret, can't I?"

McMichael face turned a dark crimson. It was the first time Olivia had seen the man embarrassed.

"Don't tell me you were foolish enough to squander your insurance money on this venture Lucy," he said. "I thought you had more brains that that."

"Evidently she does Mr. McMichael, as Lucy is an employee of the store, not one of the owners. No offence to Lucy."

"None taken Olivia," Lucy replied.

"Lucy, will you leave Olivia and me alone for a minute?" McMichael asked.

Olivia nodded to her friend, who went back into the staff room, her ear pressed against the door, just in case.

"If you were so determined to open a store in this town, you should have come to me. I'm sure we could have made an arrangement."

Olivia could see Akiko outside, waiting to come in. Akiko could also see what was going on inside, and made a hasty retreat.

"I did make an arrangement, Mr. Michael. Just not with you. Now if you don't mind, you are scaring my customers away."

"Oh, Mrs. Fitzpatrick. I have not yet begun to scare your customers away. I am making you an offer again. Come to me at the end of the month when you can't pay your lease and I'll see if I can take some of your stock off your hands. Or didn't you know I dabbled in liquidation as well?"

"I think it's time you left, Mr. McMichael," Olivia said flatly. "Good day."

McMichael paused as he opened the door.

"How could you do this to me?" he asked, the door slamming behind him.

The question sounded so personal that for a moment Olivia was taken aback.

"You can come out now Lucy," she called to her friend.

"Is the war over?" Lucy asked.

"Not by a long shot," Olivia replied. "The battle has just begun."

CHAPTER 24

The door chimes tinkled announcing a new customer, but Olivia barely noticed. She was packing some of the stock back into the original packaging, hoping they could be returned.

"May I ask what you are doing?" the customer asked.

Olivia looked up to see William standing before her.

"Dad!" she squealed, her face lighting up immediately.

"Good, then that despair on your face is a fleeting thing," he said, giving her a hug.

"Well not exactly," she sighed.

"Where's Lucy?" he asked, noticing she was not in sight.

Olivia sighed deeper. It had been a month and a half since she opened the store.

"Olivia," William said sternly, "what exactly is going on?"

"He's won, I'm afraid," she said. "I have no customers. It started with Akiko, she's McMichael's cleaning lady. Sarah told me he saw her come in here and told her if she ever set foot in here again, he'd fire her. I had a special order for a friend of her young son come in one day, and her Jimmy came to pick it up. McMichael he saw him leaving the store with the bag in his arms. Akiko got fired because he said he meant her whole family dare not enter the store, and that if the boy came in again, he'd fire her husband, the mine's assayer next. Word spread through the Oriental community and they stopped coming in first. But then it spread to the other townsfolk and let's just say very few have had the gumption to cross him. I had to lay Lucy off after only two weeks. I'm hoping I can return some of these things to get your and Uncle Aaron's money back."

"And Frank?" William asked.

"Frank's fine. I have no idea why McMichael hasn't fired him, but he hasn't. I guess he really is good at his job."

"How are the two of you getting along through all this?"

"We're not, I'm afraid."

"Then Olivia," William pleaded, "why don't you just pack you bags and come home?"

"But the store," Olivia protested, "all the money you and Aaron have put into this…"

"Olivia, it's a drop in the bucket for both of us, not to worry. Come home."

"I want to stay here Father," she said. "I can't explain it, but I like it here. I hated it when I first came here, but I've come to love the people in this town. The store was a good idea. The first morning's sales were fantastic. It was so promising. If only that blasted man had stayed away a little longer, to really give the store a chance."

"He was bound to come back sooner or later."

He saw the look of disappointment on his daughter's face.

"Olivia, are you upset about the failing of the store or upset about having to tell me about it?" he asked.

"The store," she replied. "I've had to tell you a few times I've failed. I was hoping this time would be different. It's embarrassing to tell you, of course, but you've always forgiven me before and I suspect you will now."

"We can always get you set up in a store of your own in Seattle," he assured her "if shop keeping is in your blood."

"I'm not ready to leave Britannia yet Father. I'm not ready to leave Frank yet."

"Olivia," her father pleaded.

"No, don't say it. I know what you're thinking. It's what you've been thinking from day one. I made my bed, now I have to lie in it. I don't want to put the family through the scandal of a divorce."

"It would hardly be the first Bower scandal," her father replied.

Although he tried to change her mind for over an hour, William conceded that for reasons entirely her own, his daughter wanted to stay in this community. But what she had been through with the store had hardly been fair play.

"The thing about we Bowers," he told Olivia, "is that we always have another card tucked high up our sleeve while our poker faces play the game. I can see McMichael out on the street, waiting for someone. He's asking Frenchie where that person went, and Frenchie, God love him, is pointing at the store. The man McMichael is waiting for is the man who could talk the bankers for the Canadian Pacific Railway into providing a north-south line to move his precious ore into the United States cheaper and faster. He's prayed for that more than he ever prayed for the war to end. That man he is looking for, my darling, is me."

Olivia tried as best she could to stifle the laugh that was within her.

"William!" McMichael exclaimed with genuine warmth as he entered the store, ignoring Olivia completely. There was no sense dragging a stranger into this mess, McMichael thought. He offered his hand out to the American, but it was declined.

"Is there a problem?" McMichael asked, noting the grave expression on William's face."

"There is indeed," William declared. "I'd like you to meet my daughter Olivia, the middle girl."

CHAPTER 25

"Why don't we use the new tea?" Jimmy asked old Mr. Li. "This one smells mouldy."

"Jimmy," the man explained, speaking slowly, but speaking very good English, "there is a terrible sickness in town. They call it the influenza. Thousands of people are dying all over Canada. But not just here, all over the world. Look at me, I am an old man. I should be sick, but I am not. Look at my family. My wife started to get the cough. I gave her the tea. She got better. Now, I cannot say that all people will get better by drinking the tea. But maybe it can't hurt. There are things called anti-oxidants in green tea, remember, we read that together in the Chinese medicine book. The new tea is fresh, but it is black tea. It does not have as many anti-oxidants. The green tea smells a little musky, yes. It is a little mouldy as it got a bit damp when I forgot to put the lid back on this tin. But it is my last tin. It is a big tin. I will give you some. I want you to promise me you will take the old tea, and make some for your family. I want you and your mother and father to be safe. Please do the honour of obeying an old man." He handed the lad a tin of the tea.

"Okay," Jimmy sighed. "But they're not going to like it."

Jimmy plugged his nose and drank the old tea that Mr. Li had poured for him.

"That is a good boy," Mr. Li nodded. "You may go now, little Dr. Yada."

Jimmy left Mr. Li's home and stopped off at the Beachcomber market, leaving his wagon outside as he always did. He took his teapot from it. Since the day after the avalanche years ago, he had continued to earn pocket change after school going back and forth to the mine, selling tea, pop and potato chips to the workers and passers-by on the street.

Things had definitely changed at the Beachcomber's market since Olivia's father paid that fateful visit. As suddenly as the customers went away, they now mysteriously re-appeared. Jimmy came in at the same time most days, and the re-instated Lucy was more than happy to have boiled water ready for him. Olivia felt it was the least she could do, as his mother was still without a job. McMichael had found another cleaner who would work cheaper than Akiko, so she was still without work.

Olivia glanced at the calendar on the wall. It was hard to believe it was now 1918, and she had been at Britannia for three years.

"Mrs. Lucy, Mrs. Olivia," Jimmy began, "I need you to drink some of this tea."

He poured a couple of small Chinese cupfuls for them. They obliged and drank the small amount. Its odd taste had Lucy making a face.

"I know," Jimmy admitted. "It doesn't taste too good."

"Tell you what Jimmy, why don't I give you some fresh tea to take around, hmm?"

"No," Jimmy explained. "Anti-oxidants. Mr. Li says I must use this green tea."

"I beg your pardon?"

"This tea has magic powers; it will keep us from being sick."

"Well," Olivia offered, "why don't you blend it with some fresh tea, maybe just to dilute it a bit?"

"Hmm, that would make it weaker. I would have to sell more of it to work. I could make more money I guess, but people would have to buy extra."

"Don't let McMichael hear you say that," Lucy laughed.

"He would think that it is a wise business decision," Jimmy said.

"He would at that," Olivia admitted.

"Maybe I will take some sweet cookies and offer a two-for-one deal," the lad said. "More to offer my customers and help the bad taste."

"Sounds like a plan to me," Lucy agreed. "Only I wouldn't tell them it was bad. Tell them it's exotic."

Jimmy paid for the cookies and a bag of fresh green tea and diluted the mixture he had made from Mr. Li's leaves, but only just a bit. Outside in the street, he could see his friend Lara coming across the road, and he went out side to see her.

"Lara, come have some tea."

She had been meeting Jimmy for tea whenever she could escape the hawk-eyes of Mrs. Schwindt, who since the war, carried even more prejudices with her than she had before.

"Take a sip of the tea, a bite of the cookie, like that," Jimmy explained.

"Did you hear the news?" she asked Jimmy, not waiting for an answer. "I heard the doctor say two more people have died because of the influenza since the weekend."

"I know," Jimmy said. "That is why you must meet me every day, and have some of this tea, okay Lara? Mr. Li and I think it is magic. It will keep us well. And I will make sure I go by the mine office and give some to your father everyday. I will put it on sale for him because it kind of tastes yucky. He always buys a cup of tea from me, so he should be okay too."

"Why is everyone getting sick Jimmy?" Lara asked.

"Mr. Li says it is a thing called a virus. Something like a cold germ. He says that this is a very bad one, a lot like one many centuries ago called the Black Death."

"Black Death," Lara repeated, her eyes growing wider and her voice quivering as she said it aloud.

Mrs. Schwindt came from around the corner and screamed bloody murder at the two children, knocking the cup from Jimmy's hand.

"What are you doing, you heathen?" she screeched.

Olivia came out from the store.

"What are *you* doing, Mrs. Schwindt?"

"Are you not aware the influenza is spreading through the town, Mrs. Fitzpatrick?"

"Of course Mrs. Schwindt, but…"

"Germs. The monkey is spreading germs. That's how it's getting around. Going from house to house."

"I hardly think so, Mrs. Schwindt. Jimmy sterilizes the cups in boiling water and never uses them twice without washing them, do you Jimmy?"

Jimmy shook his head.

"I never use a dirty cup. Influenza is caused by a virus Mrs. Schwindt. I am very careful. This tea is special. Mr Li, he told me his family drinks it when they are sick and soon they start to feel better."

"See," Olivia said, "there you go." Olivia poured another cup and drank it, just to side with the boy. Its flavour had improved only slightly having been blended.

Jimmy poured a cup and offered it to Mrs. Schwindt. She swatted this one to the ground as well, breaking the cup.

"You keep that concoction away from me and away from our house, do you hear me?"

As it happened, McMichael was coming down the road and saw the incident occur.

"Mrs. Schwindt," he yelled, "have you completely lost your mind?"

"It's filth, Mr. McMichael. I am trying to protect your daughter from the influenza."

"Mrs. Schwindt, I have had quite enough of your ranting these past few months. We had this conversation some time ago as I recall. Jimmy is Lara's friend. Lara and Jimmy meet every day and have tea while you are taking your afternoon nap. I know all about it."

"This tea is special," Jimmy said. "Would you like some Mr. McMichael?"

"Of course Jimmy," he said, "and here's another nickel for the cup Mrs. Schwindt broke. I will take it out of her pay."

"But Mr. McMichael..." Mrs. Schwindt began.

"Not a word, Mrs. Schwindt. Not one word."

Over the next few months, many people in Britannia fell ill with the flu, many never recovering. It eventually hit the McMichael household, Lara coming down with the flu symptoms first.

Every morning and afternoon, Jimmy, wearing a cloth mask over his nose and mouth, came and gave Lara some tea and some home made soup. McMichael had noticed that for whatever reason, Jimmy's clientele had a remarkable recovery rate, or didn't get the influenza at all. No one in the Yada household had come down with the flu, despite the fact it was passing from miner to miner. At the first sign of his own symptoms, McMichael joined the breakfast, lunch and dinner tea plan along with his daughter. He was quite ill for a week and a half, but in the end it passed. Lara also recovered in a remarkably short time, her body building the antibodies to fight the illness.

There was sadness in the McMichael household when Mrs. Schwindt, who steadfastly refused to have anything at all to do with Jimmy, took ill and died. The nanny had been hospitalized, but did not make it. All in all, seventy-five percent of young Jimmy Yada's customers survived the killer disease. His record was better than Dr. Van Den Broek's was by far. No one ever knew what was in the magic potion Jimmy and Mr. Li had conjured up. It would be into the next decade before spores, similar to those in the mouldy tea would be identified by Dr. Alexander Flemming officially as pencillium mould. What would become the wonder drug of the twentieth century, penicillin, may have been hiding in Mr. Li's smelly old tea.

One night, on his way home from his route, Jimmy was startled by Les Ferguson. Les had been trying for days to get Jimmy to give him some tea, the word of its magical powers having spread. Jimmy, not liking Les, had always conveniently run out. This time though, Les caught him before his last stop.

"Give me some of that tea, kid."

"No." Jimmy replied.

"If you don't give me some of that tea now," Les coughed, "I'll knock you senseless and take it myself." He coughed again, the hacking taking the wind from his lungs.

"With your respiratory problems," Jimmy said matter of factly, "I hardly think so. Go away Mr. Ferguson, I have no tea for you."

Les raised his fist to the child.

"Go away Mr. Ferguson," a voice said. "There is no tea for you."

Les turned around to see McMichael behind him.

"I think it's best you head off now."

Les slunk back into the darkness of the night, doing as his master said.

"I'm sure glad you came along when you did," Jimmy said.

"I'm glad I did too."

There was a silence between them for a moment.

"He's sick," McMichael offered.

"Oh, I understand that," Jimmy began, "but I only have a little bit of the dried tea left. I am saving some for Christina, in case she gets sick. I could send some down to her. Lara misses her. I don't have a big brother or sister, but I think I would miss them too if they had to go away. Lara would miss her more if anything really bad happened."

McMichael was touched by Jimmy's generosity towards his eldest daughter.

"That's a very kind thing to do Jimmy. But Christina is just away at school. Lara will see her again soon."

"That's the part I don't understand."

"What do you mean Jimmy?"

"The influenza is in Vancouver too. The tea is here. You sent Christina away. You kept the bad man here. How can we protect her when she is all alone? Soon may not be soon enough."

McMichael took a step backward. The musings of a young boy had just profoundly affected him. Again.

The next morning, McMichael walked over to Sarah's house and caught her on her way to work.

"Sarah, there are three things I'd like you to do today, in this order."

"Yes, Mr. McMichael?" she answered. He had never come to meet her before.

"Get Les Ferguson's papers in order. He doesn't know it yet, but he's going to be leaving town. Then call Christina's school in Vancouver and get my daughter back up here. Frenchie's already on his way down to get her."

"Oh, that's wonderful," Sarah sighed. "And the third thing?"

"Don't you dare say a word, to anyone, do you understand?"

"Yes Mr. McMichael?"

"I want you to go into Olivia's store, and order a new red wagon for Jimmy from that blasted Eaton's catalogue."

"Oh, Mr. McMichael!" Sarah said, hugging her boss for the first time in all the years she had known him.

"Not a word Sarah. Not a word."

A fortnight later, on a warm night, McMichael sat on the porch with a cigar and some fine cognac. He could hear the laughing voices of the re-united sisters in the background. He had relented and given Mrs. Schwindt's old room so that Christina could have some privacy. She didn't have to share a room with Lara anymore. She was a young woman now, and was going to be a handful, he admitted to himself. How he was going to handle her without Mrs. Schwindt he didn't know. Joe from the general store was coming over later that night give the room a fresh coat of paint. Christina had picked some yellow paint and some floral paper. Quite a contrast from Mrs. Schwindt's stark white room, he thought. Much more like her mother would have chosen.

Les was gone and Frank was going to have to step up to the plate if he wanted to keep his job. He wasn't sure Frank had the muscle he needed, but Frank had slowly but surely become his yes man over the past few months, which is why he didn't fire him when he landed in jail and the business of his wife's store first came up. How fortunate that had turned out to be. McMichael had not had any idea that Frank was William Bower's son-in-law.

He turned his eyes to the Vancouver paper that had arrived by boat earlier in the morning but he had not yet had a chance to read. The headline sent a bone-chilling shiver through him.

INFLUENZA CLAIMS TWELVE AT PRIVATE SCHOOL

CHAPTER 26

The night air that evening in 1921 was thick with smoke, the air echoing of the wail of sirens as Frank and Rudy made their way across the main roof of the mine plant, testing each beam gingerly before taking a step. The flames were already scorching several of the timbers, their fiery tongues licking through the cracks of the beams.

"I'm going to try to get to the far turret nozzle," Frank said, pointing towards one of the two rotating water pumpers mounted as a fire precaution on the roof.

"Let's get this one going first," Rudy indicated to the closer water fire extinguisher. "Let's try to get some of that wood dampened before you try to cross."

On the ground, all available men were aiding the fire department as they battled a fierce blaze burning through the mine's concentrator building. Starting in the crusher, the flames quickly caught a draft blowing through the building. In no time the building was engulfed in flames. It was the first time since Rudy threw Frank in jail that the men were talking to each other.

Olivia and Lucy stood on the porch of the Beachcomber store, shocked by what they saw before them.

"Not again," Lucy whispered, her hand covering her mouth. "Not another disaster."

"Let's get some food and water for the men," Olivia replied. "We could use someone to run it over to them. Where's Jimmy when we need him?"

"Probably already there," Lucy admitted, heading into the store.

Although emotions were running high in Lucy's mind, she shook her fears aside. It was her turn to try and help the community.

McMichael stood back from the firefighters and surveyed the situation.

"Frenchie," he called. "Can you cross Howe Sound and bring some men from the wood fibre plant?" There were able men just a short distance across the water. McMichael could see them gathered upon the shore, watching the scene at Britannia unfold. The flames were so high they could be seen for miles.

It was a desperate situation.

"Aye," Frenchie said. "Merde, it's going ta be a struggle ta keep de fire from de powerhouse."

"Mon Dieu," McMichael answered, taking Frenchie aback. Frenchie had never heard McMichael utter any French before. But by God, McMichael thought, the Frenchman was right. If the fire spread to the powerhouse, the whole town could go up. The rows of wood framed bungalows had been built in very close proximity.

The powerhouse itself was one of the best-equipped waterpower plants in Canada, it's nearest rival being located in Mexico. The lakes and streams located high in the mountains above Britannia provided a constant source of water for it, which in turn provided more than enough energy to power the mine. The pressure created from the water would provide the fire nozzles with tremendous power. If only Frank and Rudy could reach them.

From below, McMichael could only see the faintest outline of the two men through the thick smoke.

High on the rooftop, Rudy had cautiously managed to make his way across beams to get the first water nozzle going. The force was tremendous, and Rudy barely had the strength to manoeuvre the stream of water in the direction of the powerhouse. He prided himself that he was physically fit, but the elements were giving him a workout today even he had not prepared for. The heat was intense, and he felt himself sweating profusely.

"I'm going to try to start up the east nozzle," Frank said.

"I don't know Frank, that part of the roof looks like it's going to go any second. You're too heavy, you'll go through. There's no point. Let's keep this under control and keep the water directed towards the powerhouse."

"I'll go," a little voice said from behind the men.

Frank and Rudy turned to see Jimmy Yada behind them.

"How the hell did you get up here?" Frank asked.

"I shimmied up the drainpipe," he said matter of factly.

"Son, shimmy yourself back down," Rudy said. "Right now!"

There was a commotion on the ground as firemen tried desperately to put out a new raging fire, which had broken out when flames reached the sully oil from the third floor. The oil was an elixir for the fire.

More of the women had come to the store to assist Olivia and Lucy. Olivia had heard someone mention that it was Frank and Rudy on the roof, but she refused to look in that direction, focusing on the task on hand and saying silent prayers to God that her husband would be all right.

A portion of the first floor caved in, and Frank and Rudy tried to take another look at the water nozzle on the other side of the roof. The smoke was now so thick they could no longer actually see it.

"Forget it Frank," Rudy said. They had been up there almost an hour and could see Frenchie's boat coming with more men and equipment.

"Let's get out of here while we still can. We'll let this wheel keep going as long as it can manage on its own."

The men heard a loud crack as part of the roof gave way.

"What was that?" Frank asked. He had thought he heard a scream through the rumble of falling timber.

"Where's Jimmy?" Rudy asked.

"Oh God no," Frank said. "The shouts from the ground distracted me when the third floor went. I didn't see him go back down, did you?"

Rudy shook his head.

The wind took a slight shift, momentarily giving the men a line of sight.

Beyond where the roof had caved in, and still out of reach of the west nozzle, the men could see the collapsed frame of the boy.

"What are we going to do?" Frank asked helplessly.

Rudy took off his shirt and drenched it with water from the hose, tying it around his nose and face. He motioned for Frank to do the same. He tore a portion of his pant leg, and wet it down as well, placing it around his wrist.

"We're going to have to make a bridge," Rudy said, "see if you can pry loose some of those timbers. We've got to wedge them under that cross beam that's still intact for support."

Frank moved over to a section of the roof that appeared to still be sturdy, except for a couple of weather worn planks which freed themselves easily from the frame.

"Lay them across this portion of the roof," Rudy instructed. "We're going to have to crawl across the two, like a balance beam, dispersing our weight. We don't know what condition he's in, but needless to say we'll need to cover his face with this wet wrist cloth to keep him from inhaling any more smoke. If he's still breathing."

Frank thought about it.

"Okay," Rudy continued, "I'll go first. Throw your weight on the end of these two beams and I'll do the same for you when I get on the other end."

"What do we do when we get to the other side?" Frank asked.

"Pray," Rudy announced.

McMichael watched the silhouettes of the two men on the roof.

"What are they doing?" he asked.

Harry, who had been manning a hose line between the main power plant and the mill, offered an explanation.

"I think someone is trapped up there."

"Who went up?" McMichael asked. "I see two men. That would be the buddy system. Who would be fool enough to go up there on his own?"

"I think Frank and Wolanski were up there."

"Then who are they saving?"

Akiko came around the corner with a look of terror in her eyes. In Japanese she explained to Harry that she had found Jimmy's new wagon by the drainpipe.

"My son," Harry said, his voice choking.

CHAPTER 27

McMichael put his fist through the plaster wall in his inner office.

"That woman," he exclaimed, "will be the death of me."

"Is he talking about you?" Sergeant Wolanski asked Sarah.

"Oh goodness no," Sarah laughed. "Haven't you heard?"

She leaned over to speak with the sergeant in a low voice.

"It's the concentrator."

"He refers to the concentrator as a woman?"

"Heavens no," Sarah began, "you know how it was destroyed in the fire last week…"

"Of course I know about it. The mine's been shut down ever since."

"Well," Sarah said, barely able to contain her excitement. "They say the fire happened under suspicious circumstances."

"I know," Rudy admitted, "that's what I want to talk to him about."

"My Jason, he's Olivia's brother you know, well he thinks he saw Les Ferguson standing in the rear walkway just before the building went up."

"That's what I've heard too," the sergeant said with interest.

"Oh, but that's not the best part. The best part is that Mr. McMichael has found a man in San Francisco who says he can build him a new concentrator, a fireproof concentrator, and he can do it faster and cheaper than any competitor."

"I would have thought that would make your boss happy," the sergeant said.

"Oh it did, it did. But the man in San Francisco said he wanted to put one of his relatives in charge of the installation and running of the operation to make sure that his interests were protected financially until it was fully paid for. That seems understandable, you know, since we've had to temporarily shut down and all," Sarah continued.

"It does seem reasonable."

McMichael came out of his office.

"What are you staring at Sarah?" he bellowed.

"Nothing sir, would you like some ice for that?" she asked, nodding towards his hand.

"What do YOU want?" he asked the sergeant. "I thought we went over everything last night. I don't know what the boy was doing up on the roof, and the doctor says he is going to be fine. He suffered smoke inhalation, but with bed rest should make a full recovery."

McMichael stormed out of the office.

"The man in San Francisco," Sara giggled, "is named Aaron Bower. He's a partner with William Bower, the railroad man who's negotiating a meeting for McMichael and the Canadian Pacific Railway people."

"Olivia's father?"

"Yes. And the relative his brother wants to put in charge of the concentrator operation, is his niece, Olivia Fitzpatrick."

Sarah and Rudy snuck into the inner office to look at the hole in the wall.

"I wouldn't be calling Joe to fix it yet," Rudy said letting out a whistle. "I have a feeling he'll only be patching it up again real soon."

McMichael went hunting for Frank Fitzpatrick. It wasn't much of a hunt, since he always knew where Frank was, but this time, he was looking for him like a missile looking for its target.

Frank was sitting at a picnic table having lunch.

"Get over here Fitzpatrick," McMichael yelled.

Frank almost choked.

"What is it sir?" he asked.

"It's that damned family of yours. Your uncle-in-law, or whatever the hell he is to you, Aaron Bower, is the only man who can get us a new concentrator on time and on budget and he wants to put your wife in charge of the operation. Not you. Not your brother-in-law Jason. Your wife! Get on the phone and talk some sense into him."

Frank began to stammer.

"I'm afraid he won't listen to me sir. He doesn't like me much."

"Well, I'm not liking you much now either Fitzpatrick. I have a bit of a problem. When your wife opened that confounded store, you suddenly had a father-in-law who is standing between me and my railroad. When my concentrator burns down half the town, your wife, out of nowhere, has an uncle who has his hands in just about every business imaginable including fireproof concentrators. Her brother, the realtor, gets them whatever land they need. Good God man. What other relatives do you have hiding in your closet? Is her cousin the President?" he said sarcastically.

"Well no," Frank said sheepishly. "But go easy on the God stuff because her sister is a nun and there is an Attorney General and a C.E.O. of the Bank of America tucked into the limbs of the family tree for good measure."

"I wouldn't be smirking too much if I were you," McMichael snarled. "Unless I can figure something out, your wife is about to become your boss."

CHAPTER 28

Sarah gave Akiko a big hug.

The two women were standing outside the Beachcomber store around noontime on a sunny Wednesday. Sarah had scooted away from the mining office on her lunch hour to spend some time with her friend. She knew how important this day was to Akiko.

"You look beautiful," she encouraged the older woman.

Akiko was dressed smartly in a new navy-coloured dress she had ordered from Eaton's only a month before. It was western style, but its free flowing form suited her maturing figure well. It had been a little more expensive than Akiko originally planned to spend, but she figured she owed Eaton's a thing or two.

"Now I want you to go inside," Sarah began, "and do it just like we practiced. Go on, you can do it, I know you can."

Akiko glanced nervously at the sign in the window.

WANTED: PART TIME SALES/BOOKKEEPING-APPLY WITHIN

She patted the back of her head. Her hair was perfectly coiffed without a strand out of place. Beautiful pearl combs kept her hair upswept. As she slowly opened the door, she could barely hear the door chimes, the sound of her own heart beating so loudly. She was certain everyone else in the store could hear it as well, but they were blissfully going about their business, her level of her anxiety known only to herself.

"I'll let you know," Olivia was saying to Mary Alice. "We still have a few more people to interview for the position."

"Well remember," Mary Alice said. "I have a new line of floral dresses coming out this season, if you're not afraid of a little competition for your Eaton's business."

"Like I said, I'll let you know," Olivia said, barely containing her smile.

Mary Alice nodded to Akiko as the local seamstress left the store. Akiko in turn nodded to Natsu Miwa, a Japanese friend of hers, who was looking at some shoes on display in the store.

"Can I help you with anything?" Olivia asked Natsu.

Natsu, understanding enough English to know what Olivia meant, started to explain to Olivia in Japanese that she was looking for a size seven shoe, in brown. Natsu pointed to the shoes she liked, and Olivia went to the storeroom to get a pair for her to try on.

"She can't be much bigger than a seven, or a seven and a half," she thought to herself, reaching for the correct shoebox.

Akiko and Natsu talked together for a moment. When Olivia came back into the store area, she noticed a quizzical look on Natsu's face.

"What is it?" Olivia asked, not expecting an answer. She looked to Akiko. "Where's Jimmy when I need him?" she asked herself rhetorically. Jimmy would be able to translate for her.

"Excuse me," Akiko began nervously, "Mrs. Olivia, she wants to know the price. I told her, ladies shoes, $9.95, like the sign says."

Having just heard the woman she had known for a several years now utter her first words, her first sentence, so perfectly in English, Olivia was flabbergasted.

"I don't know what to say, Akiko!"

"Say yes, the price is right," Akiko said.

"Yes, yes it is." Olivia nodded taking Natsu's purchase to the counter.

Akiko shrugged. "I told you," she said to her friend in Japanese; "$9.95, no discount. Not on sale now."

Natsu smiled at Akiko and thanked her in Japanese. She paid Olivia for her purchase and left the store.

"Thank you for your help," Olivia said to Akiko.

Akiko bowed.

"Mrs. Olivia," Akiko began, "I come about job. I can help yes? I can make signs in English and Japanese. Make everyone happy. Your sales go up."

Olivia thought about this for a moment. Never in a million years would she have thought that Akiko Yada would apply for the job she was advertising in the window. Never in a million years did she think that Akiko Yada *could* apply for the job she was advertising in the window.

"I have resumé," Akiko said, handing Olivia some papers.

"Did you do this yourself Akiko?" Olivia asked, astounded.

"No, Mrs. Olivia," Akiko admitted humbly. "Miss Sarah, she helped me. But my work history is true. I worked for my father's silk factory back home in Japan. I can do simple bookkeeping. Arithmetic is arithmetic, no? Four plus four is eight. Even in English. I would work very hard, Mrs. Olivia. I studied your merchandise. I know a lot. I could work any hours you need. Even nights and Saturdays."

Olivia could not believe the extent of this woman's English vocabulary.

"Akiko, your English is excellent. Wherever did you learn it?"

"Miss Sarah helped me."

Akiko looked out the window and waved to Sarah, who was watching everything from outside. Sarah quickly pretended to be reading her book.

"Ladies dress. $8.95," she said proudly. "I will make sure Jimmy makes his deliveries for you on time. No stopping to talk to the girls."

Olivia's informal arrangement with Jimmy had lately become a part-time job for the lad, her customers liking the new after school delivery service the Beachcomber was able to offer.

"Jimmy's no problem Akiko, not to worry. He's bringing more girls in than he's chasing away. My penny candy sales have gone up and it all seems to be selling after school lets out."

How would Jimmy feel about his mother working at the store as well, Olivia wondered?

"He's growing quite tall now," Olivia added, trying to relax Akiko.

"He will turn 13 soon."

"I know. He's been talking about it quite a bit…about becoming a teenager."

Olivia had also noticed that his voice was changing, becoming deeper, sounding more like his father's. He had grown quite a bit this past year, favouring the height his mother had. If he weren't taller than Harry was now, he soon would be.

Akiko smiled.

"Mr. McMichael, I heard him say to Miss Lucy that you employ child labour. I don't want you to get into any trouble."

"Oh he did, did he?"

"Yes. Miss Lucy talked back to him. She said that she had seen him break a few child labour laws in his day, and to go away please."

"Oh she did, did she?"

Olivia could only imagine that conversation. She laughed. She had recently given Lucy a promotion at the store; she was now a manager, and apparently Lucy liked the new responsibilities. It was true though; she had seen some young Chinese boys, much younger than Jimmy, working in the mine upon occasion.

"I have never seen anyone talk back to Mr. McMichael," Akiko said.

"Well, stick around here," Olivia jokingly said. "I'm sure we'll have reason to do so again. I wouldn't worry. Jimmy is certainly no child, as you know better than anyone."

She could see by Akiko's eyes that this was a very serious matter for her.

"He is powerful man. You do not want to displease him. No one in your family is safe from him. I should know."

Akiko's head was bowed once again, but she was not immediately raising her head. She had hoped she had not pushed her potential employer too far by reminding her it was Jimmy's involvement with the Beachcomber that eventually led to Akiko losing her cleaning job with McMichael at the mining office. It had been a calculated choice of words that Akiko had thought about for days on end while she was trying to gain the courage to ask for the job. She did not yet know how that calculation would pay off, and she was afraid to look Olivia in the eye.

It was a gamble for Olivia to consider as well. McMichael would probably laugh his head off if he heard Akiko was a salesperson in the store. Cow-towing to the foreigners, oh she could practically hear him snickering. But Akiko had a very good point. The community was made up of many different cultures and there was something to be gained on a lot of levels if this worked. Who else would employ this woman and pay her a fair wage? And she had inadvertently gotten her fired.

"Well," Olivia said. "It looks like I've solved one of my problems, Akiko. Why don't you come back at five when the store is closed so we can talk?"

"Mrs. Olivia?"

"Yes, Akiko," Olivia said firmly. "I would like to offer you a job. I'm going to need someone to help in the store in the mornings. Would that suit you?"

Akiko smiled and bowed.

Olivia offered her hand.

"We shake hands in Canada," she said. "No bowing. We don't want Lucy getting used to that, do we? She'll have us bowing all day long."

Akiko shook her hand as she had seen her husband do.

Outside the window, Sarah clapped her hands in delight. She opened the door and stuck her head inside.

"Come along Akiko," she said. "It's time for a celebratory piece of cake from the café. My treat! I'll save mine for my dinner, but you'll know I'll be thinking about you all afternoon!"

The two friends walked arm in arm down the street, giggling like two schoolgirls.

Olivia thought about the decision she had just made. It really wasn't any crazier than the position her Uncle Aaron had just put her in. He had insisted that a blood relative look after the new fire-proof cement concentrator going in at the mine until it was fully bought and paid for and legally no longer his. He had asked her to look after it for him and agreed to pay her wages to McMichael while she was there on a part-time basis, in the mornings, supervising the installation. Not that she knew anything about concentrators, but she would learn very quickly.

"Funny how things work out," she thought to herself.

CHAPTER 29

Olivia walked into the mining office that first day with great apprehension. Frank, of course, was furious with her when he heard the news but said nothing to her. Nothing at all. He hadn't carried on a civil conversation with her in weeks. She supposed he had heard the news directly from McMichael. She had heard McMichael had been very vocal about it. But with Frank it was a conversation she didn't know how to begin and preferred just to avoid.

"Let sleeping dogs lie," she told herself.

Perhaps he felt the same way, she thought. Frank's face had held no emotion.

McMichael met her with the same stone-faced expression.

"So," he said matter of factly. "You're here are you?"

"Yes sir. I thought I'd start with Sarah today. I'd like to go over the re-billable expenses for the installation and sign off on them before they are sent to Mr. Bower for final approval."

"You thought you'd start off with my personal secretary did you? Sarah is quite capable of looking after the books herself, I can assure you. It's month end and she's a little busy to be teaching you."

"I'm sure she is, Mr. McMichael. But I'm also sure my signature on those bills to authorize their payment will ensure that David Hearn's cheque is on time for him back home for his family, while he is here supervising the construction. And as for teaching, I do run my own business Mr. McMichael, as you are well aware. I can read a ledger."

Hearn was an engineer Aaron had sent up from one of his companies in the United States to ensure the concentrator was installed safely.

"My Uncle certainly won't pay him for hours he hasn't actually worked. I am to keep an eye on him. When Hearn signs off that the concentrator is fully operational, we will be done here. That should satisfy your bosses and the insurers, not that there will be any more fires."

"I see," McMichael said.

He looked at Olivia, standing determinedly before him. Her eyes pierced right through him, and he found himself unable to look away from her.

"Don't get me wrong," he said. "I don't want you to be here, make no mistake about that. But since you are, I've had Sarah set up a desk for you across from hers. I expect you'll find everything you need there."

"So she can keep an eye on me?"

"In as much as a fashion that Sarah could ever secretly keep tabs on anyone, yes. Your Uncle isn't the only one keeping an eye on things. You have limited access to the office and concentrator area. That's it. I catch you anywhere near a tunnel and you're out of here, Aaron Bower or no Aaron Bower. Understood?"

He watched as she removed a strand of hair from in front of her eyes.

"Yes sir," she said. "I do believe you have made yourself quite clear."

McMichael found himself gazing at her. She was truly beautiful. He had heard all the rumours of how Frank was treating her, and he wondered how he could possibly do that to such a lovely woman. He had had his moments with his wife while she was alive; both of them having heated tempers, but the silence between them had never lasted until the morning, let alone for months.

"Is there anything else sir?" Olivia asked, noticing McMichael was staring at her.

Caught off guard, McMichael raised his voice.

"Just keep out of my way," he said. "Then we'll all be better off. And let Sarah get her work done. You can have her for a half-hour in the morning, once she gets me my coffee, and that's it."

So it began that Olivia started each day over at the mine with Sarah, ensuring that her Uncle's payments were met on time by the mine and his fixed costs did not run overboard. She found herself having a whole new opinion of Sarah, who she had always thought of as a likeable yet somewhat silly woman. She had attributed that to Sarah's youth and sheltered upbringing here at Britannia. While it was certainly true that she was clumsy and often spoke without a thought towards what she was about to say, Olivia quickly learned that at least part of it was an ongoing act she played with McMichael.

When he had barked at Sarah one morning for no apparent reason, Olivia took her aside.

"You shouldn't let him treat you like that Sarah," Olivia offered.

"Well, he is the boss."

"But still, he should show some respect. He'd be lost without you."

"Don't let it get to you. His bark is worse than his bite."

"Sarah, how long have you worked for Mr. McMichael?"

"Since I finished school. I was the best at math in my class, and he needed a bookkeeper he wouldn't have to pay very much, and there I was, with no experience needing a job. It was a match made in heaven. At least for him."

"How on earth do you put up with him?"

"It all blows over. I'm used to it. He doesn't stay mad for long. I know what makes him crazy and what doesn't. If he's particularly mean with me, then I'll forget to sugar his coffee. I'll listen out here while he has a fit about it in his office and I'll have a quiet little chuckle to myself. He just thinks I've been forgetful. He won't fire me. I'm very good at the books although my typing isn't that great. And I think he does know he'd be lost without me."

"I see," Olivia said.

"I know people think I'm a blabbermouth, but really Olivia, there's not much about this operation that I don't know about, sometimes months in advance. The numbers are right before me. You don't have to worry; my lips remain sealed. That goes for your Uncle's affairs as well."

Sarah read the astonished look upon Olivia's face.

"Don't look so surprised. I'm a smart cookie. If I were you, I'd be checking the grade of the bolts being used in the installation. Check inside the box and make sure they haven't been switched with a lesser grade of material. You'll probably find the good ones in a bag in the stockroom, not in the box. The foremen are always under the gun to save costs. It's not something your engineer would necessarily look out for, but then he doesn't know all of our foremen's, (including your husband's), tricks in the stockroom. He'll switch them if he thinks he can save a dollar or two. Oh, and those specialized drill bits your man Hearn wanted? Here's the purchase order Frank gave me. A little suspect don't you think? Why would he be ordering twice as many as Hearn told me he needed? Hmm, maybe so he can keep them after the job is done? He likes his coffee with double cream, Mr. Hearn does. He just mentioned the drill bit order to me in passing. Funny how it all comes around eventually."

Sarah accidentally knocked her teacup to the floor. It tumbled before she could grab it, but it did not break.

"He wouldn't!" Olivia exclaimed.

"Go," Sarah said, pulling a towel from her desk that she kept there for just such an emergency. "Do a little sleuthing. Just protect your source."

Sure enough, Olivia had the engineer do an inspection and Sarah had been right. The bolts had been switched, and Frank did try to order more bits than were needed for the installation of the concentrator. She would have to have a talk with Frank when she got home. Or not. It was probably easier just to re-write the purchase order, since Sarah still had it on her desk.

As she began to feel more comfortable at the mine, she found that some of the problems she encountered she could solve by a simple phone call to her Uncle. Busy as he was, he always made time to ease her concerns and share a little gossip. Some however, were a little more complicated.

"What are you doing?" McMichael had asked her one day when she wandered over to the concentrator site and started nosing around.

"I'm inspecting the installation sir. I'm to do it once a day."

"And you know what to inspect, do you?"

"It doesn't matter if I do or I don't sir. I rely on Hearn for that. It's just a formality. I find the men pay more attention when I come around."

McMichael stared at her. The men started to snicker amongst themselves.

"All right, enough," McMichael said to them.

"I meant that they need to be watched. They're not always focused on their jobs."

The men quieted.

"I knew what you meant," McMichael grunted. "Listen to me. Women were not meant to be at the mine. Not in this part of the mine. They cause distractions. The men focus better on their jobs when you're not around, rest assured."

"Mr. Bower says I am to do it once a day."

"Well, Mrs. Fitzpatrick. Uncle Aaron Bower or no Aaron Bower, there will be no women in dresses in my concentrator building. Safety hazard. All that material could get stuck in the machinery. Your hair could get caught in a moving part. We can't have that, now can we? Go back to the office, please."

Olivia sighed.

"I am just doing my job, Mr. McMichael," she said as she left.

McMichael addressed the men.

"If I hear any of you saying one word, one inappropriate word about Mrs. Fitzpatrick, while she's working here, there's going to be trouble."

The next day, at precisely eleven o'clock, Olivia returned to the concentrator building.

McMichael could see she had donned a pair of oversized men's coveralls, the length of her skirt stuffed down the baggy legs. Her hair was tied up in a ponytail. As odd a sight as it was, she looked stunning. The men stood there with their mouths open.

McMichael smacked his newspaper against the wall in anger. She had got to him, in more ways than one.

"What are you staring at?" Olivia asked the men. "Get back to work. Focus, focus, focus."

They glanced at McMichael who raised his arms in a circular motion, indicating that they return to work.

"You heard her," he said, mimicking her. "Focus, focus, focus."

Olivia wasn't amused.

"Get new shoes," he ordered Olivia as he stormed back to his office. "No women's heels. Regulation footwear must be worn on site. You can get some at the store. My store."

It had been the beginning of their co-existence at the mine. Most of the time McMichael just looked her over, grunted, and left, although occasionally she was sure she could hear him mutter "damn railroad" under his breath. She took guidance from Sarah and ignored most of his more personal outbursts, fortunately they were beginning to be fewer and farther between. Sarah had been right; the outbursts didn't last long. She thought once or twice he had actually been quite pleasant to her, but they were usually alone when that happened.

He was an interesting man, she admitted to herself. She found herself looking forward to at least having a good conversation with a male each day. Sometimes the chatter at the store amongst the women was more than she could bear.

Today, as she left home and went over towards the mining office, she could see a group of men outside, blocking the entrance.

"Excuse me Peter," Olivia said. "I need to get by. Should you not be on shift already?"

"Mrs. Fitzpatrick, this is nothing personal, but I don't work for you. I work for Mr. McMichael."

The group of men lined up behind him. They stood there, with their hands in their pockets and their gear on the ground, refusing to budge. She could see Frank up the hill, watching the situation from above, and choosing to do nothing.

"Oh but it is personal, Peter," she said. "And you do work for me in a sense. Because if you and the other men don't get to work, there will be no ore mined today, which means my concentrator will be empty, which in the end, means you won't get paid. You or your friends. Now stop blocking this entrance so my men can get to work. We're scheduled to run a preliminary test on it today, you know that."

"We don't take orders from women," one of the older men said. "And those men you're calling yours won't be crossing this line anytime soon. Not until we get a proper supervisor, a man, overseeing us."

"We're on a protest strike," one of the men in her unit said.

"A protest strike?" McMichael yelled. He had come out from his office to see what the commotion was about. "Did I hear you correctly? A protest strike?"

The men's bravado had suddenly been lessened.

"Well please," McMichael began, his voice being very theatrical, "tell me if I'm wrong, but in order to have a protest strike, you've got to have a union. And as far as I know, and I would know because I am the boss, there is no union in this town. So therefore, there is no strike. Do I need to remind you about what happened when the Armstrong brothers tried to form a union a couple of years ago? The Wobblies, I believe they called it? They didn't succeed, did they? And are they working here now?"

He paused for effect.

"Are they working anywhere now? No, they are waiting in the bread lines in Vancouver. Gentlemen, let me put it to you in words you will understand. I don't like having Mrs. Fitzpatrick overseeing the concentrator operations any better than you do. But in order for this mine to have a new fireproof concentrator, I had to pay that price. I paid that price to save your jobs. So you've got five minutes to get back to work before I re-think this whole deal, including why I employ you in the first place. Does anyone have a problem with that?"

There was a low grumbling as the ad-hoc protest group started to disassemble.

"Oh and Peter," McMichael said, "pack your bags. You're fired."

There was a look of shock on Peter's face.

"Well really Peter, what did you expect?" McMichael asked. "Get going. Give my regards to the Armstrong brothers should you run into them."

McMichael turned to Olivia.

"The next time someone steps out of line like that, you fire him. Or deal or no deal with your Uncle, you'll be the next to go."

"But that's not my responsibility," Olivia said. "I don't work for the mine. Peter was right in that regard."

"No, but you represent your Uncle. I'm sure he wouldn't let any other manager he had be disrespected. For the past two weeks Peter's sole job has been installing the concentrator. So technically, he was on loan to you. I want you to go up to the Chinese barracks and get two men to take his place. I don't care if it's their day off. Take two of the biggest, strongest men you can find. We've lost time with this nonsense today. I need that concentrator fully operational. I want the first load going through it today, no excuses. Don't worry, your Uncle's costs won't be raised any with the extra men on board."

"Yes sir," Olivia said.

"I see your husband watched all this from the hill. Interesting. He didn't rush down to see what all the fuss is about?"

"No sir," Olivia admitted.

"Well I'll say one thing for you Olivia. You've got more backbone than he does. I don't like my supervisors not supporting each other. Carry on."

Olivia took a deep breath and headed inside the concentrator building. McMichael stormed up the hill to Frank.

"What the hell were you doing watching all that from up here? Are you my foreman or not?"

"She seemed to be handling it."

"Well lucky for you she was. You should have stepped in and stopped it before it got started. That's your job, need I remind you. You are to ensure that there is no trouble as far as Olivia is concerned. I would have thought that would come naturally. Let's not even think about the ramifications of my railway deal going sideways if her family wants to make trouble. Because if that goes south, you'll be going south, the pair of you."

"I'm sorry sir," Frank said.

"Sorry? Do you still not get it Fitzpatrick? It's her family, your in-laws, that are holding all the cards here at the moment. If I were you I'd be holding it over my head like there was no tomorrow. What am I going to do? Fire you? Not until that concentrator is up and running. Bower wanted a relative in charge. All right, I can understand that, blood being thicker than water. God knows why he didn't leave his nephew Jason up here, but he didn't. But he didn't have to pick Olivia. She could have stayed at that confounded store of hers. There was another male family member here all along. You Frank. You! How did you lose all that control? Did you ever have it? If you were a smart man, you would have used that leverage to become a partner in the railroad we've been trying to push through. But instead, now we both have to deal with Olivia."

Frank said nothing.

"You don't know, do you? You truly don't know. Do you still talk to your wife at all Frank? Even the slightest conversation in passing? Her father William has agreed to talk the Canadian government into working a deal to extend the north-south rails from Vancouver all the way north to Squamish. The Bowers have agreed to go after the financing. Can you envision what that will mean? Britannia will become bigger than Vancouver. Everyone will want to move up here. We'll be able to move more ore out, cheaper too. They'll be able to ship more lumber from the forests. Mills will spring up everywhere. Men will have jobs for life. It will be truly amazing. But its fate all lies with that confounded woman you married."

McMichael tapped Frank on the shoulder.

"Deal yourself a new hand Frank. If you play your cards right, you could be a very wealthy man indeed."

CHAPTER 30

Sarah was spending an unusual amount of time in the store, Olivia thought to herself. Not that Sarah didn't come in often just to browse, but today, Sarah seemed a bit rattled.

It was customary for Olivia to get up early and come and open the store on Wednesday mornings so that Lucy would have at least one morning to sleep in an extra hour. Olivia didn't have to be at the mine until nine, so it worked out for both of them. They had become so busy that the store was now open from dawn to dusk, every day but Sunday.

"Is there something I can help you with?" Olivia asked her, not wanting Sarah to be late for work.

Sarah looked around the store. Margaret was just leaving with a bag of groceries and finally she would have Olivia all to herself. She approached the front counter and whispered to Olivia, even though they were now alone in the store.

"I know you work here by yourself for a bit on Wednesday mornings, and I wanted to get a chance to talk to you alone. I can't really do that over at the mining office."

"It must be important," Olivia said.

"Well, it's really none of my business, and you don't have to answer if you don't want to, but I was wondering how long you went out with Frank before, you know, he popped the question."

Olivia tried not to smile. Sarah had been seeing a lot of her brother Jason, and although she doubted marriage had crossed his mind, apparently it had crossed Sarah's. Jason had been finding excuses to come for quite some time but she doubted her eternally wandering brother was ever going to settle down despite Sarah's letters to him. Olivia saw her drop an envelope in the mail chute every day after work.

"Well, that was a little different," Olivia began, "we were childhood sweethearts, so I guess in reality, it took him years."

Sarah looked crest-fallen.

"Oh, don't give up hope Sarah. Your day will come."

Sarah was not to be dismayed.

"What about your sister Emily? She didn't know the veterinarian long before she married him, did she?"

"Well, no, I suppose not."

"Hmm," Sarah smiled.

"Sarah, what are you up to?"

"Oh nothing. A girl just can't wait too long you know, that's what my mama says. I got a call from Jason after Mr. McMichael left the office yesterday. Jason said he's coming up with Frenchie for a visit tonight and he's got a big surprise for me."

"Well," Olivia cautioned. "Don't get your hopes up. My brother has promised me some surprises in my day and they've been whoppers. He promised me a pony for my seventh birthday and he got me one all right. One of his broken pieces from his Civil War army toy set. The legs were broken off a horse piece, and that he said, was my pony. I cried for days as I recall."

"Still," Sarah smiled, brushing off the warning. "You never know. I'd like to order these white shoes from the catalogue please, in a nine. Yes I have big feet. Mama says it's a good thing I wasn't a breach baby. Aren't they lovely though, the shoes I mean? All smooth satin."

"Sarah," Olivia began.

"They're just white shoes Olivia. Every woman should have a pair of white shoes shouldn't she, you know, just in case?"

"Just in case?"

"Yes. Just in case."

Before Olivia could reason with her anymore, the door chimes sounded announcing Lucy's arrival. Sarah put a finger to her lips to silence any further conversation. Olivia gave her a cautionary nod.

"Thank you so much for letting me sleep in Olivia," Lucy exclaimed. "I don't know how you managed to get McMichael to give you the late start, but thank you."

"Ah, those would be the benefits of being a part-time employee. You remember those times, don't you Lucy? Not having to show up to work until noon."

"You look awful," Sarah commented.

"Thanks for that," Lucy said.

"No," Olivia said, "she might not have been tactful, but she's right. You do look awful."

"I just can't get any sleep these days. Frenchie has been coming over more and more and he and Margaret have been staying up until all hours of the night. I used to think his songs were charming, but I'm telling you, I'm ready to kill him."

"Oh it can't be that bad," Olivia commented.

"Oh really? Last night he was teaching her a French song. Something about dancing under a bridge, I gather. They were dancing around the room all night. 'Sur la Pont D'Avignon'. I can sing the silly thing all by myself now, and I don't know any French."

"Oh, how romantic," Sarah sighed.

"Not at two in the morning! Neither of them has to get up early the next day. Not since Margaret retired."

"Maybe you should move out," Sarah offered.

"The girl is right," Olivia said. "You don't need to be the third wheel. Sarah, why don't you ask McMichael if there are any vacancies coming up at any of the houses."

"It's a great idea Olivia, but I don't know about living by myself. I've never done it. I went straight from my family home to one with Marty."

"Don't you think it's time you left home?" Olivia asked Sarah.

"It is. But I've got my own plans!" Sarah laughed as she exited the shop. "Goodbye now!"

"What was that all about?" Lucy asked.

"Don't ask," Olivia sighed.

"Well, thanks but no thanks. Living with Frenchie or living with Sarah? I don't know which one will put me back in the hospital first."

"I have to go," Olivia apologized. "Sorry to leave you on your own."

"That's okay. Akiko will be here in a few minutes. She's teaching me Japanese. Isn't that neat?"

Olivia smiled.

"You'll be speaking three languages before I know it. English, Japanese and French. I only wish her husband were as keen to teach. I hear he's giving McMichael some trouble in that regard."

Harry had recently been given the task of teaching all the new recruits first aid. McMichael had noticed that quite a few of his seasoned staff were reaching retirement age, and wanted to be well prepared. McMichael had learned a lot from the landslide. He insisted that not only the English-speaking Canadians, but also a selection of men who spoke different languages be trained in first aid. Harry was the most experienced man, having safely attended to the men for years, so the job fell to him. That was a tough request for Harry. Olivia had overheard McMichael reprimanding him about it.

"Yes," McMichael had said, "you are going to teach Yan Li how to clean a wound. You are going to teach him, and Sam George, and Philippe LaFleur and Carlo Masteroni."

"But they do not speak English."

"You clean the wound; you stick a bandage on it. How much talking do you have to do? Do I have to remind you that until recently your own wife did not speak English?" McMichael barked back.

"Okay. I will teach the Indian, the Frenchman, and the Italian. But not the Chinese."

"This is not open for negotiation Harry. You will teach Yan Li. Or you will be on the next boat back to Vancouver. Take your pick. You know damn well Yan Li speaks English. He's Chinese but he speaks English. Stranger things have happened you know."

Interesting, Olivia had thought. Yan Li was the grandson of old Mr. Li, Jimmy's friend. The prejudice had not apparently been passed down from Harry to his son. That was a wonderful thing. It must have been Akiko's influence, and yet, she was the Yada who had not been born in Canada.

"Well good luck," Olivia said to Lucy. "McMichael sells earplugs down at his store, maybe you should go get some," she laughed as she headed out the door.

Lucy pondered it for a moment, then thought the better of it.

Over at the mining office, McMichael noticed Sarah pouring just one cup of coffee.

"Where's Olivia?" he asked. Lately he had been having a cup of coffee with Olivia mid-morning and he found himself looking forward to it.

"Wednesday," Sarah said.

"Oh yes," McMichael remembered. He found Sarah staring at him.

"Is something wrong, Sarah?"

"No sir," she said, smiling.

McMichael realized that Sarah had picked up on the fact that he was enjoying spending time with Olivia. He knew that might have appeared inappropriate to some.

"Would you like to have coffee with me Sarah?" he asked.

Never in all their years together had he asked her to have coffee with him before.

"Um, no, actually. I'm a tea drinker. I don't think it's quite the same."

Sarah, McMichael mused, could be quite the diplomat when she wanted to. She dodged that one with decorum.

"Very well then," McMichael said. "Just don't say I didn't ask."

"I wouldn't dream of it."

That afternoon, Frank asked Olivia if she would like to have lunch with him.

"I beg you pardon?" Olivia said.

"Well, according to the schedule," Frank said, "we both have lunch today at one. Why don't we spend it together, out on the picnic table? It will give us a chance to talk."

What was that all about? Olivia wondered, having agreed to meet her husband. True to his word, Frank was waiting at the table for her. They both pulled out their lunches they had made and bagged themselves.

"Trade you my apple for your cookies," he said, in a peace offering of sorts. It was the most he had spoken to her in quite some time.

"Okay," Olivia agreed, making the exchange cautiously.

"Liv," Frank began, "I wanted to have a chance to explain. Things have been crazy between us. I want you to try and understand. It was bad enough when you opened the store without telling me. Okay, maybe I didn't take you as seriously as I should have, but I didn't know it meant that much to you. I'm sorry for that. You shouldn't have had to go to your father for the money. That was my fault and I take responsibility for that and the unfortunate wedding incident. And the misunderstanding about the bolts and the drill bits."

Olivia could feel her eyebrows raising.

"But when you started working at the mine," he continued, "that was a whole new kettle of fish. The guys are giving me the business. Asking me who wears the pants in the family. I'm looking like a fool."

"Well I didn't see you rushing to help me out the other day," Olivia noted. "I wondered whether you had put them up to it."

Frank smiled.

"I wish I had thought of that, but no, I didn't. You were holding your own all right."

"I didn't ask for the job Frank."

"You didn't have to take it."

"I kind of did, Frank."

"No, you didn't."

"Well, maybe I wanted to," Olivia admitted.

"There's nothing wrong with wanting to, but did you have to actually do it?"

"Frank, we're going around in circles."

"I know, I'm sorry. Just, try to remember I'm your husband. I need respect from the men. I don't need them laughing at me."

"I'm sorry if they do."

Frank paused.

"One day, I may have to call upon them to save my life. Maybe yours."

It all made sense to Olivia. Frank was suffering from a bad case of male ego. His pride was bruised.

"Frank, this job is not forever. The installation is almost done. It will be over soon," Olivia said, offering an olive branch.

"And then what?" he asked.

"And then," Olivia paused. "I'll go back to the store, I guess."

"What about starting a family?"

That was a curve Olivia wasn't expecting.

"Okay Frank. What is this all about?"

"What do you mean? We always talked about having a family. Liv, we've been married a few years now. Don't you think it's time to give it some thought?"

"Well, I don't think that's going to happen Frank. You haven't made love to me in months. I seem to recall that is a necessary part of the equation."

"Sometimes I think you care more about your "jobs" than you do about me. I'd really like a son, Liv. Someone to pass the family name along to. A son with chestnut hair like yours…"

He ran his hands through her hair.

"Frank, this isn't the time or the place."

"No, it *is* the time and the place. Neither of us can make a scene. We've been silent to each other too long. Wouldn't you like that? Wouldn't you like to become a mother?"

It was something Olivia had wanted desperately, but she had all but given up hope. Tears started to well in her eyes.

"Just think about it Liv," he said, rising from the table.

It was hard for Olivia to concentrate on her job at all that afternoon. Even Sarah noticed that she was unusually quiet.

"Is something wrong Olivia?" she asked.

"No, I'm fine. Just a little out of sorts. Nothing to worry about."

"Why don't you come down to the dock with me at five and meet Jason?" Sarah offered.

"Oh, I don't know about that," Olivia answered. She had a feeling the night was not going to go exactly as Sarah had hoped. Still, she wasn't ready to face Frank at home yet. She had been thinking about him all afternoon and wondering, why the sudden change of heart?

"Okay," she sighed. "Maybe I'll come along for a few minutes."

Perhaps a glimpse of young love would be inspirational, she thought to herself.

Frenchie's boat had been right on time. Sarah ran down the dock to meet Jason, who was equally as eager to see her. He threw his arms around her, sweeping her off her feet.

"Maybe I'm wrong," Olivia thought to herself.

"Oh, Sarah," Jason said, ignoring his sister completely. "I have the biggest surprise for you."

"I know, I know," Sarah said. "I can't wait until you can tell me."

"I'll tell you now. Olivia will find out sooner or later."

"Jason," Sarah said, "don't you think you want to ask me in private?"

"Oh, there's nothing to ask," he said. "I've already done it."

Sarah looked dumbfounded.

"Done what?"

"Purchased the old mercantile building. I'm going to open a moving picture house here in Britannia. Isn't that great?"

"Agh!" Sarah gasped in disbelief. "Olivia, cancel my order."

Sarah stormed away in tears.

"What did I do?" Jason asked, perplexed.

"Let's just say the next time you come for a visit, you'd better be bringing white shoes," Olivia said.

"What?"

"Size nine, I believe. Yes that's right, nine. Don't bug her about it and don't stand there like an idiot. Go after her."

Jason ran up the dock after Sarah.

As Olivia returned home, Frank had the radio playing soft music and her bath poured for her. A glass of wine and soft candlelight was awaiting her arrival.

Olivia's heart skipped a beat. It had been the first romantic gesture Frank had offered in quite some time. She closed her eyes and held her breath.

"Come here Liv," he said, in a soft tone she had been longing to hear. He took her in his arms and stroked her hair.

"I know it's been rough," he said, "but I love you. I've always loved you and I always will."

They made love like two strangers, having begun to forget the intimacies of their bodies with their estrangement.

"You've lost weight," Frank commented.

"I've been under a bit of stress," she offered.

"You look great, Liv."

Again they made love. This time the nervousness fell away, and the passion they had experienced as newlyweds returned. The tension Olivia had felt in every bone in her body was cleansed away. She was almost asleep when she heard Frank's voice.

"So what's going on between you and McMichael?" Frank asked.

"What do you mean by that?" Olivia asked, desperately hoping that Frank wasn't going to spoil things.

"I've seen the way he looks at you."

"Nonsense," Olivia assured her husband. "He has called me every name in the book when there's been a problem at the mine, but he has never whispered sweet nothings in my ear. That's your job."

She tried to cuddle next to Frank but the mood had been broken. What was going to happen next between them, she didn't know.

CHAPTER 31

Forgiveness.

It really wasn't something you can do until you're good and ready, Olivia thought. It had taken Lucy Bentall all of a year to begin to forgive Britannia for what it had taken from her. It had taken Sarah all of an evening to forgive Jason for not proposing. Where she was with Frank, she wasn't quite sure.

Things had improved, she admitted. They were speaking to one another once again. At least they were communicating, she thought. Frank had moved back into the bedroom, and while there was a lot of sex, she didn't feel there was a lot of tenderness involved. Still, for Olivia, it was an improvement over the past few years with her husband.

It had been a month since the threatened strike at the mine, but there seemed to be an undercurrent of anxiety toward her, just the same. Olivia knew she couldn't trust the men completely and as the days neared towards the signing off of the concentrator installation, she found herself having to watch their every move. They were trying to get under her skin, she knew, and she was desperately trying not to let them.

Things finally came to a head one afternoon when Bobby Ashton, one of the workers, returned from work, reeking of alcohol.

"Mr. Ashton," Olivia said. "Kindly explain yourself."

"I had a beer for lunch, no big deal."

"Where were you drinking beer at this hour? The bars aren't open."

"Prohibition ended with the war, boss lady. We can have beer in our house. McMichael knows all about it."

"It is a big deal, Mr. Ashton. I highly doubt it was one beer. And I doubt Mr. McMichael knows all about it. Not on a workday. Go home and sleep it off."

Bobby picked up his welding torch, fired it up and turned, waving it in front of her. She could feel the heat from the flame on her face.

"I don't think you heard me, Mr. Ashton."

"Oh, did you say something?" he smirked.

"You, Mr. Ashton, have two choices. You can either go home and sleep it off, like I said the first time, or we can invite Mr. McMichael up here to discuss your termination. You know as well as I do he does not let men with alcohol on their breath work their shifts. And don't flatter yourself into thinking you're intimidating me with that torch."

Bobby Ashton tried to stare her down, but she stood her ground.

"Well? I'm waiting. Time is money."

Bobby Ashton put down his torch and sulked off.

"You! Ronnie Sykes! Get over her and finish this weld," she shouted.

When word of the incident eventually reached McMichael, he smiled. He'd been smiling a lot lately, Sarah noted, but she dared not mention it. The coffee invitation had been unnerving enough.

CHAPTER 32

"Lucy," Sergeant Wolanski shouted as he saw her coming out of the café, "come here a moment. Please."

Lucy smiled and walked over to Rudy.

"I was wondering Lucy, if you'd do me the honour of accompanying me to the moving picture show tonight at 7:00."

"Oh Rudy, that would be lovely!" Lucy exclaimed. "I was looking for a reason to get out of the house tonight to leave Frenchie and Margaret alone."

"I was hoping you wanted to come to the show for more than that," Rudy said.

"But still, beggars can't be choosers. I'll take you for coffee afterwards, thereby delaying your return by another half an hour, how's that?"

Lucy laughed.

"You could probably keep me out until eleven," she winked. "I won't mind."

If the truth be known, and the truth seemed to be known by just about everyone but Lucy, Lucy thoroughly enjoyed Rudy's company.

"Well, what's stopping you?" Olivia asked her one day. "Good-looking single men like Rudy don't come along every day. Just ask Sarah."

"But he's been married before," Lucy said.

"Well, so have you. What's your point?"

"The point is…we know what happened to my husband. What happened to his wife?"

"Why don't you ask him?" Olivia said. "That's the only way you'll ever find out. That's the only way any of us will ever find out. He sure doesn't like to talk about it."

Jason's moving picture house, which he had called "The Caprice" after the movie houses in the United States, had been an instant hit. And while it wasn't a marriage proposal like Sarah had wanted, it did manage to keep her man in town and she considered it a blessing.

"He'll be able to provide for a family," Sarah had noted to Olivia.

As if the picture show were his main source of income, Olivia thought. Sarah apparently hadn't thought it all through. Or maybe she just didn't know of the family's wealth. Or maybe she just didn't care. Sarah's biggest thrill seemed to be that Jason let her into the pictures free whenever she wanted, and even sprung for popcorn.

It took a long time for the films to reach Britannia. They were sent city to city by train, and when the big cities didn't need them anymore, Frenchie brought them up to Jason by boat. The film they were watching tonight was a few years old, but no one cared. No one had seen it before. Tonight they were showing "The Poor Little Rich Girl" starring Mary Pickford. Mary Pickford wasn't only a Canadian, she was probably the most famous woman in the world! In the picture, she portrayed a young girl who was sadly neglected by her social-climbing parents.

"I don't know," Rudy had said after the show, "it's a bit hard to believe a twenty-four year old woman playing the role of an eleven year old girl."

"Perhaps," Lucy commented, "but I thought she was wonderful. How glamorous to be a movie star."

"You could have been a movie star," Rudy said. "You sure have the looks for it."

Lucy kissed him on the cheek. It was the first time she had extended that type of affection towards him.

"But the poor girl," Lucy continued, "left alone in the hands of evil servants who tried to poison her. How tragic. Imagine what that would do to her emotionally."

Rudy grew silent.

"Rudy," Lucy said, "I'm fine, really, don't worry."

"It's not you Lucy. Let's go have some coffee. I'll tell you all about it."

After the crowds had left the show, Jason still had some closing up to do. Jimmy Yada came by at nine thirty each night and swept and mopped the floor for him. He said he was saving the money for university. Jason hoped the young lad made it there.

"Sarah," Jason said. "Come here, I need you to do me a favour."

"What?"

"The extra set of keys fell into the popcorn. Jimmy must have left them on the top shelf. If you find them, I'll take tomorrow night off to take you out to dinner."

Sarah giggled in delight.

"What will the people do with no show?"

"I don't know," he said. "I'm sure they can get by for one night, they managed up until now without any movie house at all. I'm just going upstairs to go lock the money up in the safe. I'll be back in a few minutes."

"Do you really want me to stick my arms in all that buttery popcorn?" Sarah asked.

"Yes I do," Jason said. "Find the keys so I can throw all that buttery popcorn out. It will go rancid in a day."

"Wouldn't it be easier just to get some more keys for Jimmy?"

"Not if you want to go out to dinner tomorrow."

Sarah sighed and started to dig for the keys. About half way down she came upon something larger than keys. She brushed the kernels away to find a little box.

"How odd," she said aloud.

She took the box out of the machine. It reminded her of the days she and Akiko used to leave presents for each other hidden under her desk. That seemed like so long ago now.

She opened the box.

Jason could hear her squealing with delight.

Thank God, he thought. She found it. He didn't want to go sifting through the garbage for it later.

"Jason!" she screamed. "I've found it."

Jason went back downstairs.

"Oh Jason," she said, daring not to hope, "look what I found."

Inside the palm of her hand was a diamond ring. The biggest diamond ring she had ever seen in her life.

Jason got down on one knee.

"So Miss Lieboldt, light of my life, will you marry me?"

"Oh, wait until I tell your sister," she cried.

Jason took that as a yes.

"Please tell my sister, I am not an idiot."

"What are you talking about?"

"Never mind," he said. "Just go order your shoes."

Sarah's smile went from ear to ear.

When they reached the door of the café, Rudy paused and turned to Lucy.

"Let's not go in yet. Let's go for a walk. Do you mind?"

"Not at all," Lucy said. It was a nice night and she could see Rudy wanted to talk.

"Was it something I said?" she asked.

"No," Rudy began, "I just found the movie a bit disturbing. Not that it had anything to do with the movie really; it just brought up emotions in…me. I find the theme of mental illness a bit discomforting."

Lucy felt a chill go through her.

Rudy felt it too. He took her hand.

"No, not you Lucy. Come, walk with me. I have a story to tell you, the story of my wife Renae."

The two strolled arm and arm towards the water.

"We had a fight one night. About nothing really. I think she asked me to help with the dishes and I said no. That was the last time I saw her alive."

Lucy was speechless.

"She had taken my service revolver out of the closet I kept it in, and went out back and shot herself."

Lucy gasped, covering her mouth with her hand.

"Suicide?" she said.

Rudy nodded. "I tell people she walked out on me, but that's not really the truth. She left me, but not like that."

"I had thought about it myself once," Lucy said, "shortly after my family was killed, but…"

Rudy had been a young constable in Regina, Saskatchewan when he met Renae LeBlanc. She was a Métis who had moved to Saskatchewan from Manitoba.

"Métis?" Lucy asked. "Was she from France?"

"No," Rudy explained "The Métis are a group of people of mixed heritage who live across Canada. They are the children of Indian women and European fathers. Their numbers have grown over the years, and they have married also amongst themselves, forming their own nation. Renae's parents were both full-blooded Métis."

Like Frenchie, Lucy thought to herself.

"She was a beautiful girl," Rudy continued. "Not unlike yourself in a lot of ways. Lively, vivacious. But she was troubled."

"What happened?" Lucy asked.

"I don't know. We had run up against a lot of prejudice. Me, being of Polish decent, marrying an Indian. A half-Indian at that. But I loved her. She was one of the kindest people I had ever met. She was very proud of her heritage. She was so beautiful. I would see the other men looking at her and it would drive me crazy. I'd get so mad. It wasn't fair to her. I was just insecure. I was young. I sometimes wonder now if that helped push her over the edge."

"Do you have any children?" Lucy asked.

"No," Rudy answered. "Perhaps that's a blessing, I don't know. I don't know how I would have raised them alone. I actually admire McMichael for that."

"Tell me about her. Tell me about her family."

"I honestly don't know much about them. She didn't talk much about them. She was taken away to a residential school when she was quite young. She said horrible things happened to her there, but she wouldn't talk about it. It must have been tough for her to leave her family."

"What do you think happened there?" Lucy asked.

"What could have happened, Lucy? It was run by some Catholic priests."

"And she just shot herself one night?"

"Yes," he said. He broke down and cried.

It was the first time he had cried since it happened almost ten years ago. The tears poured out of him. Lucy sat him down on a log on the beach and put her arms around him.

"It's okay," she said. "I understand."

"I knew you would," he said.

"Are you going to be okay?" she asked.

"Yes," he said, and took her hand. "Let's go back and get some coffee to warm up."

"I must have scared the hell out of you that Easter dinner at Olivia and Frank's. When I left the house like that."

"You did," he said. "I didn't know what I had said."

Lucy told him the story of Akiko's origami birds.

"I won't tell if you don't tell," he said.

"Promise?" she said.

"Yes," he said.

"Well, I know one way to keep your mouth shut," she said, and kissed him passionately.

CHAPTER 33

Jimmy looked at the new bicycle in disbelief.

"Is this for me?" he asked.

Jimmy, Olivia and Akiko stood outside the store, admiring the bike.

His mother lowered her head. The Yada's had not been able to afford such an extravagant gift for Jimmy's thirteen birthday, despite wanting to.

"Well, sort of," Olivia said. "Technically it belongs to the store. So if you quit…" Olivia lowered her voice, "…or if you get fired, it comes back."

"Oh, I won't get fired," he said.

The new blue bike was a big shiny two-wheeler, the nicest bike Jimmy had even seen, and certainly the nicest bike anyone had in Britannia.

"It has a basket on the back so you can carry the groceries. And a bell on the front so you won't run people over," Olivia laughed.

"Wow!" Jimmy said excitedly.

"And I think it would be all right if you borrowed it to go to school, and on weekends," Olivia added. "Just as long as you take good care of it. It is store property."

"Oh I will, I promise," Jimmy said.

"Well then you'd better get to work and deliver Mary Alice her milk. Happy Birthday Jimmy, or should we call you Jim now that you're all grown up?"

"Jimmy," Lara McMichael called from up the road. "Is that a new bicycle?"

Jimmy smiled at Lara, then turned to answer Olivia.

"No, Jimmy's still good."

Akiko heaved a sigh of relief.

Jimmy hopped on the bike and rode off. He had often borrowed the McMichael girls' bicycles and taken them for a spin. Christina had taught him how to ride. But this one was special. It was a boy's bike.

Akiko turned to Olivia.

"That was very kind."

"He's a great kid Akiko," Olivia said. "I would be truly blessed to have a son like him some day."

In that moment it was hard to tell which woman was prouder of the young man, as he rode up next to Lara McMichael. Though teenage years were upon them, and Lara was slightly older than Jimmy, (which can make a difference at that age), the two had remained best friends since their childhood. He showed off his new bike with pride.

"He is getting jealous, you know," Akiko commented.

Olivia did not understand.

"Lara McMichael. She has many young boys vying for her attentions already. Jimmy of course, loves her dearly, but it can never be. She will eventually break his heart."

"One never knows what the future will bring," Olivia said to her friend. But in her heart, Olivia knew Akiko was probably right.

"She's going to be a handful, just like her sister," Olivia said.

"Yes," Akiko agreed. "I am glad I have a boy."

Last summer, Christina McMichael had announced her intentions to enter the Copper Queen beauty pageant. The problem this presented was that none of the other girls her age wanted to enter the contest for fear of losing. The organizers spent hours convincing the girls that it would be a fun time, when they knew themselves that Christina would undoubtedly win. And win she did, surprising no one. The fact was, she was a kind, smart, beautiful nineteen-year-old woman whom everyone adored despite her last name. She had never shown any interest in running in the competition in previous years, but this year she had a reason. She wanted to impress the new young doctor Alex Thompson, who was joining Dr. Van den Broek's practice in preparation for Dr. Van den Broek's retirement. And impress him she did.

Olivia and Akiko watched the handsome young couple sharing some fish and chips as they passed by the storefront.

Time was passing quicker and quicker, she thought to herself. The town had grown, and while still isolated, it had just about everything they could want: a new school, a big library, the movie theatre, and a billiards hall. Jason even rented the movie theatre out to the performing arts group that had recently been formed. This winter they were going to present Shakespeare's "As You Like It". The whole town was looking forward to it.

"Akiko, could you do me a favour?" Olivia asked. "Could you open the store tomorrow morning for me? It's Lucy's day to sleep in, but I've been a little tired lately and McMichael has asked if I could come in early over at the mine. I would really appreciate it."

Akiko had never been asked to open the store by herself.

"It would be an honour, Mrs. Olivia," Akiko said.

Sarah came running into the store.

"Are they here yet?" she asked excitedly.

"They're in the back," Olivia said. "I'll go get them."

A few moments later Olivia returned with the Eaton's shoe box. Inside were white satin covered shoes.

"They fit like a glove," Sarah exclaimed as she tried them on. "I just can't believe it! Everything is going perfectly! I can't thank either of you enough!"

Her wedding was less than two weeks away and the talk of the town. Sarah had asked Akiko to be her Matron of Honour, with Olivia taking the less glamorous role of bridesmaid, but Olivia didn't mind. It meant so much more to Akiko Sarah had taken Akiko with her down to Vancouver to shop for her wedding dress, and Akiko had stocked up on a few dresses for herself while she was away. She firmly announced to Harry upon her return that she was taking at least one trip down to the big city each summer. Akiko had discovered the Hudson's Bay department store.

"You will be a beautiful October bride," Akiko said.

"I hope it doesn't rain," Sarah sighed. "October can be so chancy. I don't want anything to spoil my wedding day."

CHAPTER 34

McMichael stood on his veranda, sipping the last of his coffee before he headed off to work. It was going to be one of those days, he thought to himself; he could just feel it. He had awoken with a headache that despite taking aspirin, was not going away. He could see Olivia making her way over to the office, dressed in blue. He liked her in blue, he thought to himself, knowing by the end of the day such glimpses would be fewer.

The price of copper had dropped considerably the past six months, dropping from twenty to fourteen cents a pound. Although he delayed this day as long as he could, it had finally arrived. He was going to have to cut his staff by about forty percent. It meant drastically reducing the new concentrator shifts. It meant shutting down the mine's tramway and the new electrical railway that had been installed. The writing had been on the wall for weeks but the men had been blissfully unaware. That was part of the reason he had recently given a rather generous donation to help complete the new recreation hall. He wanted the townspeople to have some form of inexpensive recreation in case the situation worsened.

"At least we don't have to shut the mine down totally," he thought to himself. The ore at Britannia had silver and gold in it, enough to keep the other sixty percent employed. For now.

His first appointment of the day was coming up the street.

"What is it McMichael?" the sergeant asked.

"We need to do something about Ruby."

Ruby's house of ill repute had been functioning behind blind eyes ever since the officer had first arrived, so Wolanski was confused by McMichael's sudden interest in it.

"What exactly are you asking?"

"It's time to get her to leave town. She and her girls and that hulk of a man she uses as a bouncer."

Wolanski had always thought McMichael had a financial interest in Ruby's establishment, making him turn a blind eye.

"Rudy," McMichael started, using the officer's Christian name for the first time, "I might as well let you in on it. There may be some trouble over the next little while. I've got to lay some men off today. Let's just say more than one or two. I want the bar to stop serving alcohol for the next month. I mean that. You catch anyone drinking, you throw them in jail."

Rudy's expression turned solemn. He knew what layoffs would mean to the community. The mine was the employer that all the other businesses relied on. There would be a lasting trigger effect if the layoffs were as big as McMichael was letting on.

"When times were good," McMichael started to explain, "as much as I abhor Ruby's line of business, it kept the men for the most part, happy and out of my hair. It helped them deal with their depression and loneliness that the isolation of Britannia Beach often spawns. But they could afford it then. And Ruby and her girls would spend the money for the most part here in Britannia. But the men, they're not going to be able to afford it now. I'm not going to have families starving because the men are throwing their money away on unchristian opportunities. Ruby's time to vacate the premises has arrived."

He handed Wolanski an envelope.

Rudy looked at it cautiously. Was McMichael trying to bribe him?

McMichael had read Wolanski's mind.

"The envelope is for Ruby," he assured him. "It seems the bank has taken this opportunity to foreclose on her mortgage. It's all laid out there in black and white."

"How convenient," Wolanski said.

"Funny how that happens. Still, it's a legal eviction notice. And just to make it clear, I'd like you to escort the occupants of the house to Frenchie's boat this evening. There will be no room for them at any of our hotels. I think Ruby will get the message."

Olivia walked into McMichael's office.

"You wanted to see me sir?" she asked.

McMichael motioned to Wolanski that their conversation was over. Rudy tipped his hat to Olivia as he left the room.

"No coffee?" Olivia asked, peering into the canister where it was normally kept.

"Sarah says she's run out. I don't know what the hell is wrong with her lately."

"The upcoming nuptials, I presume."

"Please, have a seat," McMichael motioned to her.

She sat in the big oak chair he had pointed to.

"Olivia, first let me say that this conversation is to go no further than this room."

"I understand Mr. McMichael," Olivia offered.

"I want to commend you on the job you did with the concentrator. Not just for your Uncle's interests, but also for the mine and myself. You and Sarah worked marvellously together. And on-site…I would not have believed you would have been able to handle that rag-tag group of men I gave you to install the damn concentrator. God knows they weren't my best workers, I couldn't spare the good ones to give you. But you pulled it off, and for that, I take my hat off to you."

"Thank you sir," Olivia said.

"Now, please, let me finish. Now that it's installed and working properly, I really can't afford to keep the men working any longer."

"I understand sir. I didn't think it would last forever."

"I said let me finish, Olivia."

Olivia became silent.

"I meant what I said. I really can't afford to keep the men working any longer. The price of copper has dropped so much I'm afraid I'm going to have to lay off all the men who have been working on the concentrator."

Olivia sighed. If only her men were laid off, then they would attribute their downfall to her.

"And you want me to do that for you?" Olivia said. She supposed that would be part of her job.

McMichael paused. If it had been one of the men interrupting him, he would have thrown him out of the office. But instead he found his voice becoming gentle.

"Well, I could do that and then bring you back in here and tell you that you were next out the door. I suppose that would be rather cruel, but it would get the job done."

Olivia's face remained expressionless. She had known her job was ending soon and it appeared now was the time.

"I have a problem Olivia. With fewer men on shift, I also need to reduce my supervisory positions by one. All the remaining supervisors are going to have to step up to the plate and give one hundred and ten percent. It's come down to you and Frank. It's a toss up for me, quite frankly, and I never in the world would have imagined I'd be in this position. You're better at the job than he is, no doubt about it. The men hate working for you, just like they hate working for me, and there's something to be said for that, although it's probably for far different reasons. But Frank, he's a man."

Olivia's blood flowed nervously in her veins.

"So here's the deal Olivia. I'll fire all the men, if you decide who goes or stays, you or Frank. I can't let you continue on as a supervisor, but you can be my assistant, with all the same responsibilities. You'll never be bored."

"And do the same work? Manage the men?"

"Yes. I'll pay you a fair wage. More than I do Sarah."

"Mr. McMichael, you know I've enjoyed working here at the mine. You know what I can do for you. Sarah and I managed to save you thousands of dollars by re-scheduling the concentrator shifts. We saved several hundred man-hours. Surely you recognize my contributions were more than 'assisting' you."

"But you have to understand Olivia, while your Uncle could call your position whatever the hell he bloody well wanted to, I don't have that same luxury. I can hold open a job for you, and it will be a respectful job for you, but I can't give you a job title that would belong by rights, to a man."

"Did you notice that your injuries were down?"

"Yes, Olivia."

"Did you notice that on several occasions on the late shift the men stayed an extra hour without pay so that things would be ready for the morning crew? Not bad loyalty to a boss they hate working for, as you said."

"Olivia…"

"I'm sorry Mr. McMichael," Olivia said. "I have to refuse your kind offer."

"Olivia," he began, "please reconsider. I promise you I will find Frank a job in town somewhere. Maybe at the general store. On second thought, perhaps that wouldn't be appropriate. I will find him something…I promise you."

"I can't," Olivia said.

"You're sure?"

"I'm sure. I'm pregnant, Mr McMichael."

The news shocked McMichael. The emotions that ran through his mind were surprising to him. He wasn't at all sure this was right for Olivia, but it was none of his business. He bent down to her.

"Well, I suppose congratulations are in order," he said, not convincingly.

He stood up and walked over to his desk, pulling out his rye, and pouring himself a stiff shot. He did not offer Olivia any, not that she would have taken it.

"Shall I leave?" she asked him. She could sense the news had upset him.

"Perhaps it's best," he admitted.

Olivia moved quietly towards the door.

"Olivia," he paused, "you can rest assured I do not say this with any frequency."

Her eyes rose to meet his as he continued.

"Take some time off. Raise your child, or children as it may be. Go back to your store when you're ready. But if you ever find you can't get the ore out of your veins, my door is always open. There will always be a job for you here at the mine as long as I'm in charge." He would never admit it, but he knew he would miss her.

"Thank you, Mr. McMichael, that's quite kind."

"Kind nothing. I'd rather have you working for me than against me."

That much was true, McMichael thought to himself. She competed against him with the store, and that had been a success. She had tackled the unfathomable job with the concentrator with a finesse he hadn't seen in many of his men. Not any since John Cruickshank had retired. And through it all she had managed to hold onto her pride, her dignity, and, he thought, her femininity. Even in the overalls, he recalled.

He escorted her out the door, his hand resting on her shoulder.

While Sarah noticed this, she made nothing of it, as she was well aware of what McMichael was going to do today. She assumed Olivia had been given her news.

"Sarah, get me Frank," he said. His head was still pounding and there was so much yet to do today. He'd make Frank fire the men.

"Certainly, Mr. McMichael. Mr. William Bower phoned while you were with his daughter. Shall I get him on the line for you?"

McMichael sighed. Not today, he thought. Not more bad news.

"Yes, thank you Sarah. Please do call him back for me."

McMichael went into his office and waited for Sarah to get William on the line.

"John," William began, "I've got some news for you."

McMichael didn't like the tone of his voice.

"It appears the Canadian government has run out of money as far as railway expansion is concerned. They're having a hard time making their existing financial commitments as it is. Cashing in bonds left and right or so the banks are telling me. The rail line to Squamish has been delayed indefinitely. And without them securing the loan, I'm afraid we'll have to pull out as well, at least for the foreseeable future."

"Delayed? Again? How long?"

"They're saying it could be decades. We can't afford to have our portion of the money tied up that long. I'm sure you understand."

McMichael's hopes and dreams of the coastal railroad collapsed in an instant.

"John? Are you there?" William asked.

"Yes William. Damn disappointing, that is."

"Indeed. But there's something else I'd like to talk to you about John. I'll see you next week. We're all coming up for Jason's wedding. Grace, the whole clan, and me including Aaron. We'll talk then."

"Of course."

Great. McMichael thought. I can hardly wait. I just went through months of your daughter under my feet, and now this. He could think of a million places he'd rather be than in a room with the Bower clan now that the railroad had fallen through.

The word "your daughter" lingered in his mind for a moment. Perhaps he was wrong, he thought. Perhaps there was nowhere else he'd rather be.

"William," McMichael said, "I understand you're about to become a grandfather. I just thought that maybe you should know."

He wasn't sure why he said that. Perhaps it was to keep her safe. He had fallen in love with her, he admitted to himself. Slowly, gradually over the seven years he had known her she had taken his heart. But she was a married woman, blissfully unaware, and he was a decent man. At least in that regard.

As he hung up the phone contemplating this, Sarah's fists pounded on the door.

"Mr. McMichael," she screamed. "Oh my God, come quickly!"

"Has something happened to Olivia?" he asked, not waiting for an answer.

CHAPTER 35

"What the hell happened?" McMichael asked.

"There's been a cave-in," Frank said.

"How? Where?"

"In the southwest tunnel. We're not sure how it happened."

"Is anyone down there?"

McMichael started to head off towards the tunnel entrance. The scene was chaotic as the men tried to organize themselves.

"We're not sure sir," Frank said, following him. "The men were just coming off shift. The cave-in happened as they were leaving. The walls fell in behind them."

"Then we've got to do a head count."

Olivia approached McMichael.

"I heard the news."

"Good news travels fast, bad even quicker."

"Here's the roster sir," she said, handing him a clipboard. I brought it over from the office. We can check the scheduled attendance. Sarah said no one called in sick. I know I don't really work for you anymore…"

"It's quite all right Olivia. I need your help."

"Frank," McMichael called. "Come get this list, do a roll call."

"Olivia, go find Harry. I'm going to need a full report on this. Tell Sarah to call Wolanski and the doctors. I need every available man on the scene. Tell your man Hearn I need his expertise. Ask him to work for me until we sort this out. I'll pay for him."

"No problem sir."

She left to look for the men.

A crowd had begun to form at the base of the mine.

"Is it true?" Akiko asked.

"Yes," McMichael said. "There's been a cave-in. Now you know about as much as I do," he snapped.

"Forgive me," Akiko said, and bowed her head in respect.

"Forgiveness is up to the Lord, not me," McMichael said. "Akiko, I need you to be a translator. I promise to keep you informed as soon as I know more. Stay close so I can get you to assure the Japanese workers that we will do everything we can. Pass the message along to the other bilingual people. We need more translators. Can you do that for me?"

"Yes. I will do what I can to help," she said humbly.

Tragedy. It comes in threes, she thought. First the landslide, then the fire, now this. At least they would be safe after this. Her sentiments were shared by most of the community.

"Can I help?" Jimmy asked, standing alongside his mother.

"I don't think we have any magic potions for this one," McMichael sighed.

Jimmy stood firm.

"All right Jimmy," McMichael said. "You're an experienced man. I need you to help co-ordinate the rescue efforts. You'll be my liaison with Dr. Van den Broek. Tell me what I need to know about potential medical needs. Are you up to it?"

"Yes sir," he said.

"You're a fearless lad; I'll give you that."

Akiko looked at her son with pride.

Frank approached McMichael, his employee list in his hand.

"Well?"

"Everyone is accounted for except for two," Frank said, glancing at the Yadas.

"Well then, let's have it," McMichael said.

"Yan Li, and Harry."

Akiko's hand clasped her mouth, stifling a scream.

"Good God," McMichael sighed, placing his arm around Jimmy.

Jimmy closed his eyes for just a moment.

"I am fearless, Mr. McMichael. I must go to work," Jimmy said, turning to his mother. "Be strong, mom." He held her hand until she regained her composure.

Jason Bower came over to McMichael.

"I gather people won't feel much like going to the movies tonight. How can I help Mr. McMichael?" he asked.

"We're going to need to be working day and night until we get those workers out. If you could just report to Frank, I'm sure he can use all the help he can get."

Jason was silent.

"Jason," McMichael began, "I know there's no love lost between you and your brother-in-law but if I could get you to set aside your differences for the time being. He really is the best man to organize the work crews. He knows everyone's skills. We'll need to get them out as fast as we can."

"So it's true then. There are people trapped inside?"

"Yes, it's true. Two as far as we know."

"How long can they last?"

"I don't dare make a guess at this point. I don't know if they're injured. I hope they got to the safety room, but I just don't know."

"Safety room?" Jason asked.

"We have safe spots throughout the tunnels that carry a supply of food and water, medical kits, axes, shovels and other things that could be of use in an emergency. The men know where they are."

"And what if they didn't make it to the safety room?"

"Then they've probably got a few hours to a few days at best, if they're lucky. But I wouldn't go spreading that around."

"I'd better get to work then," Jason said.

"Thank you Jason, I appreciate it," McMichael said.

He took a deep breath. He didn't know Yan Li all that well, but he knew he was one of his best employees. Yan had never given him any trouble. Never late. Never missed a day's work. And Harry…thinking of Harry brought a lump to his throat. Harry was such a diverse man, with all his idiosyncrasies. He had been a good friend to him over the years. Or at least as close to a friend as any of his employees were. He would miss him.

CHAPTER 36

"I could use the assistance of your first mate getting this equipment on board," Aaron Bower said from the wharf. There were two large crates at his feet.

The Captain motioned for his sailor to come over to help Aaron.

"Permission to come aboard Captain?" Grace asked.

Frenchie smiled.

William Bower helped his wife Grace step aboard the Northern Mary. The rest of his family were already inside the cabin. It was a wet day in Seattle, the winter rains having come early this year.

"Frenchie!" William said, extending his hand to the Captain. "It's good to see you, my friend. You remember Grace and the rest of the clan?"

Frenchie shook William's hand.

"How could I ever forgit such a delight to de eyes? Welcome aboard Mrs. Bower. You're welcome to anything ye find onboard. Tea, coffee, hot cocoa. I tink dere's some biscuits in de galley. If der's anything else ye fancy, well then we're kinda outta luck until we get to the 'Couve."

"We're stopping in Vancouver?" Grace asked.

"Aye. I've got to pick up Father Fernier along de way."

"He's coming up a few days before the wedding?" Grace enquired. She knew Father Fernier was coming up from Vancouver to perform Jason's wedding.

"'E might have one or two people 'e needs to see first," Frenchie winced.

"I see," Grace said, smiling at the Captain. "I'm sure everything will be fine. Anne says he comes highly recommended. Lovely weather we're having, isn't it?" she said sarcastically.

"'Dat time o' year again. Maybe we should turn de Northern Mary around and head for Hawaii. It's been doin' nuttin' but rain fer days now."

He noticed Grace's smile fade.

"Oh but it'll be fine fer yer wedding. I put in a special order."

He winked at her and her smile returned. He could see where Olivia got her own beautiful smile. As he studied Grace's face he could envision Olivia in twenty years or so. He realized he was staring and turned his gaze to the dock.

"Do you need a hand boys?"

"No, I think we've got it," Aaron said. He and the first mate finished loading the cargo and disappeared below deck themselves.

"Go on down and git out of dis rain, lovely lady," Frenchie said to Grace.

Grace went inside the cabin to join the rest of the family. They had all made the trip up for Jason's wedding: Billy, Emily and her husband and Sister Anne. And Daniel. Olivia hadn't seen her baby brother since Emily's wedding. How he had grown! She was going to be surprised! William helped Frenchie untie the boat from the dock.

"You've got a fine looking family," Frenchie said.

William nodded with pride.

"So my friend. Aside from the weather, what else is happening in your fair town?"

"Well," Frenchie sighed, "since ye asked. Der's been a mine cave in. Looks pretty bad. Dey've been down der for two days befer I left to come get you."

"My Lord," William said. "How many men are trapped?"

"Two," Frenchie said.

"Frank?" William asked.

"No, Yan Li and 'arry Yada. Ye might know 'arry. 'E's de head assayer."

William let out a sigh of relief.

"I'm sorry, that was rude. Of course I feel for the families involved, I just thank God it wasn't mine. I don't recall meeting the men before. Although the name Yada seems vaguely familiar."

"Well 'arry's wife, she works for Olivia at de store."

"Oh," William acknowledged. "Akiko. Olivia has told me about her. I'm sorry to hear that. Grace was quite looking forward to meeting her. She's quite an amazing woman, I understand. Do they know what happened?"

"If dey do, der not tellin' me," Frenchie said. "'arry's and 'is family are Catholic. I've got to pick up Father Fernier early in case dey 'ave to give 'im de last rights. Jimmy Yada, de son, 'e works at de Beachcomber too, doin' de deliveries and runnin' errands."

"I presume the town's not in much of a mood for a wedding. This certainly puts a damper on things."

"Well," Frenchie pondered. "Whadda ya gonna do? Life goes on, n'est pas? But if der not rollin' out de red carpet for yer family, it's because der kinda busy right now. Jason shut the picture show down for a bit. He's been working on de rescue crew like de rest of de men. Dey need everyone dey can get. Runnin' twenty-four hours a day dey are."

"I may as well go in and tell the others," William said. "It sounds like they can use some fresh blood. Billy will be able to help once we get there. I'll send Anne over to Akiko's to give her some pastoral care. How's Olivia holding up?"

"Well, I 'aven't ad to kidnap 'er lately if dat's what yer askin'."

William gathered Frenchie knew nothing about the pregnancy.

Aaron poked his out from behind the cabin door. William told him briefly what was happening at Britannia.

"Well then," he said. "It appears we have uncanny timing once again don't we?"

William nodded.

"Frenchie. Do you have any hootch on this vessel?" Aaron asked.

"I'm in international waters I tink, so I tink the answer is yes. Although I was hopin' dat was what you had in de crates."

"No worries. My cargo is legal," Aaron answered

"I'm not talkin' about de U.S. and Canada border sir. I'm talkin' about de Canada and McMichaelville border. A bit finicky 'e is lately."

"Well, we'll see what we can do to change that," Aaron laughed. "I have a feeling we'll be just what the doctor ordered for our friend McMichael."

"You might as well go show him where the booze is," William said, "before he ransacks the place. He's read a few too many pirate stories, has my brother. While you're at it, you'd better pour the mother of the groom a stiff one too. She's not big on surprises, my Grace."

CHAPTER 37

McMichael found himself gazing towards the heavens. The rain had refused to co-operate with the rescue workers at the mine. It had been pouring down hard all night and didn't show any indications of letting up.

"What's happening now Frank?" he asked.

"We've got water pouring into the emergency shaft. With all this rain the earth and rock have become water soaked, and the debris is turning into a muddy mess. It's not helping any. It's got to be seeping into the safety room, if that's where they are. They've been down there a few days now. It's not looking good."

"I know," McMichael had to agree. "You and your men have been going non-stop, I know that. And I sense the men's spirits are breaking. But just think of Harry and Yan, and think that it could have been any one of you trapped down there. You're all to be commended for your efforts."

"I'll pass along your thanks to the men. We just wish Mother Nature would co-operate a bit more."

"She has been a bit nasty here over the years," McMichael commented, looking up at the slide area. That seemed like a long time ago now.

"I mean it though Frank. You've done a hell of a job organizing the rescue."

"We're getting closer," Frank acknowledged, "but it's been a tough forty feet to bore through."

"There are these new drills that use a combination of air and water," McMichael began, "Aaron Bower has got a line on some. Ironically he's bringing one with him for us to try out. I'll probably never say this to you again Frank, but Frenchie can't get your relatives here fast enough for me today."

Frank smiled. "If there's a dollar to be made anywhere, the Bowers will do it. But if that drill works, I might even kiss Aaron Bower myself."

"It's supposed to be quite something, but I won't hold you to that. He tells me the process greatly reduces the silicon shards, which will have us all breathing easier, and I mean that literally. Silicosis might be a thing of the past. If it works as well as he says it does, I've got the go ahead to order more. We'll be able to get rid of the old widow-makers. This will be one hell of a test."

"It looks like they're docking now," Frank said.

The Northern Mary had indeed reached the shores of Britannia Beach.

"Well let's get down there then," McMichael said. He noticed Frank hesitate and knew Frank was not looking forward to seeing his father-in-law. Given the fact he had truly been working non-stop since the cave-in, McMichael decided to give him a break.

"Go find Hearn and tell him that new drill should be up to him in a few minutes. I understand he's used them before so he'll be able to show you the ropes. I'll go meet the boat."

"Thank you sir," Frank said.

"Jimmy," McMichael whistled, placing his hands between his teeth. "Come on son, I need your help."

Jimmy had been bringing fresh drinking water to the rescue crew.

"What is it Mr. McMichael?"

"Put the water down. Frenchie's boat is in now."

"Do you want me to help carry their luggage up?"

Jimmy had heard that Olivia's family was coming up for the wedding.

"No son. I think they can manage their own luggage. I want you to help carry the new drill that's going to potentially get your father out of there. Think you can handle that?"

"Yes sir," Jimmy said. His face remained solemn but his heart started to race.

McMichael could hear Mary Alice and Maggie talking as they passed by.

"God have Mercy on their souls," Mary Alice said.

"Now Mary Alice," Maggie began, "don't give up hope."

"Well that's the horror. We don't know whether they're dead or alive."

Jimmy's face went ashen.

"Son," McMichael said, "I know these past few days have been hell for you. If you need to let it out, go ahead. I won't think any the less of you."

"No," Jimmy said. "I must be strong because my mother can't."

McMichael took a deep breath. The Yada's were such a nice family. Every last one of them was full of character.

"I don't want you to listen to gossip. I'm going to be honest with you. It's true, we don't know if your father is dead or alive. But I know your father. He is a stubborn man. If there is any way in this world to cheat death, he's going to do it. Harry's no quitter. I think we need to get down to the docks and help him with his cheating, all right?" He put his hand on Jimmy's shoulder as they made their way down to the wharf.

Frenchie nodded to McMichael. He had young Daniel by his side. McMichael could see a lot of William in Daniel's six-year-old face.

"Any news?" Frenchie asked.

"No," McMichael said. "Nothing's changed since you left. They're still trapped."

"Mon Dieu," Frenchie sighed, shaking his head.

"What did you say Frenchie?" Daniel asked.

"I said you made as fine a first mate as der ever was, young Daniel."

William and Aaron came on deck and nodded to McMichael.

"I understand you've got a bit of a problem John," William said.

"That's a bit of an understatement. Hello William, Aaron."

"Well then," Aaron offered, "we'll save the pleasantries. We'd better get Bertha up and running."

William looked at his brother.

"Bertha?"

"She's not a big girl, this drill. But she packs a lot of whollop. Reminds me of a woman I knew once down in El Paso. Fiery sort, spent a lot of time…"

Frenchie covered Daniel's ears with his hands.

"Well, you get the picture," Aaron said.

The three men shook hands briefly.

"I'm sorry about the railroad John," William said.

"Let's not worry about that now," McMichael said. "There'll be time to talk before the wedding, I'm sure."

"It's still on then?" Grace asked as the rest of the family came on deck.

"Hello Grace. Yes. There was some talk of cancelling the wedding at one point, but we won't have that, will we?"

"Well, under the circumstances…" William began.

"Under the circumstances nothing. You don't know your future daughter-in-law very well do you? I'd never hear the end of this." He waved them off the boat. "The crowd may be a bit smaller than Sarah planned. Some of the men will need to keep working, but the show as they say, must indeed go on."

"Where's Olivia?" Emily asked.

"You must be Emily. Olivia told me about you. I'm John McMichael. The store has been operating as a makeshift command centre for the rescue workers and she's up to her ears in it. I know she's thrilled you're all here. Come with me and I'll take you up there. I'm sure she can use your help."

"Jimmy isn't it?" William asked. "You're certainly taller than the last time I saw you. When you're finished with Aaron, take Sister Anne over to see your mother will you? Billy, help these men with the drill."

"Yes sir," Jimmy said. "But I must help with the drill first."

"Frenchie can take Sister Anne to Akiko," McMichael nodded to William. It was important to Jimmy, he knew, that he helped with the new machine. "Ah yes," McMichael continued, "Billy. I understand you're a carpenter. Welcome to Britannia. I'm sorry about the circumstances."

"It can't be helped," Billy said.

He looked around at the scenery.

"These trees are a carpenter's dream."

"They are indeed. I'd like to do some remodelling in my house. Perhaps when this all settles down we can share some ideas."

"That would be my pleasure," Billy replied.

"Frenchie, where's Father Fernier?" McMichael asked.

"I'm afraid 'e couldn't make it. We were met at de docks in Vancouver by one of the clergy who sent 'is regrets. 'Der lookin' for somebody else."

"The Cardinal has passed away," Sister Anne said.

"Well," McMichael said. "Let's take this as a sign we won't need any last rights. I'll get on the blower and see what we can do. There's another boat coming up tonight and if we're lucky another priest will be on it."

Sister Anne touched his sleeve and whispered in his ear.

"If it's an emergency, I do know them, the last rights I mean. We wouldn't want anyone denied a safe passage to heaven. I'm sure God will look the other way under the circumstances. Rumour has it I know a thing or two about Catholicism."

"You may get a chance to say them yet. But if I'm not mistaken you don't do marriages. If I don't get a priest to marry Sarah on schedule, she'll kill me and then you really will be put into action. I'm going to need all the help I can get before I make my own final journey."

"The Lord does work in mysterious ways," she laughed.

She followed Jimmy up the road.

"Your daughters," McMichael laughed to William, "they don't take no for an answer, do they?"

"Not very often," William agreed. "Not very often."

CHAPTER 38

Yan Li held two candles in his hand. That's all that were left from the supply in the safety room and he knew he should keep them until help came. At least they had been able to make it that far, to the safety room. For eight days now he had been trapped in the mine in the tiny enclave with Harry Yada, and he could hear the drills getting closer and closer, the men's voices becoming louder hour by hour. He now could distinguish some of the rescuer's voices, giving him a sense of time and day as the workers went off shift, rested, and came back again. He thought he could hear Frank Fitzpatrick, so it was probably morning again.

There had been a steady trickle of water through the crevices in the rocks since they had been trapped, indicating to Yan that it had most likely been raining for some time. It was a welcome source of water if he needed it. He would be able to trap some water into the canteens he had found once they were empty. There had been enough water stored in the safety room for an entire crew, but still, Yan was rationing it, not knowing when or if they would ever be rescued.

While his clothing was cold and damp, and he was tired and a little hungry, there was little else physically wrong with him. Being of a very slender build, food was something he could take or leave, so he rationed the food he had found, eating when he felt it was absolutely necessary. Emotionally though, the time he was trapped seemed endless, and inside himself he harboured a fear of never getting out at all.

The man next to him groaned.

Yan looked over at the man, who was twenty years his senior. How suddenly frail he looked to him, as he lay there, his body stretched out on the rocks. Yan had moved him into a dry spot when then walls started to leak, so that he could rest.

"Sleep," he said to Harry. He would wake him in a little while and make sure he had some food and water.

When the walls caved in around them, Harry had been hit in the head by falling rock, knocking him unconscious. Yan had applied pressure to the wound, as Harry had begrudgingly taught him, cleansing it and wrapping his head in gauze he had found in the first-aid kit. He was concerned that Harry may have suffered a concussion, so he kept waking him up every little while for what he believed was the first day they had spent down there. It had been so hard to keep any sense of time. While Yan didn't get much sleep himself, taking care of Harry gave him a focus, shutting the predicament they were in from his mind.

Harry's eyes fluttered awake.

"What's happening?" he asked weakly.

"They're coming," Yan said. "They will be through soon."

Harry tried to sit up.

"No," Yan said. "Lie down, save your strength."

"I want to tell you something," Harry said, undeterred. He reached up and felt the bandage on his head. "I want to thank you, for saving my life."

"That's not necessary."

"I think it is Yan. You know, I did not want to teach you first aid. I did not want to teach you anything."

Yan remembered how Harry had patiently taught others the basic skills, but grunted his way through it with him. His grandfather had told him that Harry held some funny beliefs about his fellow Orientals. He explained it was a lot like sibling rivalry, the more alike they were, the more they wished things were different, each one trying to find their own identity.

"I did not like you," Harry admitted.

"I think that was obvious. What did I ever do to you?"

"Nothing," Harry said. "I like you now."

Yan smiled.

"Jimmy kept telling me, you're a good guy. I didn't listen. He likes your family. Perhaps that was part of it. He spends more time with your grandfather than he does with me."

"Well, we are twins now, yes? Like brothers. You pushed me into the safety room. A little too hard maybe. See, I have a gash on my leg where I hit the ground. I wasn't paying attention. That wall almost crushed me when it came down. Look, you can't see the place where I was standing before you gave me the shove."

Harry saw the bandage underneath Yan's ripped open pant leg. He then glanced at the pile of rubble that had once formed the wall of the tunnel. It was as if an earthquake had ripped through it.

"This mountain is awake," Harry thought to himself.

"You saved my life by doing that," Yan continued, "and then the rocks came tumbling down and that big one over there hit you on the head. You passed out. I took care of you, just like you trained me. I wonder, if that had been me, unconscious, would you have saved me?"

Harry looked into Yan's eyes and saw his own.

"I believe so," he answered honestly.

"I believe so too," Yan answered, "so now we are twins like I said. We were not born at the same time but we escaped death at the same time. We owe each other our lives."

"Humph," Harry grunted. He would have to think about that.

"You need more training," Harry said, placing two fingers under the gauze and stretching it a bit. "The bandage is too tight on my head. It's giving me a headache."

"You must be feeling better," Yan answered. He passed him some water.

"Here, sip slowly."

Harry suddenly realized how thirsty he really was. He eagerly took a few gulps.

"Do you not listen to anything I say?" Yan said smiling, passing him a wet rag. "If you start to feel sick, don't blame me."

"What's this?" Harry asked.

"The rest of my pant leg. I have soaked it in the water leaking through the walls. Use it as a cold compress. It will help that bump on your head go down."

Yan thought for a moment he almost saw Harry smile.

"Very good, thank you."

"Where did you learn English?" Yan asked him.

"I learned it as a boy. How about you?"

"Me too. We have that in common. My grandfather, he also speaks English, but he doesn't like to do it in public. He thinks people will laugh at him."

"Jimmy understands him," Harry offered. "Jimmy doesn't always understand his mother, but he understands your grandfather."

Harry paused for a moment.

"It was difficult for my wife to learn English," he admitted. "Perhaps I was not patient enough with her when she was first trying. It was hard to see her struggle. But she was determined. She is learning more and more words every day. But we have to work on her pronunciation."

"I think perhaps Jimmy understands more of your wife's English than he admits."

"True," Harry said. "He is a teenager. He understands what is convenient for him. In English, one word can have many meanings. That confuses my wife. When Jimmy is mad at his mother he will try to confuse her. And what is that saying? The apple does not fall far from the tree as they say. Maybe I do a little of that myself."

"So when we get out of here, are you going to tell your wife how proud of her you are?" Yan asked.

"No," Harry laughed. "The yin and the yang, yes? I am the boss of the Yada household. It would upset the delicate balance of the home if I said something like that."

"Harry Yada, you are full of it," Yan said. "I know you are proud of Akiko. She does not have to work long nights anymore. She educated herself in a new language and got a good job with daytime hours. My daughter Diane, she looks at your wife and knows her future will be full of more hope. She does not have to be a cleaner. She wants to be a teacher. She knows it is possible. I am proud of your wife."

He took a sip of water.

"And your son...Jimmy has a friendship with an old man. Do you know how unusual that is? Particularly for a teenager? He never misses lunch with him on Saturdays. They sit on the back porch having soup whether the weather is hot or cold. I think it's what's keeping my grandfather alive. Even I do not see him that much. I am proud of your son."

The drills above them suddenly stopped, sending an eerie silence into the space inhabited by the two men. The men held the silence for a few moments, each of them deep in thought in his own private world.

A shiver of dread passed down Harry's spine as he considered the fact that after all this time in the mine; the rescue may have been called off.

"If we get out," Harry whispered, following the quiet, "I will tell them both how proud of them I am, I promise."

"When we get out," Yan insisted, "I will have lunch with my grandfather. Maybe even every other week. I promise."

The two men shook hands.

As if on cue, the silence suddenly was broken by the sound of more activity.

"Listen," Yan began, "the voices, they're close."

The two men started to yell.

On the other side of the pile of rubble, the same conversation began to play out.

"Listen," Frank said. "Can you hear them? They're alive! Just on the other side of this pile of rock. Jason, go back up and tell the others. I need all hands down here. We've found them, and they're alive! Billy, bring Bertha over here!"

"Hearn should take a look at this wall of rock before we start her up," Billy said.

"Good man," Frank said. "You're absolutely right. I wouldn't want to kill them this close to getting them out of there!"

Jason headed back up the tunnel as fast as his feet would take him.

Outside the shaft, the solemn crowd prepared for the worst. Sarah had come by bringing some breakfast for Jimmy. He had continued to refuse to go home, preferring to try to sleep on the ground outside the shaft with only a few blankets and pillow. He was only sleeping for a few hours at a time, she noticed, and now she could see that he was getting a cold.

"Jimmy, please," she began, "go home and get some rest. I'll call you the minute I hear anything, I promise. You need to change out of your wet clothes. You'll catch pneumonia. Go on, off you go."

Before Jimmy had a chance to protest, he could hear Jason calling to everyone from within the tunnel.

"We heard them," Jason said excitedly as he stepped outside the mine.

"Them?" Sarah asked.

"My father?" Jimmy hoped.

"Yes, them. Two voices. They're both alive!"

"Sarah, quickly, go get Akiko!" Jason said.

"Did you see them?" Jimmy asked.

"Jimmy, listen to me. We did hear two voices, but we don't know what kind of shape they are in. They're behind a thick pile of rocks. They may be injured. I need you to go get the doctors and bring them here. In the meantime, I need to find Hearn so he can take a look at the rock wall and tell us how to best clear it with the new drill."

"The drill from the boat?" Jimmy asked.

"She's a beauty Jimmy; she'll have them out of there in no time."

I'll go get the doctors," Jimmy said, running off towards the hospital. "And I'll go tell Mr. McMichael. It's my job."

Sarah thought that just for a moment, she saw Jimmy start to cry.

"This is good news, no?" she asked Jason.

"It sure is a lot better than silence."

Frank emerged from the tunnel, completely covered in mud.

"That Bertha," he stated, "she's one hell of a drill. She got us through twice the rock today. We should have them out by morning."

Sarah clapped excitedly.

"In time for the wedding," she sighed. "It's going to be a glorious day after all."

CHAPTER 39

As the dawn broke over the majestic mountains, Britannia was waking up with a new found hope.

The Beachcomber opened a little earlier than usual. Lucy carried over some cheese scones that Maggie had baked the night before.

"You take these up to the store," she said, "and make sure those wonderful Bower women get some. I met Grace at the café last night and we chatted for hours like old friends. I said I'd look after the lad for them during the reception. Let the family have a good night to remember. They've been a Godsend."

Olivia already had the tea brewed. She expected her mother and Emily to arrive any minute. Sister Anne had gone to Akiko's with Daniel. Akiko had been so touched by Anne's kindness that she invited them over for some origami lessons.

"The infamous Beachcomber," her mother said, the door chimes announcing her arrival. "It certainly caused quite a stir when it opened, didn't it? There were so many people here during the rescue, I didn't have a chance to properly look around. It's quite wonderful darling!"

"I am quite proud of it," Olivia beamed.

"And so you should be. Emily, look at all these spices!"

"We bring them in from Chinatown in Vancouver. We've got quite a selection of teas as well. We're drinking chamomile today, it's Jimmy Yada's favourite."

"It's really wonderful Olivia," Emily chimed in. "It makes me wish I had a head for figures so I could do something like this myself."

"Well I couldn't have done it without Lucy here, and of course Akiko."

"I still haven't met Akiko," Grace said. "Maybe after the wedding, when she's had a chance to catch her breath, we can have a little chat. Anne says she's delightful. Goodness we've all been so busy here; we haven't had a decent chance to talk ourselves. How are you, Olivia?"

"You know, tea is fine and dandy, but I could murder a cup of coffee. Lucy, could you take me to this café I keep hearing about? I'm not very good at directions, I'm afraid. But do save me a scone for later mother."

Sensing that Emily was trying to give her mother some time alone with Olivia, Lucy took the hint. "I suppose I could sneak away from work this once. I think Olivia and Grace can manage." The two women left the store.

"Your sister does not know the meaning of the word discretion," Grace announced. "Still, it gives us a few moments together. How are you feeling Olivia? I understand you're expecting."

"Do I show that much?" Olivia asked.

"No, but your father found out. He finds out everything."

"I'm fine thank you. I haven't had much morning sickness."

"Is Frank happy about the baby?"

"Of course."

"And are you?"

"Yes of course, why do you ask?"

"Olivia, I would have to be blind and stupid not to have noticed the change in your husband over the past few years. I am neither. I worry about you."

"I know that we were going through a tough time, but things are...well things are just a lot easier now that I'm not working for Aaron at the mine."

"I told your Uncle that was a bad idea. He should have had more sense. Are you planning on staying on here at the store after the baby is born?"

"Yes. Lucy and Akiko have agreed to be flexible with their work hours, so everything should work out fine."

"Well my darling, your life is certainly going to change. I hope it turns out to be everything you ever hoped and dreamed. We're always just a phone call away, you know that. If Frank gives you any trouble, you just holler, and I'll be on the next boat up. At least with Jason living here, you'll have some family support."

"Mother, really, everything will be fine. Can we please change the subject?"

"That John McMichael is a nice man."

Olivia laughed aloud.

"What?" her mother exclaimed. "He's polite, he's thoughtful..."

"Maybe to you."

"Well, he certainly can keep his wits about him in a crisis. And he's quite handsome too. If your sister weren't a Sister, I'd be doing a little matchmaking!"

Olivia laughed some more.

"Have another scone mother. I do think you're beginning to lose your mind."

Grace laughed.

"It is good to see you Olivia, and you do look happy."

Olivia smiled. She was content.

Later that morning, a crowd had gathered outside the mine entrance as word of the imminent rescue spread. It had been eight long days since the men were first trapped. The fact that they were alive was regarded as a miracle.

As Olivia and McMichael stood outside the mine entrance awaiting word of the rescue progress, they heard cheers coming from beneath the ground. Jimmy, close by as always, grabbed a helmet and ran into the tunnel.

"My son!" Akiko cried, looking at McMichael helplessly.

"Let him go Akiko," McMichael assured her. "He'll be safe enough."

"Can you hear them?" Olivia said excitedly. "It's good news! I can't believe it, it's good news!"

Jimmy was gone barely a few minutes before he was back at the mine entrance. He was grinning ear to ear.

"My dad. He's okay!" he said, running into his mother's arms.

Akiko eyes swelled with tears. She hugged her son tightly as the emotions ran from her.

Overcome with emotion himself, McMichael turned hugged Olivia.

"Thank God," he said. "It's truly a miracle."

Realizing what he had done, he released Olivia from his embrace.

"Pardon me Olivia," he said. "I was overcome."

"I understand Mr. McMichael," Olivia said, herself overcome with relief. "No harm done. This is the most wonderful news we could have hoped for."

But from the corner of the mine entrance, Frank had witnessed the brief embrace. His breathing began to quicken and he found it hard to contain his rage. While the other men were bringing out Harry and Yan, Frank turned his back on them, staring blindly into the rock.

"I'll get him," Frank vowed.

CHAPTER 40

At Sarah's home, Lucy was pinning up the loose strands of the bride's hair.

"You look stunning," Akiko said.

"I know!" Sarah said excitedly.

Lucy rolled her eyes, but she had to admit that indeed, the bride was beautiful.

"I am about to become Mrs. Jason Bower," Sarah sighed. "I never thought this day would come."

"Well it has," Lucy smiled. "And you'll only be missing two people from your guest list."

Harry and Yan had been brought out of the tunnel earlier that morning in fairly good condition, but were being hospitalized as a precaution. Yan had been able to walk out, but the men had carried Harry out on a stretcher, as his strength was weaker than the younger man's was.

The dark cloud of doom that had hung over the community had been lifted and there was an immediate celebration.

Rudy stood on the street observing as people were openly raising their spirit glasses to good tidings. Then men had come out of the tunnel a few hours ago, but there was an ongoing impromptu parade in the streets as neighbours celebrated with neighbours.

"You want me to do anything about that?" he asked McMichael.

"I'm sorry Wolanski, what were you saying? The sun seems to be in my eyes."

"And the money from the beer is lining your coffers," Aaron Bower laughed.

"Well then, everything worked out for the best, didn't it?" McMichael added, and raised his own glass of rye to the heavens. "Frenchie," he said as the

Captain walked by, "come. Let me buy you a beer for transporting this wonderful family and our new Bertha so safely to the mine."

Frenchie stopped dead in his tracks. Did McMichael just offer him a drink? He had known the man for many a year and that had never happened before aside from the one night long ago when he and William had saved the life of the sailors.

"I suppose I could find it in my heart to drink to the rescuers," he said.

"Well come on then gentlemen. Please join me in the bar. You too Rudy, I do believe you're officially off duty."

McMichael's rarely seen burst of light heartedness was brought to a halt as Frank, having drank more than his fair share of ale, had him in his sights.

"You!" Frank said, pointing at McMichael. "Come here you bastard!"

The street was suddenly silenced.

"Frank," Wolanski said. "You've had enough, turn around and go home."

"I wasn't talking to you," Frank said. "I was talking to that slimy, money-pinching boss of mine."

McMichael stared blankly at Frank.

"I said go home Frank," the sergeant said.

"That slimy, money-pinching, wife-stealing boss of mine," Frank continued, staggering towards the two men. "I saw you. I saw you with your arms around my wife."

Wolanski looked at McMichael.

"Are you out of your ever-loving mind Frank?" McMichael asked.

"I saw you. And you weren't even slinking around. You were embracing my wife in the middle of the street where the whole world could see. I knew you've been after her for some time. I just couldn't catch you."

He started to come towards McMichael, the hatred burning in his eyes.

Wolanski put his hand on his gun.

McMichael realised that Frank must have seen him hug Olivia in the excitement of the rescue.

"It wasn't what you think Frank. I was excited that the men were alive. Akiko was hugging Jimmy. I hugged your wife. I would have hugged Sarah if she was beside me, but it just happened to be your wife."

"Just happened? I've seen you looking at her. You look at her like Les looked at your daughter. You're about to get what's been coming to you for a long time."

"Okay Frank," Wolanski said. "That's it. You're under arrest."

"No," McMichael said. "Don't arrest him. He saw what he saw. But it was innocent. Think what you want about me Frank, but have some faith in your wife."

"That's right, she's MY wife. You keep your hands off my wife. Olivia's mine. Do you hear me? She's MINE!"

"Frank, because I respect your wife's family and I don't want to have to explain to them that you've been arrested for being an idiot on the day of your brother-in-law's wedding, I've asked Rudy to let you go. He doesn't have to do that, but I'm hoping he shows some compassion and let's you off the hook. But now you're officially fired. Your days at my mine are over."

Frank took a swing at McMichael, but he was far too drunk for it to land with any accuracy.

"Frank," Wolanski said. "I'm officially escorting you home to sleep it off."

"You are drunk Frank," McMichael said, "and I have a vehement distaste for that. I suggest you do what the sergeant says before I change my mind and charge you with attempted assault."

The crowd in the street remained hushed.

"All right people," McMichael said. "The show is over."

A thunderclap exploded, breaking the tension. Wolanski pushed Frank towards his home, escorting him up the hill.

"He's been chasing after her for months," Frank said.

"You just keep your mouth shut Frank," Rudy said, "before I re-acquaint you with your room at the jail. It's pretty much as you left it."

Olivia had gone home to change before the wedding later that afternoon. She had purchased a green velvet dress for the occasion and its empire waistline hid the slightest sign of her pregnancy. She rubbed her stomach. Emily had decided that Olivia was having a baby girl and told, not asked, her to name it after her. Olivia had not given any thought to a name for the baby. She started to explore the possibilities in her mind when she was awoken from her daydream by the sound of pounding on the door.

Rudy, not waiting for her to answer, opened the door and threw Frank inside. Her husband fell to the floor.

"What is going on?" Olivia asked.

"He's drunk and he accused McMichael of making a pass at you."

"He did WHAT?"

"And he's lost any hope of ever working at the mine again. I think that's enough for one day. He's all yours."

"Oh Rudy," Olivia sighed. "Why today of all days? Help me get him into bed will you?"

Rudy looked at Olivia as she stood helpless. She couldn't lift Frank's deadweight if she tried.

"There isn't anything to it, is there? You and McMichael?" Rudy asked.

"Rudy! I'm surprised at you. Of course there isn't."

"One never knows," Rudy said. "I see a lot of things in my line of work."

"Mr. McMichael has never been anything but civil to me. Well, as civil as Mr. McMichael can be. He has never in his life made a pass at me. Everyone knows Mr. McMichael loves…"

She was about to say "Lucy", but caught herself in time.

"…only himself."

"Just so you know, Frank saw him hug you."

"Oh," Olivia said. "So that's what this is all about. Trust Frank to be around to misinterpret the only time McMichael showed an ounce of human compassion in public. He hugged me when he heard the men were safe. It was just a reflex action."

"That's what he said," Rudy agreed.

"What on earth am I going to do with this man?" Olivia asked, looking at Rudy. "That's a rhetorical question, I don't expect an answer. But Rudy, what on earth am I going to tell my father when Frank doesn't show up at the wedding? What is it about my husband and family weddings? What is it about my husband?"

That one she needed help with.

CHAPTER 41

By mid afternoon, on-again off-again rainstorm was on again. Sarah's eyes started to mist up.

"Do not worry Sarah," Akiko said. "The rain is a sign of good luck. It rained on my wedding day and look how long Harry and I have been married. And so happily too."

"Is that true Akiko?" Sarah asked.

"Yes!" she said, giving Sarah hope. But Akiko had crossed her fingers behind her back while saying it, and had given Lucy a disheartened look.

"Come on Sarah," Lucy said glancing out the window. "The carriage is outside to take you down to the church. Mr. McMichael hired it special to take you, and look how wonderfully it's decorated with white bows. I'll go tell your parents it's here. Hurry outside, will you? We can't have you late for your own wedding."

Akiko took a long slender box from where she had placed it in the corner of Sarah's room earlier in the day.

"Here," Akiko said, "I have something special for my special friend. It will take your tears away."

Sarah opened the box to find a beautiful white, handcrafted umbrella.

"Oh Akiko," Sarah smiled, "you truly think of everything. You're a wonderful friend. I can't thank you enough."

"You are welcome. But we must hurry. We can keep your future husband waiting because he is a patient man. But if we keep Miss Lucy-boss waiting we will be in trouble."

Sarah giggled.

True to Lucy's word there was a handsome black horse-drawn carriage, decorated with satin bows waiting to take the bride and her family to the church. Sarah smiled and waved like a queen as she passed by well wishers themselves enroute to the wedding.

Lightning flashed illuminating Sarah's beaming face.

"Maybe you'd better put the umbrella down," her mother said. "You won't get wet in the carriage. We don't want anyone struck by lightning."

The thunder that followed the flash almost covered the light knock on Olivia's door, but she recognized the distinctive rapping from her childhood. Knockety-knock-knock. She went to answer it.

"Billy!" Olivia said. "Where have you been hiding on me?"

"I was helping down in the mine," Billy said. "I'm sorry I didn't get to see you at breakfast earlier, but I needed to clean up."

"You look handsome," Olivia smiled. "It's good to see you."

"Handsome I may be," he said, "but sadly I don't have a date to the wedding. I understand you may be in need of an escort."

"News travels fast."

"Get your things," he said, giving her a hug. "We've got a wedding to go to." He took her by the arm.

"It's quite a storm out here," he said, taking off his long formal coat and opening it wide. "Here. Let's put this big coat over and heads and run."

With Father Fernier away attending the Cardinal's funeral, the diocese had sent up a young priest to perform the nuptials, Father O'Donnell. It was his first wedding and to say he was nervous would be an understatement. He did however, have the exuberance that youth can have, and Olivia found the wedding service quite moving. Prayers were said at the beginning for the blessing of the mine rescue.

"Do you, Jason Bower, take this woman to be your lawfully wedded..."

The next word seemed to have slipped from the young priests mind. He looked like he was about to faint.

"Wife," Sarah assured him. "I have been going over this in my head for days."

Sarah was beside herself with happiness, and Jason was lovingly supporting her through her special day. It was only when Olivia reached for Frank and saw her brother Billy beside her, that she was reminded of the frailness of her own marriage. Olivia wiped tears from her eyes. She wished nothing but the best for Sarah and Jason, but she couldn't help but remember how full of hope she had been on her own wedding day.

McMichael sat at the back of the church. Although he had been invited by both sides of the wedding party to sit in the front pews, he had decided to allow the families their own space. He had known Sarah since she was a teenager and was pleased that she had finally found her man to love. He remembered fondly the many times he had been forced to console her when she was lovesick, even though he complained bitterly at the time. So far he hadn't had to console his own daughters, but he would be experienced when and if the time came. He could see Olivia sitting with her brother. He hadn't expected to see Frank, but he knew it must have been hard for Olivia to come with her brother, nonetheless.

Hearn snuck in the back of the church and tapped McMichael on the shoulder. McMichael turned around.

"I thought you should know," Hearn said, "they've issued flood warnings all along the coast from Vancouver to Prince Rupert. Squamish, Pitt Meadows and Port Coquitlam are sandbagging."

"What's happening at the dams?" McMichael asked, keeping his voice down.

There were three dams about eight miles away that provided water power to the area.

"I understand they've put extra watchmen on," Hearn said.

"Good," McMichael said. "Keep me posted."

Hearn turned and left the building as the priest was pronouncing Jason and Sarah husband and wife. The engineer was scheduled to leave Britannia and return to Aaron's employ in Seattle after the wedding. He would miss him, McMichael thought, he was a good worker. Maybe he'd make him an offer to stay at Britannia.

Sarah beamed at him as she and her husband made their way down the aisle, out of the church. The rain was still pouring down, but the lightning had stopped. Akiko passed Sarah her umbrella as everyone made their way to the community hall for the reception.

"We seem to be without an emcee," William said to McMichael. "Frank was supposed to do it, but…"

McMichael looked at him unapologetically.

"Would you care to step in?" William asked.

"No," McMichael stated emphatically. "I don't think stepping in for Frank would be a wise thing at the moment. Besides, I have a bit of a history emceeing weddings and I'd rather not tempt fate. Let's just say the last time I did it, at my niece's wedding, things got out of my control."

"I knew there was a reason we had Billy. He'll do it." William laughed, heading off to find him.

"Mr. McMichael," Sarah said upon her entrance, "I just want to thank you again for everything you've done to make this day special."

"My pleasure Sarah," McMichael said. "And if you don't mind Jason, I'm going to kiss the bride." He kissed her on the cheek.

"Now that you're married, don't you go running off on me."

"Oh I won't Mr. McMichael, don't worry. Jason and I are going to stay here in Britannia. But I may need a raise in a year or so."

"Lucky for the rain," McMichael laughed, "I don't see a blue moon tonight."

"Thank goodness the thunder has stopped," Sarah said. "I was worried the band wouldn't be able to play in the electrical storm."

"We've been fortunate with a few things today. You and Sarah have a wonderful life," he said to Jason, shaking his hand. "Treat her well, because I'll know, by God I'll know, if you don't."

McMichael caught sight of Olivia and walked over to her.

"Apparently I owe you an apology," he said to her.

"Don't be ridiculous," Olivia said. "You didn't do anything wrong. Frank's just had a jealous streak in him where you're concerned."

"Still, I didn't mean to cause you any trouble. For that I'm sorry."

Perhaps her mother was right. John McMichael *was* polite.

"Would you like to come sit with us? Lucy and Rudy are at the table."

"I think I'll keep my distance Olivia, no offence. I'd like to have a quiet word with your father and your uncle. I'll catch up with you some other time."

"Of course. I understand." Olivia said.

Perhaps John McMichael *was* nice, like her mother had said.

McMichael wandered off to a corner table at the back where William and Aaron were sitting.

"Gentlemen," he said, "may I join you?"

They motioned for McMichael to sit down.

"Thank you for your help this week," he said. "I'm sure you didn't expect all this excitement to go along with the wedding. Aaron, that new drill is something. I'll put in an order on Monday."

"Good to hear it John," Aaron said. "Because you've definitely bought that one."

"John," William said. "About the railroad. Aaron and I are sorry that your government didn't see fit to push through the northern line at this time. It certainly wasn't through the lack of your efforts."

Aaron nodded.

"What are your plans John?" William asked.

"My plans?"

"Beyond Britannia."

McMichael wished he had a stiff drink in front of him, but he didn't.

"You're not thinking of staying here all your life are you?" William asked. "You're too good to be stuck here."

"That depends on your definition of stuck," McMichael said. "I happen to have a good life for my family and myself."

"Still," Aaron said, "your girls will be grown soon and leaving for the big city. What will Britannia have to offer you then?"

McMichael knew there was truth in what the men were saying, but he wasn't ready to face that day, not quite yet. He glanced around and saw Christina dancing with the young doctor Alex Thompson, and Lara and Jimmy in the corner, sneaking sips of beer.

"They grow up so fast," he said.

"When the time is right," William said, "we'd like you to consider coming to work for us in some capacity."

McMichael smiled. "Gentlemen, I am flattered. But what would you want with an arrogant, demanding mine boss?"

"We'd like an arrogant, demanding boss to work with us and handle our employees. You've got a knack for that."

"What did you have in mind?" McMichael asked.

"We're not sure yet," Aaron said. "But we like your style. You don't crack under pressure. You're a real leader. We're exploring a few ventures. There's a family in Toronto that's getting into the liquor business. We may open a few breweries with them, we don't know. If not, there's always our railroad operations. We know you'd like that."

"And automobiles," William chimed in. "We're buying stock in car factories. We've got big plans for starting a Canadian factory down the road. We're looking at the Toronto area, on Lake Ontario. Maybe even a little east of there. Land is cheap. Aaron thinks the area is a golden horseshoe in the making."

"Well then," McMichael said. "Why don't I go get us some champagne so that we can toast our endeavours, past, present and future?"

Across the Hall, Olivia sat at the table dumbfounded.

"No," Lucy was saying, "I heard he took a swipe at him."

Rudy nodded.

"He tried to hit McMichael?" Olivia asked.

"Mary Alice, who happened to be in the street at the time," Lucy continued, "told me he called him a slimy, money-pinching, wife stealing…"

Rudy kicked her under the table.

"Ow!"

"And he did it in the middle of the street?" Olivia said. "I will kill him."

"Okay," Rudy said, "this is the part where I ask you to dance Lucy, so you don't tell Olivia anything else you heard." He quickly pulled her onto the dance floor.

"She has to know," Lucy said.

"But she doesn't have to know right now," Rudy replied.

McMichael saw Olivia sitting at the table by herself and approached her.

"I was just going to get some champagne Olivia. Why don't you come join your father and I?"

"No thank you, my stomach is a bit upset."

"Of course." McMichael said. "In that case, I'll take the champagne back to the table. Perhaps I was hasty earlier. Would you care to dance? One dance, in front of all these people who will witness nothing untoward?" He looked at her hopefully.

Olivia smiled.

"I appreciate the offer John, you were probably right the first time. I'm sorry. It's not you."

"Well, another day perhaps," John said.

I'll wait, he thought to himself.

CHAPTER 42

Mother Nature loves playing hide and seek. Between her majestic mountains and wondrous rainforests of the Pacific Northwest lay many hidden lakes and streams. Way behind the peaks of Britannia, the watchmen who manned the power facilities were unaware that one particularly large lake was about to carve her own path through the mountains to the ocean. The natural driftwood dam that held her waters in place was no match for the heavy rains that had been occurring.

It was a cold damp night, and the two watchmen from Britannia, Russ Keeping and Marco Mazzotta had gone inside the equipment building to warm up.

"So, I wonder how things are going at the big shindig?" Russ asked, referring to the wedding.

"I suppose it will be quite the party, what with the rescue over and all," Marco replied.

Russ lit up a cigarette.

A thunderous cracking sound filled the air.

"Did you hear that?" Marco asked.

"Probably thunder," Russ answered.

The noise came again, this time louder.

"Doesn't sound like thunder," Marco said.

"I'll go check it out," Russ said, donning his gloves and heading back outside.

He had only taken a few steps when he saw water heading towards him.

"Oh my God, Marco," Russ yelled. "Let's get the hell out of here. The damn's going to go. We've got to call down there and warn everyone." He started to quickly telephone the mine operations.

Hearn answered the phone. His face grew grim.

"I'll tell them," he said.

McMichael, William and Aaron stood outside the community hall with their champagne glasses in hand.

"To our futures," William said, raising his glass. The other two men raised theirs in unison.

"To our futures."

"It's a nice night except for the rain. I like it cold. But does the damn rain ever stop?" William asked.

"Yes. In February." McMichael said. "Although I must admit I find it a bit chilly this evening."

"Keeps the champagne at optimum temperature," Aaron added philosophically.

William looked up the mountain.

"What the hell is that?" he asked.

McMichael looked up the mountainside.

"I don't see anything."

"The noise," William said. "Listen."

The men were silent. A rumbling was coming from the mountain. McMichael instantly thought of the landslide.

Hearn came running up to him.

"We just got a call from the watchmen. The dam has let go."

"The dam's given way? We've got to get everybody out!"

"What are you talking about?" William asked.

"An entire lake is about to empty itself on our town. I'm going to the mine to sound the alarms."

"What?" William said.

"I have no idea which way the water is going to go. Get everyone you can up on the rooftop of the hall. It should be safe. We're going to have a flood like we've never seen before. I have about five minutes before it'll be too late. Move gentlemen. Now!"

McMichael and Hearn ran up to the mine. Aaron and William went back inside the community hall, with William making his way to the microphone.

"Ladies and gentlemen," he said, "this is an emergency. I need everyone to make their way to the rooftop of the building. Don't ask questions, there's no time, please, do not go into the street. Just get up to the rooftop."

Rudy made his way over to Aaron.

"What's happening?"

"McMichael says the dam has given way. Listen, you can hear the water coming."

Rudy headed towards the door.

Aaron grabbed him.

"No, don't go out there."

"I'm an officer of the law," Rudy said. "Please, handle everyone in here for me while I find out what's happening."

Aaron let go of him.

Rudy stepped outside and to his horror found that Aaron was right. There was a wall of water heading towards the town. The sound was becoming louder, closer.

The mine's emergency sirens came on at full blast. It brought the people who had not been at the wedding into the street. McMichael ran from the mine with bullhorns in hand, looking for help.

"THE DAM HAS BURST!" he yelled. "EVERYONE, GET TO HIGH GROUND!"

He saw Rudy.

"Get on the rooftop," McMichael said. "Get on the rooftop and yell to everyone to do the same."

"Where are you going?"

"I'm going to knock on as many doors as possible. We have to do something."

"I'll do that," Rudy said. "You go back to the wedding. I can handle it."

"Rudy," McMichael began, "you weren't here in 1915. It was at a wedding, on a night like this when Lucy lost her entire family. I don't want that to happen to her again. I don't want that to happen to anyone else ever again. Please, get up there. Get up on the roof. Tonight you're off duty. Tonight, for the time being, you're just one of us. I need you alive for later."

McMichael saw the young doctor standing in the street.

"Where's Christina?" McMichael screamed.

"What?" Alex yelled.

The sound of the rushing water was now almost deafening.

"Where's Christina?"

But it was too late for the doctor to answer. The rushing water was now upon him, hurling him forward with all the force of a giant wave, and sending him crashing into a tree, where he held on for dear life, dazed but alive.

The water missed McMichael and as he turned to run out of its path he saw his youngest daughter Lara, alone on the front porch of their home.

"Daddy!" she was screaming, but he could not hear her.

With a rush of adrenaline he had never experienced before, he ran to his home, grabbed his daughter and went to the top of his roof. He turned her eyes to the unfolding tragedy taking place. The flood was upon them. He watched several of the small bungalows being washed out into Howe Sound, the strength of the water being too much for their foundations to hold.

Olivia stood on the rooftop of the community hall and watched as the torrent of water ripped apart what had been her home. She could see her bathtub, floating into the sea. Lucy held her tightly.

"Frank," she cried. As drunk as he had been, she knew he would not have awoken until it was too late, if at all. "Oh God, no," she screamed. "Frank!"

Sister Anne made her way over to her.

Olivia's eyes were glued to the horror. She watched her house flowing piece by piece into Howe Sound. She saw the quilt that Frank had given her, which she had washed and hung out on the line to dry, being carried out to the waters. She wondered where Frank was and kept looking for some sign that he was alive.

Anne turned her gently away from the view.

"Why?" Olivia wailed.

There were some things, Sister Anne admitted, that God did not provide an answer for.

Jimmy Yada noticed a small child in the sound, hanging onto what had probably been the park picnic table, afloat in the water. He ran from the roof.

"Jimmy!" Akiko yelled, "You get back here!"

Jimmy sensed the worst of the flood was over. It had happened in a flash, but now the waters were slowing. Within seconds he was out on the street running towards the ocean. As he swam out into Howe Sound and grabbed the little boy, he passed the floating body of his friend old Mr. Li. He was face down in the water, and Jimmy knew instantly Mr. Li's time on earth was over. Jimmy brought the boy back to the beach and safety. As he gave the toddler back to his panic-stricken mother, he turned to the waters once more.

"I can't leave him out there," Jimmy said to himself, and wadded through the now shallow area where his friend had drifted. By this time, Yan, who had been on top of the roof, spotted Jimmy and his grandfather. His heart sank as he realized his grandfather was dead. He went to the waters to help bring them both back.

It was later estimated that the wall of water had been from three to five feet in depth and over seventy feet in width. Everything in its path had been taken with it into the salt waters of the ocean.

Lara cried into her father's arms, unable to look into the street.

"It's over," McMichael said. "It's all over now." He could see Christina waving at them from atop the community hall. He said a silent prayer of thanks.

The young doctor, still confused, came down from the tree and started tending to the injured.

He went over to Yan and took his grandfather's pulse.

"He's gone," he confirmed.

Yan broke down and cried. Jimmy looked silently on.

"I need your help," the doctor said.

"I know what to do," Jimmy replied.

"Good," said Alex, still shaken from his ordeal. "Because I don't."

The flood had knocked out the power lines, throwing the lower town into darkness, making rescue attempts difficult. People started making their way slowly into the street.

Christina, unable to find her boyfriend the doctor, ran up to her home where McMichael was waiting for her. She ran into his available arm, her sister refusing to leave her father's side.

"I am never getting married here," Christina said.

McMichael thought that would be just fine.

Still up on the rooftop of the community hall, Lucy began to cry as she noticed the Northern Mary, her stern having been ripped apart by the force of houses crashing into it.

"Frenchie!" Lucy screamed, fearing the worst. She had not seen him at the wedding.

"God please," Lucy begged. "Not Frenchie."

And then she remembered, Maggie had said she was going to take care of Olivia's little brother.

"Oh please," she begged, "not the child. Not again."

Lucy turned around looking for Grace. She found her. Daniel was in her arms, safe and sound. He had been quite well behaved at the wedding and Grace had told Maggie it would be okay if he stayed, but thanked her for her generous offer. And then Frenchie and Maggie had left the reception.

"We're gettin' too old fer this," he had said, and Lucy had laughed in his face.

"Sur la pont, D'Avignon," she had sung, taunting him.

Jason held his new wife tightly as he looked down the street from the rooftop. The movie theatre stood alone, undamaged. He knew deep inside, that if the movies had been running, at nine o'clock when the flood happened, many lives would have been saved. Saturday night was always their busiest night of the week. But of course it had been closed for the wedding. He couldn't help thinking that the flood had been selective in its destruction, much like a tornado would have been. While the bar and the general store were now demolished, Olivia's store, the Beachcomber, remained intact. So had the café.

Then as if Mother Nature had decided her game was over, the rain stopped and an unseasonably warm wind began to blow in from the south. But not before she had taken the lives of thirty-seven people and injured several others.

McMichael sniffed the air. The worst was over.

CHAPTER 43

A week later, McMichael, rising early after another sleepless night, saw Olivia sitting on the porch of the Beachcomber as he was heading to the office. He could see she was crying. There had been a lot of crying in the town since the flood. But the steadfast community had picked themselves up once again, and started rebuilding the town site. The mine itself was still operable, so there was work to be done to help people get their minds off the tragedy, but they were a long way from healed. A long way from forgetting.

He brushed some dirt off the step and sat down beside her.

"Is there anything I can do to help?" he asked her.

"I didn't even get a chance to give him a proper funeral," she said.

Frank's body had been claimed by the Pacific ocean. They never found him.

Father O'Donnell had presided over a mass burial at sea, and Sister Anne had indeed helped him.

McMichael could not find the words to try and comfort her.

"I'm sure the Lord understands," he said.

She nodded.

McMichael could see her nose running. He handed her a handkerchief.

"So what are your plans?" he asked.

"I don't know," she said. "My family wants me to come back to Seattle with them, but there's the store."

"Jason can look after the store for you," McMichael said. "Hell, I can look after the store for you; I don't have one anymore."

Olivia smiled.

"Thank you John. I know you've wanted to get your hands on it, but at least this time you asked," she laughed. "If it were just me, I'd stay. I love it here. But I've got the baby on the way."

"Oh and God forbid you be a single parent bringing up a baby in this place," McMichael said. "All these people around to fuss over it, to love it. Akiko will have it speaking Japanese before you know it."

"I know it worked for you John," she said, patting his hand. "But I don't think it's in the cards for me."

She hung her head in her hands.

"What am I going to do John?" she asked.

"You're going to go put those darn overalls on. You're going to wear them during your pregnancy because they were always too big for you anyway. They'll remind you of Britannia while you're back in Seattle with your family. Then maybe one day, after the baby is born, you'll come back to Britannia for a visit and maybe, just maybe, you'll fall in love all over again."

"I feel like I've aged fifty years since I've been here," she sighed.

"Yes, you feel like that now, I know. But give it some time."

"It's been one disaster after another."

"I suppose that's one way to look at it. But it's been one miracle after another as well. Lucy and Sarah each found love. Christina and Lara survived the plague. Jimmy escaped the fire, and Harry and Yan lived through the cave-in. If you add them all up, I'm sure there will be more good times than bad. And in less than a year you'll have your own little miracle."

"I don't know how I'm going to say good-bye to everyone."

"Then don't. Say, see you soon. It's less final. Or better yet stay."

He looked at her for some time, but he knew in his heart her mind was made up.

CHAPTER 44

June 1924.

The mainsail was coming down on the sailboat as it approached the dock marked Northern Maggie Charters, at Britannia Beach.

"Are we there yet Uncle Frenchie?" the little girl asked. Her curly auburn hair was in ringlets and she wore a green sweater and light cotton plaid skirt.

"You're always in such a rush to get places lassie," Frenchie said, "you're worse than your mother is."

Olivia came out from the cabin.

"It was a wonderful sail Frenchie," Olivia said. "It's a beautiful boat."

"Well, I've got your father to thank for that. It was a blessing the Mary goin' down that night. I was getting too old for it anyway. This charter business, now that's the life for a retired married man like myself. Nobody wants to go out when the weather is bad. It suits me fine."

On the night of Sarah and Jason's wedding, Frenchie had proposed to Maggie. They had snuck off to see the new house down the road that they were buying, which happened to be Ruby's old house. It had lots of rooms for Frenchie's charter guests to stay overnight, that's for sure. And it had been far enough up the road to be safe from the flood. They had been saved that night.

"Nervous?" Maggie asked, coming out behind her.

"A little. It's been a few years."

"Nothing's changed much."

But it had. Everything was new again.

John McMichael came down the dock to greet the boat. He noticed the little girl.

"Lucy," he said, picking her up and swinging her around. "You're just as beautiful as your mother."

Frenchie pulled Olivia aside.

"Are you sure about dis? I can still take you back."

"No Frenchie, I'm sure," she said. "My mother says he's nice."

"And polite," McMichael said. "She told me so."

"And good in a crisis," Olivia added.

"Not to mention handsome," he said.

"Of course my father says he's arrogant."

"Actually, I said that, if my memory serves me right." McMichael said laughing.

In the three years that Olivia had been living with her family back in Seattle, McMichael had kept finding excuses to travel down to the States. How he convinced Christina and Alex to get married down there, she didn't know. But he had, and of course the Bowers had been invited.

"My rain check," he said to her, after the bride and groom had their first dance.

"I'm sorry?"

"You owe me a dance. I asked you to dance at your brother's wedding and you turned me down. I said I'd take a rain check."

They danced the night away, laughing and talking about old times, and when the reception was over, McMichael went over to William for a quiet little chat.

"I might as well tell you now," he said, "I'm going to wait an appropriate amount of time, maybe a week, and then I'm going to ask Olivia out. And if I get my way, which I usually do, I'm going to ask her to marry me. I will raise your granddaughter. I will provide for them both. So get used to the idea, DAD!"

"Oh really," William said. "And you think I'm going to let you marry my daughter and put her to work? I think not."

"Do you really think I'll have any say in the matter?"

They laughed. Olivia and her mother joined them.

"You know, you two are a lot of fun when you're away from business," Olivia said.

"Olivia," John said, "I'm not quite the tyrant I'm made out to be. I have the welfare of several hundred people on my shoulders. I have to make some rules and I have to enforce them. That doesn't necessarily mean I have to abide by them myself, particularly when I'm out of town."

"Did I mention he was smart?" Grace said.

And here she was again, back at Britannia. As the smell of new growth Douglas Fir filled her soul, Olivia glanced around the seaside, her memories reforming.

"That can't be Jimmy," Olivia said. She could see him up the road.

"He's Jim now. He's off to University in the fall. He skipped a grade. He also won a scholarship to the University of British Columbia. He's going to be a doctor. I promised to help him set up a practice here if he still wants to come back when he's graduated. I somehow doubt that. That's his girlfriend Kim."

"Kim? What happened to Lara?"

"Well, my daughter two-timed him and he dumped her. She was heart-broken. I found myself saying to her all the things I had said to Sarah."

He tweaked little Lucy on the nose.

"So you just wait little one, I'm ready."

"There's Lucy! Your Aunt Lucy!" Olivia squealed. "And Rudy. And Mark."

Lucy and Rudy had eloped the summer after Olivia returned to Seattle in a quiet civil ceremony in Vancouver.

As she was running the Beachcomber in Olivia's absence, they spoke often, and Lucy had visited the Bowers in Washington State a few times. She had also stayed in touch with Sister Anne, who had told her about a beautiful baby boy who had been dropped off on the doorstep at St. Theresa's Shrine.

Lucy held Mark in her arms. He had flaming red hair just like hers, and Rudy had been unable to say no when Lucy asked if they could adopt him.

She ran and gave Lucy a big hug.

"I've missed you so much," Lucy said. "Rudy, grab her bags and take them home."

"I am home," Olivia sighed.

John McMichael took her by the hand.

"You're coming for dinner aren't you?" Lucy asked.

"Are you cooking?" McMichael said.

"No. Rudy is."

"Good. Then we'll be there."

Lucy and Rudy waved good-bye and left the three of them alone on the beach.

"She still can't cook?" Olivia whispered.

"Can't boil water."

Olivia laughed.

"I love you Olivia," John said. "I never thought in a million years that I would fall in love again, but I have. You made me the happiest man on earth when you gave me a chance."

"The last time I moved up here I was a newlywed," Olivia said. "And now I'm about to become a bride again. I never thought in a million years that would happen."

Little Lucy ran ahead, playing along the shore. She had a fascination with rocks.

"She's a miner all right," Olivia commented.

"Have you decided where you'd like the wedding to take place?" John asked.

"I've given it a lot of thought," Olivia said. "We don't need to make a big fuss. It's the second time for both of us. We don't need a church wedding. We don't need a wedding here in Britannia, or down in Seattle. Frenchie's still a Captain. He does have boat. Why don't we charter his boat up Desolation Sound and ask him to marry us along the way?"

John kissed her.

"That sounds perfect."

"Mommy!" little Lucy said, pointing to an object in the sand.

A tiny origami bird was poking its head out from some sand. She unearthed it and handed it to her mother.

A wave of emotion came over Olivia.

"What is that?" John asked.

"It's a paper bird," Olivia said. "Akiko used to make them for Lucy, I think."

"For me?" little Lucy asked.

A gust of wind arose and took the bird from Olivia's hand. It flew up towards the street, eventually landing high atop a peach rose bush. Little Lucy ran after it.

"I can't get it. It has pricklies," she said.

"How strange," Olivia thought. "This bush is just like the one in my father's garden." She felt totally at peace with herself and her world. The disasters at Britannia were over for Olivia.

Life is a lot like a tiny piece of origami paper, she thought to herself. It's colourful. It's light. It bends and folds and cuts you if you're not careful. It takes shape and becomes something spectacular. It wrinkles and creases and tears. It is often beautiful. It is always delicate. It is to be shared.

THE END

ABOUT THE AUTHOR

Janine McCaw lives in Vancouver Canada with her husband Paul.
　　Having worked in the Canadian television industry for many years as a producer and distributor of television programming, writing novels is somewhat of a new venture.
　　"Olivia's Mine" is the first of several novels currently underway. You can read excerpts from this and other novels by visiting www.janinemccaw.com. Please take a moment to sign the guestbook.

978-0-595-37924-8
0-595-37924-9

Printed in the United States
44865LVS00004B/130-153